Praise for Valerie Bird

'I love Valerie's writing. She paints such a beautiful picture with her words.'
D Barton

'a compelling read, well-plotted and constantly vivid'
D Penrose

'as always with this author, a wonderful sense of season and of place'
J Desborough

'what cannot be denied is the complete artistry'
P Valentine

'very well-drawn, credible characters'
W Jones

Also by Valerie Bird

Incident on the Line
Ladybird, Ladybird
The Angel Child
A Retrospective
The Eye of God
An Allowance of Small Noises (with Innes Richens)

www.valeriebird.eu

In memory of the gardens and gardeners of my childhood,

all inspiring my life-long love of gardens and gardening.

Canst thou not minister to a mind diseas'd,

Pluck from the memory a rooted sorrow,

Raze out the written troubles of the brain,

And with some sweet oblivious antidote

Cleanse the stuff'd bosom of that perilous stuff

Which weighs upon the heart?

Macbeth Act 5 Scene 3

The Greenhouse

Gina turns the door knob as if in the process of defusing a bomb. It's an old door, stout wood, inclined to jam, the accumulation of year on year paint. A gentle push, an intake of cool air and it is done, the slight movement releasing glass to fly free on to the greenhouse floor. A sound too delicate for the damage done, damage that has let the cold spring in and the heat out.

The glass lies in scattered shards, whole and half panes. This is no accident, freak weather, a stray tile or blinded bird. It is deliberate, an act of purposeful destruction. The perpetrator of the deed, 'this wanton act' as Ivan would later say, is not her first concern. It's the unholy memory brought back to haunt and unsettle all that had been laid to rest.

To fear to step inside is ludicrous; the distance, the time span since, two generations. It's   not unreasonable to wonder why she's been tricked back to witness again that appalling scene.

That is what Gina is thinking as she steps down onto the concrete floor and stands amongst the sharp fragments crunching under her slippers. She only came out on this bright blue morning, a sharp nip of frost in the air, to check her seedlings, gloat over the plants pricked out the day before. She grips the sides of the staging. Panic sucks all strength from her legs, runs tingling down her arms, leaving her as limp as the discarded seedlings in the compost bin. It is cruel, too cruel that they hid what they'd done all those years ago, and have suffered for it. The despair of lives blighted, the residual anger that they allowed her ignorance, bites more keenly than any other pain she's ever borne.

There was no warning. Nothing woke her last night, sleep undisturbed. Her bedroom on that side of the house, where the evening sun settles in the west, looking out over the garden, the terrace beds and beyond the lawn to the greenhouse, is far enough away to block the sound whenever it happened.

She walks on in to pick out the bits of glass that lie on top of the trays. All the tiny and tender plants, nothing robust, being nurtured with light and heat.

The searing beauty of a robin's call makes her turn. Blood drips from a cut already opening up in the palm of her hand but the real hurt is for what has gone before.

There was blood then, sixty years ago. Arms crazed with cuts, deliberate wounds, her mother's face china white, eyes pleading, weeping words that were too shocking to offer an eleven year old child. And her grandfather slumped on the floor as if fallen asleep, too tired to go back to the house, to find his armchair or bed.

Elspeth

Elspeth 1938

Elspeth Smith was ambitious and clever. Elementary school and a shorthand and typing course had given her the tools to earn a living. Money and marriage, to be socially better than her Ma and Pa, however, were what she wanted to achieve.

Madge, her mother, she considered no role model, with little love to give. Once a lady's maid now a drudge, in Elspeth's opinion. Ernest Smith adored both women, but was unable to bring peace, to lessen their animosity. Elspeth's feelings for him were complex; as a child she'd loved him because he so obviously demonstrated his love for her. But as she grew older she began to see him as a nonentity, content to be a dogsbody. He was a shop assistant with the commonest surname.

Kenneth would be a catch, netted at a tennis club dance. Not that Elspeth played tennis, the racquet and fees to join were beyond her reach, and white wasn't her colour. 'Auburn hair, pale skin, one needs to wear bright colours,' she informed Maxi, the friend from the course that made her a shorthand typist, the girl who played at everything with parents who could afford for her to do so. For Elspeth, she was a useful contact.

'Glasses, you've fallen for a man who wears glasses!' Maxi tweaked Elspeth's curls, the ringlets from rags. 'Looks a bit sort of intellectual to me.' She was piqued at the extortionate cost of her own Marcel wave which was much less effective.

Elspeth ignored her; the Max Factor Rose Red lipstick, worth two week's wages, needed careful application. Pressing her lips together she pouted at the mirror. Slinky and slender in lilac taffeta, the frilled neckline emphasised her neat breasts.

To be ladylike; there was so much to learn. Other girls took elocution lessons, Maxi too. She spoke extravagantly, thought it a lark.

Kenneth asked her to dance; a poor dancer but then so was she. He held her, she clung on. He asked if she came there often, if she played tennis, if she liked going to the flicks. He spoke impeccably, sounding like the man who read the news on the wireless. He wore a dinner suit with black bow tie, his hair was slick with Brilliantine, the scent of luxury. His eyes never quite caught hers. Even when she looked up at him to say, 'Thank you for the dance,' he glanced to one side. He thought she was a sweet girl; he wanted a wife.

The Smiths owned a wireless. A prized possession, it sat on a table beside the mantelpiece, taking precedence over all the other knick knacks. A lamp placed beside picked up the sheen of the wood. A domed creation with an intricate cut out pattern of wood to let sound through the cloth covered speakers, it became the most prestigious object in the house. It was switched on as soon as Ernest came back from the shop in the evening. Never a talkative man, unassuming, the prospect of war changed him, made him articulate and more forceful. When Chamberlain came back from meeting Hitler flapping a piece of paper offering. 'Peace in our time,' he was outraged.

The family - though Elspeth never thought of them as a family - were having tea when he announced to his wife and daughter, 'Whatever they say, we're in for it. War's coming, times are going to be hard.'

Elspeth wanted none of it. What had it got to do with her? Seventeen and intent on sloughing off the remnants of her origins, even her pleasure meant hard work, constant wariness in case her manners and attitudes betrayed her; fun and freedom were her due. She didn't want to accept his opinion.

'You're not one of those frivolous creatures, are you, Elspeth?' her father continued as if reading her mind. 'I've been proud of you, making your way, learning how to stand on your own two feet.'

Which was when she boasted of her new acquaintance, Kenneth Simms. 'He's a solicitor, working in his father's firm. He said they have vacancies for shorthand typists; I might apply.'

Ernest and Madge exchanged a look which she didn't understand; it was as if they'd been talking behind her back. 'It's worth a go, Elspeth,' he said. 'But don't you go losing your heart, 'cause we're going to lose everything else before you know it.'

'Oh, Pa, why do you have to be so glum! It's people like you who'll wish it on us.'

'Don't you speak to your father like that,' her mother snapped. 'He knows what's what even if we don't want to believe it.'

What a relief that she has the prospect of getting out from under his pessimism and her mother's dull subservience! 'Well, I'm going to get this job, war or no bloody war!'

'Don't you use that language, Elspeth!' Madge raised a hand as if she was about to slap her but seeing Ernest's face shook her head instead. 'And if you think that'll get you on in this world, I can tell you you're much mistaken. When I was in service …'

'Oh shut up!' Elspeth scraped back her chair and flounced out, pausing at the door to say, 'I'll better myself, you'll see, I'll be nobody's slave!'

Madge shrugged, 'Well don't come crying to me and Pa if nothing comes of it.'

It was George Simms, joint partner in the firm, Simms and Furland, who interviewed Elspeth. 'You'll be aware, Miss Smith, that your employment will be temporary for a month. If your work is helpful to our firm we will be pleased to offer you a permanent place on the staff.'

'I understand.' She would have said more, was planning to remind him of the praise she'd received on completing her shorthand and typing course and the reference from the garage where she'd worked for six months. She wore a turquoise suit lent to her by Maxi, elegant and eye-catching with matching beret. But as she sat with her legs carefully crossed at the ankle, she knew it was a mistake. In this austere room, facing this man in his impeccable dark grey suit with stiff collar and black tie, Elspeth was out of place. Far too showy, she knew that she should have chosen brown, been Miss Dowdy, played the demure mouse, which is what her mother would have advised. Under his silent observation of her, which could have been described as forensic - if Elspeth had known the meaning of the word - she shrank.

'I believe your father has applied to become an Air Raid warden,' he said, his voice less formal.

Elspeth looked back at him, helpless; had he?

'A good man; we'll need all the help we can get. This building will become an ARP recruiting post for the time being so you may encounter men arriving at the office who will not be wanting our services as such. Miss Bowker will instruct you on all the procedures.' He smiled for the first time but Elspeth could see no likeness to Kenneth. This man had dark, almost black hair, was tall and broad. Kenneth was blond and short with pale blue eyes, the eyes which never quite met hers.

'Have you any questions you'd like to ask me, Miss Smith?' George Simms' voice was benign.

Was it her father who'd helped her get this job? Had she been chosen above the other applicants not due to Kenneth's influence, but because of her father?

She recovered herself. 'I'm interested to know who runs which department, Mr Simms. I believe you are in charge of constitutional law and your son is head of conveyancing.' Was this what she should be asking? 'Who will I be working for?'

Although the hesitation before he spoke was infinitesimal, it was enough to give the impression that it was the wrong question. 'Miss Bowker will be in charge of your duties; she will assign you to whoever needs your services.' The distance between them was established and as he stood, holding out his hand for her to shake, the cool and brief touch reinforced this.

Outside the room Elspeth shivered wishing that she could lean against his door, let it hold her upright. It was hard to fathom why she was upset. She had the job, a real ladder to climb, people she could impress.

George sat back in his chair. A pretty girl, eager, but maybe too flighty. A bit of spirit was good, and her credentials had been excellent. Miss Bowker would cope with any silliness; Miss Bowker was the glue that held the firm together. The end of an afternoon, the room had lost some of its brightness; he switched on the desk lamp looking over to the door from where the new girl had left. He knew nothing of her connection with Kenneth; her application arrived in the post with all the others. His son was away training with the Observer Corps.

Elspeth waited to hear Kenneth's voice, thought he might ask for her, even poke his head round the door of the room where she worked. She couldn't mention his name to Miss Bowker; after her first encounter with Mr Simms Senior - as she learned to refer to him - she knew that questions unrelated to her work were inappropriate. Miss Bowker usually set her to type up shorthand notes of dictation which she had taken herself. She was hidden away in an office with another girl so rarely saw the men and women who entered the building.

She didn't tell Maxi of her lowly status but boasted of how well she was progressing and how 'beastly Miss Bowker is.' Though that wasn't how she felt. The woman was fair and motherly offering praise and tips on how to improve. Miss Bowker's motto repeated frequently was 'vigilance, courtesy, reliability, watch words for the prefect secretary'. Perfection was Elspeth's ambition.

It was Miss Bowker who eventually announced that, 'Mr Kenneth is away training in case of war'. Elspeth felt equal chagrin and relief; at least he wasn't ignoring her, but would he ever come back?

In the meantime she asked Maxi, 'Will you be going to your Pa's golf club dance again this year?' angling for an invitation.

Maxi shrugged. 'Don't know. Daddy's in such a mood these days. Moans about money being tight and going to get worse. Nobody'll be buying jewellery. Says, what good's a diamond ring when Hitler gets here? But I said, good for giving him a black eye! And he had to laugh, said he'd put it in the window, sort of advert!'

Elspeth didn't find it funny; why were they all giving in to these morbid thoughts. It was her life that was being ruined.

Maxi said, 'Where's that man with the glasses gone?' Which riled Elspeth as she didn't know and it was what she cared about most. Not that she'd tell Maxi.

'Away on business,' she said.

And then Kenneth appeared.

He didn't seem to have come specially to see her when he came to the door of their office. He greeted Miss Bowker who introduced Elspeth and the other girl. He remained on the threshold, acknowledging both girls as if he knew neither of them. She was mortified until later when she found a note asking if she'd like to accompany him and friends to the pictures the following week. Chagrin turned to ecstasy. She would be eighteen at the beginning of December with the world at her feet.

Elspeth's bravado vanished when she was sent into George Simms's office for the first time to take dictation. She'd seen him rarely, once going out of the building as he was coming in. He'd nodded and said, 'Good evening,' but he wouldn't have heard her stammered reply.

Acting for Miss Bowker, who was absent with 'flu, filled Elspeth with as much pride as receiving Kenneth's invitation. Which didn't make sense. What was work in comparison to a man wanting the pleasure of your company and to spend money on you - which was the way Kenneth had so gallantly described his offer?

Elspeth knocked on the door and waited before entering, as taught by Miss Bowker. Her hands trembled which would be useless when holding her pencil, and swallowed the lump in her throat for the umpteenth time. It was the first time that she'd been into this room since her interview. Today it seemed quite different. A low sun filtered through the sash windows lifting the polished floor to a deep sheen; Elspeth saw it as a pathway lit by the beam of a searchlight. George Simms sat as if in its shadow with his back to her, looking out at the street beyond. 'Mr Simms, excuse me,' she said, 'I've come to take dictation. Are you ready for me or …' The words came in a rush, too loud for the hush they were filling.

He swivelled round to say, 'Of course. It's Miss Smith isn't it?'

'Yes, sir,' she said.

'Please, take a seat,' and he stood to indicate where she should sit. It was like a scene in a movie.

She liked his voice, it didn't have the hard twang of so many of the young men she knew including Kenneth; the fashion to sound American.

It was peaceful and purposeful sitting taking dictation, listening to his measured language. He rarely needed to change anything he said, apologising when he did so. Six lengthy letters later, it seemed no time had gone by before she returned to her own desk.

Two hours passed, having worked through her lunch break, she went back to ask for his signature, all the letters neatly arranged with their envelopes inside a leather-bound blotter. The door to his office was open and Elspeth hovered unsure whether to knock or peer in to see if he was inside. As she waited a voice behind her called out. 'Can I help you?' It was Mr Furland, the senior partner, speaking from the doorway of his office further down the hallway. He came out to greet her. 'Don't worry, lass. He's upstairs talking to Mr Kenneth.' Elspeth felt herself blushing, hoped the dim light would conceal her red cheeks. 'Put the letters on his desk for him to sign,' he said, smiling down as if she were a sweet child. 'You can come back later, in time for the post.'

'Thank you,' she said recovering her poise. 'I'm deputising for Miss Bowker, sir. She's unwell.'

'Dear Miss Bowker, it's sad news but no doubt she'll be back with us soon.' And with a knowing nod he disappeared. She thought how good it must feel to be thought indispensable.

She felt the thrill of a desire to please walking in to place the correspondence on his desk, her work for him to approve or if necessary correct. The sun still flowed into the room, warming all the dark wood of the panelling, his desk. The long velvet curtains at the windows hung to the floor, a deep gold. The piles of brown manilla folders bulging inside their tape ties were stacked on all the surfaces without giving the impression of desperation or untidiness. All was in order and the air breathed a lush scent of polish. And the final touch, which she thought quite exquisite, was the plant in a pot on his desk. The pale green leaves clustered around the stems which stood nine inches tall holding a floret of the palest pink flowers, a flower that she'd never seen before. It was so elegant, a room where she wanted to stay, would be content.

George Simms sat opposite his son, the smell of tobacco disturbing his good intentions. 'Stop criticising him,' his wife would have said. 'You never see any good in the boy.' Looking at him now he saw a replica of Marjorie. The round cheeks, the pretty pout. 'Why shouldn't he enjoy himself?' had been her usual rebuttal of any discipline he'd wished to impose. The time when the boy caught butterflies in order to pull off their wings to see what made them fly. The truancies from school which he, as father, was forced to defend. The endless unkind pranks he played on their live-in maid, Ruby. 'Please be kind to him, George,' Marjorie had begged on her death bed. 'He's your only child, our dear boy. Let him be true to himself.'

'So how was the training?' George said to Kenneth, quashing his irritation, hoping his enquiry sounded enthusiastic.

Kenneth lounged back in his chair blowing another cloud of smoke at the ceiling. 'Ripping, Dad.' And as if spurred on by the words, jerked forward, stubbing out his cigarette and beaming at his father. 'If I can't fly, this is the next best thing.'

'Well done, Ken. I'm very pleased.'

'We're going to need people like me, our organisation, aren't we? Especially after the latest news.'

'Is that the feeling in the Corps?'

'Rather. Nobody's fooled by Hitler's supposed promise to Chamberlain. So much waste paper, they say.'

The boy's blonde hair fell over his forehead, the discipline of Brylcreem to no avail. How young he looked. George leant forward too, clasped Kenneth's shoulder with a rush of affection.

'Your mother would be proud of you too, if she were still with us. You know that, don't you?'

'Sure,' Kenneth pulled back. He looked away to find his packet of cigarettes, took one out, lit it with a fancy lighter behind a cupped hand. George sank back. Was he wrong to have mentioned Marjorie?

'When do you need to go back for more training?'

Kenneth shrugged. 'A month, maybe. It depends doesn't it?'

'Right.' George eased a finger between his collar and neck. The reek of the newly lit cigarette stuck in his throat. 'You might have time to look at …' he noted the lack of documents of Kenneth's desk. 'There is some outstanding conveyancing - John's been attempting to keep on top of the work, but he's not fully trained and …'

'Okay, Dad. I'll look at them tomorrow.'

'Tomorrow? Why tomorrow? We've some unhappy clients …'

'Yeh, sure. Don't worry, I'll sweet-talk them tomorrow. No rush.'

'I don't think you understand the reputation which we're trying to maintain.' George heard the aggrieved tone of his own voice, and her disapproval, 'stop nagging the poor boy.'

'Why on earth are these people buying and selling houses anyway?' Kenneth rocked back on his chair again, inhaled deeply. 'Don't they understand it'll all have gone belly-up before they've set foot in those precious properties.' And despite his languid pose there was a glint in his eye, a thrill in what he'd said.

George stared at his son. The boy should never have been pushed into becoming a solicitor. But his poor eyesight failed the test for him to join the RAF, his dream. What else was there to do? He wasn't an ogre nor was Ken a fool. 'It doesn't look good, I agree,' he said. 'I've become an Air Raid Warden - this building is an ARP recruiting post.'

'Well done, Dad,' a playful tone, the relaxed pose.

George sat on, regarding Kenneth. The boy's tweed jacket splayed open to show a striped green shirt and patterned braces. He could think of nothing else to say.

As if aware of his father's assessment of his apparel Kenneth sat forward to lean on his desk. The old boy was such a stickler, stuck in an era long gone. He offered an amiable smile; it wasn't his fault that Mother Mine was gone. He'd called her that since letters home from boarding school. She'd written Darling Son of Mine so he'd responded similarly. She'd loved it too, in fact had been quite ecstatic; signing off 'With oceans of love from Mother Mine'.

'Well,' George rose, stood uncertain though knowing there was nothing more to be done. He leant across the desk again to clasp his son's arm but there was no response to this act of affection. 'See you at dinner,' he said and left.

Elspeth was called back, the letters signed, one letter needing to be altered for an addition he wished to make. His thanks were sincere. 'I am most grateful and impressed. Miss Bowker will be relieved to hear, on her return, of the way in which you fulfilled her role for me so satisfactorily.'

Elspeth walked home as if on a cloud of warm air. Perhaps he would ask for her again tomorrow.

Next morning she got up early to give her shoes an extra polish. Her mother was already in the kitchen ironing. 'Well, who's the early bird!' a chirrup in her voice. 'I've got something for you, Elspeth. That's if you'd like it.'

She slid the garment off the ironing board and held it up. It was a skirt, black with pinstripes. 'And there's a jacket to match.'

'For me?'

'Yes, I think it'll fit. I just thought with your new job it might be suitable.' Madge looked away from her daughter to hang the garments on a clothes hanger. 'The lady I used to work for up at the big house asked me to find a good home for some things she was throwing … passing on, is what she said.' Elspeth could hear her mother's casual tone, as if she were offering the option to refuse. 'They're too small for her and her daughter didn't want them.'

Elspeth wasn't sure what to say.

'Do you want to try them on? Have you time?'

'Well, they look just right, I will, yes, thank you, Ma.'

Five minutes later when Ernest came into the room there was Elspeth preening herself and Madge with a look of such pleasure on her face it was hard to take in.

'What's happening here?'

'Ma got me this suit, doesn't it look good, it'll be perfect for work,' the words came in a rush as she stood for both her parents to admire.

Elspeth walked to work in her new pencil skirt, her brogues slipping on the frosty pavements. A mood of uplift as bright as her blue blouse and the morning sky. She'd only time to take off her hat and coat by the time the bell rang from Mr Simms' office. Seeing that Miss Bowker hadn't arrived, she picked up her pen and pad and strode towards his office door. Again she knocked and waited to enter. 'How can I help you, Mr Simms?' Her tone masking how nervous she felt, but when he said, 'I wish I knew,' she was confused.

He held a small watering can and had obviously been tending the flower on his desk. He looked up at her and smiled. 'Fussy plants, primula, Miss Smith; too much water and they become sick, too little and they die. And it's the same with temperature, too hot they wilt, too cold they shrivel.' He laughed, 'You must think it odd that I bother.'

'Oh, no, sir. I think that's lovely, such a delicate flower. I've never seen one before.'

'Thank you,' and he put the watering can on to the windowsill. 'I have a greenhouse full of them; pampered creatures.'

Elspeth was enchanted, that he should share something so personal and that he should possess such a place. 'How wonderful,' she said.

He nodded indicating that she sit down. 'So, it's a month since you joined us and Miss Bowker and myself have been very pleased with your work and hope that you will stay with us, your position is permanent. Does that suit you?'

'Oh yes,' she said. 'I'm very happy here. Thank you.'

George Simms looked at this pretty girl dressed so smartly, her blue blouse setting off the colour of her hair, hair bound at the back in a neat bun, a girl who'd proved not to be frivolous. Her pleasure upon receiving the news also pleased him. Such a contrast to Kenneth's attitude to the firm. For one inappropriate moment he wanted to give her the flower she'd admired.

Kenneth 1939

Kenneth couldn't tolerate living at home any longer. Going away, training with the other officers, had made him realise that the situation was unbearable. Dad was such a bore. None of the other fellows lived with parents. They were either married with a home of their own or in digs. Either way they were free, could be their own man. And here he was, a twenty-four year old, tied to a stuffy job, going back to a house which held no affection for him. How could he expect that it might be any different? At boarding school you got used to pretending not to need creature comforts, be self-reliant. When Mother Mine was alive it was different. She wept when he went away making him feel wanted, that she cared. Coming back to her joy in seeing him was nice, the cosseting too, though it got a bit overpowering if he was honest. And the house still reeked of her, a glum loss, nothing changed since her death. A mausoleum. And it wasn't as if they'd been happy, Marjorie and George; it had always struck him as a pretty miserable marriage; she complained about 'your dear father' constantly, and Dad put up with it, kept out of the way, at work or in his damned garden. That's what she'd said, 'He's happier with his silly plants than with my company.'

Elspeth had asked that they meet outside the cinema; she didn't want him coming to see where she lived. And it'd been a nightmare to think what to wear. Her dress for the dance was long, too formal. Anyway it wouldn't do on a cold evening in December. Maxi wasn't any help; swore she was going out that night too and didn't know what she'd want to choose, so had nothing to lend. Elspeth was desperate; she couldn't wear what she wore for work and her only coat was too long and shabby. All the animosity she'd held towards her mother had to be put aside. She asked whether 'your lady' had given her anything else.

'What for, Elspeth?' was Ma's guarded reply.

'It's a date, I'm going to the pictures. I can't wear my work clothes.' Elspeth made it a statement, expecting to be told that she was lucky to have any decent things to wear.

'Is it a coat you're after?'

'Yes,' Elspeth couldn't believe Ma'd not even questioned her about who she was going with and why her other coat wouldn't do.

'Well, there was a cape I could cut down. It's a bit fancy but a good colour, royal blue so it would suit you. When do you need it?'

'Tomorrow.'

It was a miracle. Was it something Pa had said? Why this change in her mother? On the next evening when the garment was produced, a perfect fit, something really lovely to make her feel good, she had to say, 'I'm ever so grateful, Ma.'

And Madge huffed a little laugh and smiled. 'I can see you're doing well, Elspeth. Only a month in and this job seems to really suit you. Your Pa and I are proud of you.' She didn't say, which they both thought, that Elspeth was growing up, the job doing her good. Elspeth had spoken with respect of the man she worked for, this Mr Simms, had even asked about what they could grow if they had an allotment, 'with the war coming.'

Kenneth stood on the steps of the Odeon, a cigarette cocked in one hand, the other on the shoulder of a man whose arm circled the woman beside him. All three were smoking and as Elspeth approached they tilted their heads in unison to blow smoke rings under the portico of the cinema. Elspeth stopped; Kenneth had said 'with friends' but she'd not appreciated the implications. They were strangers. The girl was much older, wore an expensive looking coat with a fur collar and nipped in waist. The heels on her shoes were high and narrow, perhaps even suede. Their laughter as she reached the trio might have been about her. She looked up at the poster advertising the film, 'The Lady Vanishes'. 'Kenneth,' she called out trying to assume a merry tone as if she was already part of the fun.

'Hello,' he called back, 'come and meet these chaps.' But no one shook hands with her, they didn't even offer her a cigarette. though she could see that there was an interest in this girl Kenneth was dating. The other man, Jack, looked her over approvingly, and the woman, Lizzie, hid behind a screen of smoke.

There was an uncomfortable silence. So Elspeth said, 'I'm sorry, I interrupted what you were saying.'

'No,' Jack smiled down at her, taller than Kenneth, his dark oiled hair gleaming under the street light. 'It was a silly joke Ken was telling us. Been living with all these rough types this last month. Ghastly crowd.'

'It's what you'll encounter in the army, Jack. That is, I take it you'll join up?'

Then there was some banter about kilts and different regiments which Elspeth didn't understand but, by following Lizzie's laughter, hoped that it appeared as if she was one of them. They drawled their plummy accents as if it was all too tiring, seeming to speak in code. She was glad when they went in to see the film

Elspeth was told to lead the way into their row of expensive seats, Kenneth next to her. His attention was on the other two, though, so most of the snatches of conversation she couldn't hear; talking all through the Pathé News, laughing at film footage of Hitler saluting his troops, cheering the launch of some ship, made her feel ignorant and disturbed. The film, though, was thrilling and they all agreed when they came out, that Jack was the spitting image of Michael Redgrave. 'Just grow a moustache, old boy,' Kenneth joked, 'then they'll all be falling at your feet.'

Elspeth was relieved and disappointed when Kenneth didn't offer to walk her home and he hadn't even tried to hold her hand during the film; she might as well have vanished like the lady in the movie. If he asked her out again she might say that she was already doing something else, play hard to get. Did she like him that much anyway?

Kenneth asked Jack, 'What did you think of her?'

Jack laughed, 'Why ask me?'

'You and Lizzie. You seem to get on.'

'Sure. She's a chum. No complications.'

'And you think women are a complication?'

'I didn't say that. Elspeth's certainly a looker. Why are you thinking of getting serious?'

'I thought if I got married it might help.'

'What?'

'Well, living at home with my father is ghastly. And I'm that sort of age.'

'Odd reasons by my reckoning,' Jack said. 'And aren't you going to be away a lot if there's war?'

George was nonplussed when Ken announced one evening at the end of March, 'I'm going to marry Elspeth. You know, Miss Smith, the girl who works in the office.' He stared at Ken, unable to comprehend as he carried on with, 'I asked her a week ago and I gave her the ring last night,' Ken was sitting with his feet up on the sofa in the drawing room of their home. Marjorie would have mildly admonished her son, 'Feet off, Kenny,' to which her reluctant son would've sulkily done as she'd asked. And as if to score a point, she'd have looked across at George to show that she could control their son, that it was she he obeyed.

George said gently, though wishing to shout, 'Ken, you can hardly know this young woman.'

'Oh, we've gone out lots of times.' Ken examined his cigarette. 'Cinema, the odd meal. She's a great girl.'

George wanted to say, 'I know And you'll be depriving me of an efficient and pleasant secretary,' but that would have been inappropriate. 'You've told me nothing of this,' he said instead. 'I had no inkling …' but he didn't finish. What did he know, what did they talk about? Only this new interest, the Observer Corps, but of his social life there had been nothing. Who had Ken ever referred to, except Jack Fenton. He had met Jack; a likeable young man, similarly working for his father, Robin Fenton, known through Rotary.

George tried to sound reasonable. 'You haven't been here much of the time these last few months, back and forth training. He didn't say, 'and little work done in the office,' for fear of an unpleasant retort. Instead he said, 'How can you know her, or vice versa, after such a short time?'

'Dad, just calm down,' Kenneth's feet remained on the pale blue brocade cushions. 'She's pretty, she likes me, we enjoy the same films.'

'Those are not reasons for marriage, a life-long commitment. Love?'

'And is that what you and Mother Mine had?' Kenneth's retort flung with the same force as his leap and escape from the sofa and room.

George was aghast. Had the strained atmosphere of his own marriage so badly affected their son? He'd always assumed that his care of Marjorie proved their bond was true. The room floated in wreaths of smoke. He got up to follow his son, calling out, 'Ken, please, you can't go, we need to talk. This is serious.' But the front door slammed and he was left staring out of the window to the drive, hearing a revving engine and the crunch of gravel as a car swerved out on to the road.

A slight sun slid between the heavy velvet curtains showing the deep blue had faded, the folds appearing as stripes. They had been new twenty odd years ago when Kenneth was a baby, a pretty pink faced child. What a joy his arrival had been! Such a healthy body in comparison with Marjorie who was often sick; a fragile woman with an iron will. They had been an awkward couple. A romance of adoration, gentle caresses and kisses was enough for Marjorie. The look of horror on her face when after several weeks of marriage she succumbed to his sexual overtures, considering them an assault, had wrecked any hope of physical closeness in their future life. That one occasion had produced their dear son, which George hoped would bring them together. That wasn't to happen; if anything Kenneth became a battleground.

George looked out to where the first murmur of spring could be seen on the trees, the pink buds, the citrus green of immature leaves. He'd mown the grass, the first cut of the season, and trimmed the edges of the lawn. To keep those strict lines and shapes under control gave the garden structure while the rest could abandon itself to bloom and blossom. He'd once said this to Marjorie who'd wanted to know why the gardener couldn't do that job. 'Because I want perfection, or as near as damn it; and to show him how it should be maintained.' She'd laughed, 'That's what he's paid for.' And now Reg Pearson was getting too old anyway. A replacement wasn't a pleasant thought; would there be any men available?

The light was fading, the drawing room losing colour to the dark. George switched on the standard lamp, its glow picking up the sheen of the gramophone. Where had Ken been all day? He'd heard him playing his jazz records on the record player - as the young man insisted on calling it. George resisted the temptation to tell him how fortunate he was; there would be no such machine in the house if he hadn't needed the balm of music too. Though he'd never mentioned to Ken his preference for the classics, finding the latest modern music brash, 'a cacophony of notes and agitating rhythm' as he'd once remarked to Jim Furland.

An awful realisation began to occur to him. Had Miss Smith, or Elspeth as he'd now need to know her, applied for the job because of Ken, angling for this attachment? The thought sickened him. The tea tray sat with stewed tea and the remainder of the fruit cake from which he'd cut the two slices. A lump the size of that piece of cake blocked his throat, tears, ridiculous tears, trickled down his cheeks. This girl, Elspeth, whatever her motives, was clever, bright and personable; how would she cope with being shut up in a house merely overseeing the cleaning and cooking of meals? It was clear she enjoyed working in the office; out loud he said, 'And I don't want to lose her.' Why the hurry, was she pregnant?

He was twenty three when he married Marjorie, she two years younger; acquaintances through their fathers' work. His father, Albert, then senior partner in their firm, Marjorie's the owner of the most respected building company in the county. A match arranged but then hadn't they found each other agreeable? She expressed an interest in horticulture, liked to boast her knowledge of wild flowers. He'd delighted in taking care of her, at the time taking pride in her fastidious nature. Ruby had come to them as a girl to clean and help the cook who left after a disagreement with Marjorie. Several more came and went but Ruby remained their stalwart. Ruby, who had made the cake, would be expecting the remains to be put back in its tin 'to keep moist like'; Ruby who would arrive tomorrow morning at 8 o'clock to make their breakfast, expecting him to have left their dirty dishes for her to wash-up. 'That's not a man's job,' she'd say. However she never expressed surprise when she found that the kitchen was clean and tidy, the bread and cheese left for supper gone.

George gathered up their cups and plates. There was no point in becoming maudlin, Ken wasn't stupid nor it seemed was the girl. Halfway across the hall to the kitchen he heard the sound of a car turn into their drive, the wrench of the handbrake being applied. He waited as footsteps approached the door which was flung open by Kenneth. 'Sorry, Dad. I needed to cool off.'

The ring 1939

Kenneth said, 'Elspeth would you like to marry me?' adding, 'We get on awfully well so it seemed a good idea.' No down on one knee, no protestations of undying love, no gazing soulfully into her eyes, merely a hand held, a ring in a box. She said, 'Yes', for what else was there to say? Hadn't it been her idea? Wasn't it what she wanted?

The ring was a sapphire, a vivid blue stone encircled with tiny diamonds, winking up at her, but still he could not look her in the eye.

'I told my Ma and Pa,' she said to him the next day. A walk along the shore was his suggestion, but much of it was barricaded with barbed wire, the mudflats drained as if even the water was too fearful of the future. 'I know that I'm old enough to make up my own mind, which I said,' she told him. 'All the same they'd like you to come and ask.' She'd been dreading saying this to him. On the other hand it was proper to do that sort of thing. It was protocol. She smiled to herself; all these new words she was learning, becoming a real know-all.

'Yep, of course.' He fancied presenting himself as the dashing young man of the world who had swept her off her feet with the means to support her.

Ernest and Madge welcomed Kenneth into the front parlour. No fire had been lit in that room for many months, even possibly the whole of the last winter. It was decidedly chilly, as was Madge in her response to Kenneth's suave manners. Ernest was merely dumbfounded. Elspeth had said little about this young man who she'd already accepted as a fiancé. Once or twice she'd mentioned the films they'd seen, speaking of 'going to the flicks with friends', never of being in love. Was this the new-fangled attitude to marriage?

'I hope that you're happy with Elspeth's choice,' Kenneth said. The smell of his Brylcreme and cigarettes overpowering the polish that normally pervaded the room. Neither Ernest nor Madge approved of smoking and Elspeth too disliked the smell and even more the taste of his breath when he kissed her. But it didn't count as a reason to refuse him; with time it might not matter.

He boasted of his position in the firm, even outlining his mother's connections and the income she'd left him. Madge was used to the upper class, having worked from a girl of fourteen at the 'big house', rising to the rank of lady's maid. People like that didn't flaunt their wealth; she was suspicious of Kenneth Simms' need to brag. Later Ernest would insist, 'the lad was only trying to let us know that he'd look after our girl.'

'Are you sure you want to marry this man?' was Ernest's first question to Elspeth after Kenneth had left.

'He's really very nice,' was her reply.

'And love?' Madge said. 'Does he love you and you him?'

'What's love got to do with it?' was Elspeth's gay reply but as the words left her mouth the doubts crept in. 'I'm sure we do,' she added for even if she wasn't, there was no going back.

'It's a shame that you'll have to give up your job,' her father said as if sealing the contract.

'Married women don't work, not when you're married to someone like him,' Madge added. 'He'll want you to be at home looking after him and the house.' She didn't mean to sound scornful but she was disappointed. All that money she'd saved especially for Elspeth to learn shorthand and typing, to have a skill, to be able to have a respectable job, to make something of herself. Her own marriage was happy but she'd like to have been back working for Mrs Briggs Fanshawe with all the excitement of the lady's lovely wardrobe and the companionship of the other servants. It could be lonely stuck at home and doing more menial work.

'Ma, I'll go on working,' Elspeth put in quickly, shocked at such an awful prospect. 'After all I'm in the firm with his father. It's not like …' but she couldn't finish. Here in the back parlour the fire was glowing, but the cold of the unheated room they'd sat in with Kenneth crept back in. What was Mr George Simms going to say? Had Kenneth told him? What might he say to her on Monday? And Miss Bowker? She looked down again at her hand, the stones sparkling, their beauty undiminished. What was it worth?

Kenneth apologised to his father. 'It's all a bit sudden, I know, but, with how the world is at the moment, I didn't think we should wait.'

To George these were exactly the reasons to be cautious. Wasn't this what had happened to himself and Marjorie; married at the beginning of that war to end all wars. 'You'll be away a lot of the time, Ken. What's she going to do with herself?'

He shrugged.

'A married woman isn't expected to continue working after marriage,' his father said. 'And children?'

'Glory be! Give us a chance, Dad!' Kenneth's cheery response belied his horror at the possibility. A pretty woman on your arm was a long way from creating a family.

'Where will you live?'

'Well,' and again it was apparent that he'd no idea but quickly covered with the proposal that they'd live there until he could find a house, maybe build one.

Kenneth perched on the edge of the sofa, his glass empty of whisky. Last night he'd gone straight on to join Jack in the Barley Mow after meeting Elspeth's parents. They'd had a merry time together trying to forget the enormity of what he was doing, at the same time as pretending it was all a jolly good idea. 'For the life of me I can't imagine what you two have in common,' Jack had said as they swayed down the road holding each other upright at the end of the evening. He'd laughed that lovely guffaw which always made Ken join in. 'Nor can I,' he'd said.

The snowdrops George had cut and put in a vase that morning shivered as he walked past the hall table. Above, there was his favourite picture, nothing valuable or fashionable, but a watercolour of a country fair. The bright stripes of the tent awnings, the big wheel with the simple family groups strolling amongst hoop-la stalls and toffee apple sellers, with a backdrop of a blue sky strewn with strands of pink cloud. It represented an open, happy life, simple and untroubled. Looking at it brought tears to his eyes. He did mourn Marjorie for the cruelty of her life being cut short but also for the marriage they'd never managed to make good. And to hear Ken talk so casually of his relationship with this girl seemed another blow.

Somehow he'd have to face it all in the morning. At no time had Miss Smith seemed to be covering a secret that might embarrass both of them. True, he only saw her when taking dictation, bringing in files and arranging them in order of the need for attention. Miss Bowker found her 'intelligent and discreet'. She'd praised her on several occasions. 'Miss Smith will make an excellent secretary in a few years time'. Tactfully the girl had even suggested a different way of dealing with the daily filing. To have achieved that without offending Miss Bowker was a small miracle. It couldn't have been an act.

Elspeth woke early having slept a fractured sleep. Outside was dark, the blocks of houses in the next street black shapes, no lamps lit, no one else awake. She stood at the window of her bedroom watching between the curtains, waiting for some light. Light to give her courage, to lift the gloom which rested on her whole body. Was this really how it should be? Worrying that she'd said, 'yes', before she was ready? Worrying that to be married was going to prevent her doing a job which she found so satisfying? Worrying that she would displease Mr George Simms and Miss Bowker. It was they who'd made her feel important, someone worth their trust. Being at the firm of Simms and Furland created opportunities for advancement, a way to rise up that ladder that she'd not realised before. If she could no longer work there, what would she do with herself? A housewife? She turned to her bedside table to see the ring, picking out the first glint of dawn. Should she wear it to go to work? Kenneth hadn't suggested Elspeth meet his father at their home which had sort of been a relief. In fact he'd merely muttered vaguely about 'going to the flicks on Friday' but that was five days away. She looked down at her bare hand, ringless fingers. Nobody need know yet.

'You look a bit peaky,' Madge remarked when she came down for breakfast 'I hope it's excitement,' which Elspeth knew neither of them believed.

'I think I'll leave the ring here today, Ma.'

'Yes, that might be the best idea.'

It was as if her mother knew how she felt, was on her side though nothing could be said out loud.

George drove to the office the sun spiralling on the windscreen, flickering between the branches of trees, a Peter Pan spirit, playing with his few resources of energy. The office was bright with spring sun, the air clear where you would have expected dust motes. It was as if this place, knowing of his turmoil, called to him with fresh safety. The thought gave him a jolt; such sentimentality. A clear view was needed to cope with these new circumstances. Before he encountered Miss Smith in the office, Ken should have brought her to meet him in their home, introduce her as his fiancée, it was only fair to the girl. He'd make that proposal tonight.

Miss Bowker said, 'You don't seem yourself this morning, Miss Smith.' A statement that was both kind and questioning. It was well past midday but Elspeth hadn't taken any time to eat her sandwiches. 'It's a nice spring day, dear. Why don't you take your lunch in the garden at the back, sit on the bench? Mr Simms never minds us doing that.'

Elspeth looked up at the woman, worry rising in waves, a flood wanting to drown her. She clenched her teeth. 'Thank you,' she didn't dare say any more. but put on her coat, picked up her bag, and again said, 'Thank you.'

The grass was still damp with morning dew. It was like walking on a deep soft carpet. The bench faced away from the building down to a jumble of bushes and fence. To be out in the fresh air was a relief. She breathed in deeply, letting out the air as far as her lungs would let her. She nibbled at a sandwich before wrapping it back into its greaseproof paper. Engaged, a bride-to-be, marriage, no job. Closing her eyes, she let it all swirl around, a dizzying effect of things which she didn't want to think about. Bird song pierced the silence, sweet and forceful. Even with her eyes shut she caught the movement that brought the bird to her feet. She opened her eyes to peek without lifting her head. And there it was, hopping closer and closer to find invisible crumbs. How pretty, how round and brown, the tiny sleek feathers and red breast. Could she open up the package of leftover sandwiches without causing it to fly away?

George got up from his chair to stand at the window, shrugging his shoulders, his neck tight with tension. It was turning into a lovely day; the grass like green velvet. And then he saw her. A small brown figure bent forward, sitting alone on the bench.

Was she all right? Her posture suggested not. Should he call Miss Bowker, ask her advice? No, it was his duty to see her. Why wait for Ken to introduce her formally? To ignore the situation was cowardly.

She didn't hear his footsteps. The little bird was all she wanted to think about. It still hopped closer and closer, pecking up those infinitesimally small crumbs. How perfectly peaceful it was out here; the building that had begun to feel like a second home, even a more exciting home, and then to come out here, to find a garden in which to sit and belong, it was so special. Tears were a relief, she let them fall, didn't wipe them away.

'Hmm,' he coughed in an effort to warn of his approach. 'A lovely day. Do you mind if I join you?'

Elspeth's indrawn breath, her startled turn to face him, told what he suspected. Her eyes were swimming with unshed tears, her cheeks wet with those that had fallen.

George took out his handkerchief and handed it to her. 'It is clean,' he said and sat down beside her. The robin watched from the closest tree. 'That little chap thinks he owns this place and I suppose he's right. After all what are bricks and mortar, and letters and deeds to him. Worms and a few fine nesting places are all he requires. This is his territory quite rightly.'

Elspeth wiped her face, the softness and laundered smell of his handkerchief so soothing. Clutching it tightly she said, 'He was after the crumbs from my sandwiches. I haven't finished eating and was going to give them to him. But unwrapping the paper is going to make too much noise.'

George smiled. 'Try now, he'll know it's worth hanging around.'

'They're only marg and marmite.'

'A feast for the likes of him.'

'I'm not so sure. I think worms are probably a better diet.'

'But then neither of us eats worms.'

She managed to laugh. He was right. She crumbled the bread and sprinkled the crumbs a few feet away. They sat still and silent and within a minute or less the bird was back pecking as if they weren't there.

And it didn't feel embarrassing any more either to Elspeth or George. The sun shone, the grass grew greener and greener and the only sounds were of other birds chirruping in the bushes, waiting their turn.

'Miss Smith,' George finally said. 'I hear that my son, Ken, has asked you to marry him and you've accepted.'

She bowed her head.

'That is true?' he said gently.

She looked up, a grief stricken expression on her face and nodded. 'I ...' and again tears ran down her cheeks, which she wiped away frantically, pressing her lips tight, trying to keep back the shuddering sob which wanted to overwhelm her. 'I'm so sorry,' she cried. 'I'm so sorry. It's just that ... well, I can't bear to think that I won't be able to go on working here.' Like the tears her words came out unstoppable. 'I love being here, it's what I enjoy most, and my Ma said that married women can't work, not in places like this. It's not what's expected. I just ...' She stopped with a gasp of breath. 'I'm so sorry.'

George was stunned. And touched. He'd been right; she was a girl dedicated to her job. That at least was a relief. There can have been no calculation on her part. But what of now? Was this young woman happily contemplating marriage to his son?

'You don't have to stop working here,' he found himself saying. 'I'm sure that an exception can be made. We ought to move with the times. And with war ...' then he stopped. 'Do you want to marry my son, Elspeth?'

He'd spoken her name. It sounded so much prettier when he said it. But did she want to marry Kenneth? How could she say 'no'?

He didn't wait for her answer though, carrying on with, 'I have wondered whether my wife, Marjorie, would have been happier if she'd been able to pursue a career - botany perhaps? She was very interested in that sort of thing. Unthinkable at the time.'

'I want you to be happy, Elspeth.' Madge stopped turning the wheel of the sewing machine. A brief pause to look at her daughter, a daughter turned away and bent forward, intent on the needle and thread in her hand, the crumpled pile of white silk lying in her lap. The girl's hair shone a deep copper, a few strands escaping the tight bun nestling in the nape of her neck. It was strange to see her vulnerable and pliant. For all the years of her childhood they seemed to have been at loggerheads, sparring in opposing corners. Seeing her like this, though, accentuated the tiny worm of worry which had burrowed its way in and wouldn't leave.

'Your Pa and I have been very happy,' was the best way to say it. 'You might not think that sometimes when I scold him, let my bitter tongue rage against some petty thing. But we've always been close, loving each other, enjoying that loving.'

Elspeth didn't look up, hearing the words follow on from the whirr of the machine, the sound of another threaded needle dipping down to a turning spool, picking up a different thread, taking hold to make a stitch and another stitch, a quicker stitch, an easier stitch than the ones she is attempting.

'I want you to know that there is nothing to worry for on your wedding night; you can love him as he will love you.' Whatever else she'd ever say, Madge knew this was important. 'Women don't need to be shy, to hold back, we are made for the pleasure too.'

Elspeth gripped her needle, startled by what her mother was saying. The mechanics of sex Ma had imparted when her first period came. This was something else.

Madge, seeing that she had her daughter's attention, looked back to her own sewing, adjusting the position of the garment before turning the handle slowly to begin again the cogs turning cogs, thread meeting thread. 'It's what our bodies were made for, to be appreciated, stimulated to the greatest excitement and pleasure. That loving,' she accentuated the words, 'is special, a great bond. It's like a sort of glue that holds a marriage together.'

Elspeth stared at the fabric bunched in her lap, astonished as much by the words as the length of the speech. Madge usually delivered ultimatums. To be speaking openly of her and Pa as lovers like in the movies, was extraordinary and embarrassing.

'Don't be put off by all that women's talk of a wife being submissive in bed as well as in the home. You know what I mean?' Madge didn't stop for an answer. 'All the talk of how painful it can be the first time is exaggerated. Anyway,' she gave a little laugh, 'it'll be worth it.'

Elspeth saw, even though her mother was half turned away, her smile, the twinkle in her eye, as she eased the garment with one hand, guiding it slowly and precisely under the needle's point. A pride and warmth washed through her, something she'd never felt before. Ma was offering herself as a friend, hiding her hostility to the marriage, as if wanting to make the marriage a success.

Madge glanced sideways at Elspeth as if about to share a secret. 'Your father thought me quite a catch when we were first courting, and I felt the same about him. Me being older than him didn't matter, we fancied each other. He brought the groceries up to the big house and although I was no longer working in the kitchens by then, cook used to give him a cup of tea on a cold winter's day before he rode back on his bicycle. I just happened to walk in on them one day. It wasn't quite love at first sight as I was a bit toffy nosed in those days, couldn't be associating with tradesman.' Again she laughed at her silliness. 'But a good-looking man, like your Pa was, gets noticed, and he says he was smitten from that first day.' Madge teased out the gathers on the sleeve, smoothing the seam before cutting loose the thread from the garment. 'Though I didn't want to leave my work which is why we were engaged for such a long time.'

Elspeth sat transfixed by her mother's free flowing speech. Not only was Madge restyling her own precious dress, a gift from the staff at the big house on the occasion of her own wedding in 1913, it was as if she was talking to a friend. Elspeth admitted to herself for the first time that her mother who'd also been given the sewing machine, an expensive gift, by Mr and Mrs Briggs Fanshawe, her employers for sixteen years, was thought of as someone special.

'I don't want to leave my work, Ma,' Elspeth found herself saying, pleased with the opportunity to share her worry. 'I spoke to Mr George soon after we were engaged and he said that perhaps I could carry on, something could be arranged.'

Madge turned abruptly. 'Is that so? Well!' And the two women sat looking at each other as if meeting for the first time. The clock on the mantelpiece ticked loudly, and through the open back door the sound of a cart being driven by could be heard, the clip clop of the coal man's horse, a regular rhythm to seal them in. 'That's good, Elspeth. I'm pleased for you. It's a changing world.'

'Thanks, Ma.' And looking down at her own stitching she found herself again blinded by tears. 'I hope I'm doing this right.'

Elspeth and Kenneth were married on June 30th, 1939.

This is what she was remembering on her wedding night as Kenneth sat hunched and morose on their bed. He was fully dressed in the grey striped suit he'd worn for their marriage at the registry office. There'd been no need for a church service, he'd told her; there wasn't time with the fear of war hotting up. This prospect seemed to excite him more than being married to her.

'Are you all right?' she said feeling no desire to go near him. She was still wearing her going away outfit, a pink jacquard jacket, a gift from Maxine, with her own grey skirt and a new lace blouse with pearl buttons that Ma had somehow rustled up. Standing on the other side of their room in this London hotel, she could see herself in a long mirror. The spray of pink roses pinned to her lapel were beginning to droop. 'Would you like a drink of water, Kenny?'

Kenneth shook his head. 'Got a headache. Don't feel too good at all,' and he kicked off his shoes and loosened his tie.

'Can I do anything?'

He didn't respond but sat slumped forward as if studying the carpet.

It was a fine carpet, thick and cushioned to walk on. Three days at this expensive hotel was an exciting prospect, a dream really. She'd never been 'up to town' and never stayed in a place where you paid for the room. Never slept in any other room than her own small bedroom.

Kenneth got up unsteadily. 'I'll just go to the bathroom,' he said.

And this was a wonder too. Attached to this big room, a bedroom with windows down to the floor, was their own lavatory with bath and basin. Whatever else, he was providing her with unbelievable treats.

She sat on the bed to wait. The coverlet was shiny satin, a deep red. The quilted pattern of swirls and circles made the colour change from every angle under the chandelier light. She stroked its sleek silkiness before folding it back to see the sheets beneath. Crisp and soft, the whitest white. A perfect setting for the first night of marriage. But what ought she to do? Take off her dress or would he want to do that himself? Isn't that what she'd seen in the movies, the man kissing the girl as he slid his hands under her jumper before the camera faded discreetly to another scene?

She checked her watch, a tiny watch in a marcasite bracelet which had been given to her by Mr Simms, who she must now call George, he'd said. It was the prettiest thing which had been adjusted to fit her perfectly and she loved it. The time was 11.30 and there was no sign of her new bridegroom. Should she knock on the door? He'd been sullen all evening.

There was a telephone across the room, positioned on a table with notepaper and blotter. Could she phone someone? But who? The only person she knew with a phone was Kenneth's father. She got up and went to sit down at the desk. Perhaps if she wrote a note and slipped it under the door of the bathroom. But that was ridiculous, he'd come out any minute and she must be ready for him.

The fur cape that he'd given her and she'd worn to come up on the train, lay on another chair, curled as if in its original animal form. She stroked its fine fur which stirred with her breath, her pet as she sat alone on her wedding night.

Soon she would need to go to the lavatory herself. She tapped on the bathroom door, calling out, 'Are you all right?' There was no reply. She rapped harder until her knuckles hurt. There was no response. Could he have fallen asleep? 'Kenneth, please, I need to use the …' but she couldn't bring herself to say the word. 'Please, Kenny!'

'Go away …' was followed by the sound of retching.

She drew back. He was being sick. That must be why he'd been so grumpy all evening. But she mustn't be upset, not her, Mrs Kenneth Simms, married to a well-to-do man, with her dream come true. With this thought she wrapped the fur cape over her shoulders and slipped out of the room to a guest toilet along the corridor of soft silent carpet.

But coming back to their room she found the door not only closed but locked. It was a latch lock. She hadn't thought to take the key. Where was it anyway for Kenneth had opened the door when they'd arrived? She knocked on the door, called his name softly but of course he wouldn't hear as he hadn't heard her when inside the room. What could she do? She squashed a flicker of panic and walked back to the lift and on to the stairs. She'd go down and see if there was anyone at the reception, except what if Kenneth came out to find she'd gone? Waiting was the only answer so she sat on the floor, tucking her legs under her skirt, snuggling her head into the fluff of her cape. She was cross for he ought to be looking after her, his bride, making her feel as if she was floating on air, like her mother had said, *'We are made for the pleasure too.'*

Then again how amazing it had been to walk around London that evening, arm in arm, seeing the lights in Piccadilly Circus, Trafalgar Square, walking past famous theatres and shops where he'd kept telling her they would go next day to buy her new clothes. 'I want to treat you, Elsy, my pretty wife,' he'd said which was something wonderful to look forward to. She wished though that he wouldn't call her, Elsy, making her sound like a common maid. And calling him Kenny, 'Like my mother,' sounded silly.

She woke to a heavy hand on her shoulder. 'Chucked you out has he? Done your bit, eh, but not paid you?' The man was huge, a giant above her and his laugh was only half amused. 'I'll take you and pay good money, little miss redhead. You're just what I need tonight. Come on.'

'I beg your pardon,' she managed to say despite being struck with the horror of what he meant. 'I'm a married woman.' She held up her hand to show the ring on her finger, 'my husband fell asleep and …'

'That's what they all say, sweetheart,' and he leaned forward, his smile grotesque in the dim light.

Elspeth shrank back as the man took hold of her arm, pulling her to stand close beside him. He slipped his arms round her waist, saying, 'Whoa there, little lady!' He was even about to pick her up, but she wrenched free, fury giving strength to her cramped body.

'Don't you dare!' she spat the words. 'I'll report you for assault.' Surprised by this quick reaction he didn't try to stop her as she strode down the corridor without looking back. Terror, though, clutched her chest as he called after her. 'Take the lift, missy, if you're that keen to escape,' but she was already at the stairs where grabbing the banister and despite her tight skirt she flew down the two flights. The corsage jostled foolishly on her jacket, her fur cape cosseting her throat so that for a blink of a second she saw herself as the heroine in a film, tripping down this grand staircase to escape the villain.

The reception desk was empty. It was as grand and austere as when she and Kenneth had signed the register but she was not afraid to bang the bell calling out again and again, 'I need help.'

A receptionist finally appeared, looking her up and down as if she might be something that had just snuck in from the street. A rush of anger hit her, pulling every nerve in her body to a point where she was scared of no one. Precisely, imitating the way that Miss Bowker spoke when a client was expecting more than he deserved, Elspeth told the weaselly man that she had inadvertently left her key in the room, that the door had closed too quickly behind her, and demanded him to, 'Accompany me back to my room immediately for I fear you have a predatory man lurking in the corridors of your hotel. I'll be reporting the incident to your manager in the morning.' The fur cape fluffed up, as she stared the young man down.

Back in their room Elspeth was exultant that she, and she alone, had dealt with such a disastrous situation. Kenneth would be proud of her. There was no sign of him though and for a few blissful minutes she didn't care. *'I want you to be happy,'* Madge had said. And although this triumphant feeling wasn't what she was talking about, it was, in some ways, better than relying on the love of a man, the man who'd locked himself away and was probably asleep in the bath. Kicking off her shoes, she unpinned the flowers which badly wanted water, took off her jacket and cape and slid between the sheets. She closed her eyes. Mrs Elspeth Ann Simms. What did it matter if her skirt and blouse were creased the next day? Kenneth was going to buy her new clothes, that was the least he could do.

A marriage 1939

On waking in the morning Elspeth found the curtains were drawn back and could hear that he was having a bath. Pillows from the bed were now on the couch with his dressing gown and a blanket where he must have slept. Sitting up and bolstered by the pillows she waited for him. The sun streamed into the room, illuminating and harsh. She could feel her hair was nested in tangles and was about to get up to find her brush when he came out of the bathroom wearing a towel round his waist and another over his pale shoulders. Her husband having cleansed himself ready for their love making. 'Hi Kenny, are you all right now?' her cheeks blushing prettily. Could she say come here? 'This is a lovely comfy bed,' she tried, 'You shouldn't have slept on the sofa.' She turned back the coverlet and sheets on his side of the bed.

'Not my best night, ghastly in fact. Thought I was sickening for something.' He made a sad puppet face. 'You okay?'

'Well, no, something awful happened when you were shut in the bathroom.' Was this the time to tell him? It would spoil any chance of intimacy, wouldn't it? 'I was worried about you but …'

'So was I,' he sniggered not letting her finish. 'But I think I'm okay now.' He gathered up his clothes. 'Do you want a bath? There's plenty of hot water. Breakfast's served till ten. Plenty of time to make yourself pretty.' With his back to her he pulled on his pants under the towel. 'I'm going to chuck my glad rags on and then we can go out and have some fun.'

'Fun!' She snapped back at him. 'Do you want to know what happened to me last night? While you shut yourself in the bathroom? Something has to be done, that's if you care for my safety and honour.' It didn't matter that it sounded a bit pretentious as she ploughed on with the whole story, adding that her knuckles were sore from trying to attract his attention.

He stood and listened, though she could see he was impatient for her to finish.

'I was truly terrified.' She held out her hands to show her red knuckles.

'Poor little Elsy,' he said continuing to put on his clothes. 'But you're okay now, aren't you?'

But she wasn't prepared to be the fluffy pet, the wife whose prettiness made her a trophy.

'You need to complain to the manager,' she swung her legs to the ground. 'It was mortifying. Think what might have become of me?'

'Oh, Elsy, I'm sorry. What a bore I am!' ignoring her question. 'I'll make it up to you, I promise. We'll have a dashed good day, you'll see.'

'No! You have to complain to the manager, I was humiliated.' That she had to pursue this and that he hadn't wanted to ravish her last night, or even approach her lovingly this morning, furthered her feeling of humiliation.

'All right, if you insist,' all conciliation forgotten, annoyance apparent as he took up his two brushes to smooth his hair into place. Shrugging on his jacket he left her saying, 'Meet me in the breakfast room, and don't forget the key this time.'

Kenneth avoided the reception desk. To have done what Elspeth asked would make him look ridiculous for after all it'd been obvious they were bride and groom with Elspeth arriving in her jacket with corsage, the coy eye she'd turned on the young man who registered their arrival. He'd never be able to use the hotel again and it was a favourite; he'd stayed here a couple of times when coming up to see a show with Jack and the crowd.

It was Jack who'd tried to soothe his nerves when he'd mentioned his worries about the honeymoon. He'd made it jokey, man's talk. 'I don't want to shock her; I'm not sure if we'll make it together.' And Jack had said, 'Don't worry, old chap, your truncheon will rise to the occasion,' which had caused him then and there to have that marvellous engorged sensation, his penis rising huge with desire. Sitting at a table drinking their usual whiskies in the bar of The Dolphin, he'd been able to hide the bulge in his trousers with his hat. Though the horrible craving for someone to take him in hand, suck him out, wouldn't go away. That wasn't something he could do with her, didn't want to do with her. He gazed at Jack, dear handsome Jack.

Kenneth left the hotel to find a newsstand. He lit a cigarette, that first drag of tobacco calming his annoyance at Elspeth's demand and his concern for what was still to come. He did love his Elsy, she was the loveliest girl he'd ever met. Even Jack had called her a stunner. 'You'll be the envy of all the chaps in the mess,' he'd said.

She needed a decent wardrobe; that tiny case couldn't contain much more than a brush, comb and lipstick. He was buoyed up by the thought; he fancied himself as a having an eye for the latest fashion. He'd take her to Selfridges, go on a spending spree. Yes, and tonight he'd remember what Jack'd said.

'I think it's the drink, Kenny,' Elspeth said that evening as she helped him stagger up to their room where he'd immediately dashed into the bathroom and been sick. Again he'd consumed far too much alcohol but how could she stop him?

They'd had such a jolly day. He had bought her lots of lovely clothes and a big suitcase, to put them in. And there she was dressed in her new silk nightgown, her new Lily of the Valley perfume splashed behind her ears when he emerged from the bathroom, saying, 'I think I must be sickening for something, Elsy.' He climbed into bed and was asleep and snoring before she could even say 'goodnight'.

She was wide awake and heady with the fabulous show they'd been to in the West End, 'Me and My Girl'. It had seemed so appropriate and she tried to believe that perhaps their love making would happen later when they were more settled with one another.

Her father had given her his treasured copy of Jane Austen's 'Mansfield Park' as a wedding present. It had been a prize he'd won at school before he'd left at fourteen. 'You'll learn a lot about people from any of her novels,' Pa had said. 'It'll stand you in good stead.' Madge told her, 'You're a lucky girl, that book is his pride and joy.' It wasn't a gift that she'd mentioned to Kenneth, or to anyone else. She took out the copy from the bottom of her little suitcase. The gold tooling on the red leather cover was wearing away with time and use, and there was a kind of comfort in holding it in her hand. Opening it to the first page, she read of the good luck of a young woman in captivating a rich man who would bring her luxury and raise her rank in society. She laughed to herself; isn't that what she'd done?

On the third and final night of their honeymoon, Elspeth asked him not to drink so much. At first he'd protested, 'Alcohol is never a problem for me. I think it was the water they put in the whisky.' She hadn't laughed or argued, just said, 'I'm having such a lovely time, Kenny, I want you to feel like that too.' He'd been cajoled and finding a club again where jazz was being played he agreed and all his swagger disappeared as the beat and the snarling threads of tunes absorbed his being. Together they skipped back to the hotel like real honeymooners.

The room looked especially inviting, the covers turned back on the bed, the sidelights lit and low, casting pools of light on to the pillows. A lingering trace of Elspeth's new perfume hung on the air. It was a stage set like in the movies

He didn't try to undress her or suggest that she do the same to him. Decorously he put on his pyjamas and waited, not looking at her as she slipped into her nightdress. Focusing his mind on what Jack had said. '*It'll all come naturally, old boy,*' he put his arms around Elspeth and laid her on the bed, kissing her cheeks and neck. The silk of her gown was a delight to touch and he tried putting his hand on her breast. Was it embarrassment that held him back? She was making little sighing noises so perhaps this was all right. She stroked his back, lifting the pyjama jacket to find the flesh underneath. Flesh that was clammy, pocked by a rash of tiny moles. 'Oh Kenny!' she sighed. 'You do love me, don't you?' He lifted her gown and undid the ties on his trousers. Where was 'Jack's truncheon'? And even as that came into his mind, he felt himself rising, a stiffening in his cock, urgent. Not to lose the moment he pushed his hand between her legs, prodding with his fingers to find a hole, and then holding himself tight pushed as hard into her as he dared. She seemed to rear back, arching herself which didn't seem right. Swiftly he pulled out letting his spunk dribble down her thighs. As swiftly he rolled away from her.

Elspeth kept her eyes closed. This couldn't be what her mother had spoken of. She'd felt pain which was good, the marriage had been consummated, an important point in law, she knew. Would there be blood on her nightgown or sheets? The stickiness on her legs was unpleasant. 'Are you all right, Kenny?' she said.

'Yes, thanks, Elsy. I'm tired though.'

No words of love, or concern for her. She lay quietly wondering what else she could say. 'I think I ought to give myself a little wash.'

'Yes, I expect you're right.' And he gave an exaggerated yawn. 'It's good having our own bathroom, isn't it?'

'Yes,' that couldn't be denied. 'Will you be awake when I come back to bed?'

'Don't expect so, old thing. I'm all in.'

'Goodnight then,' and she leant over to kiss his forehead.

Mr Kenneth Everley Simms and Mrs Elspeth Ann Simms came back to live in the house in Glebe Avenue. The taxi bringing them from the station pulled up in the driveway of the house Elspeth had visited only twice before.

Kenneth had brought Elspeth to meet his father a fortnight after the engagement, a stiff occasion due to Kenneth's nervous and aggressive manner. Was he ashamed of his fiancée? She readily showed her pleasure in the garden, marvelling at the crocuses which grew purple and yellow swathes in the front lawn and on seeing the greenhouse asked George, 'Where your plant comes from?'

The second occasion had been a dinner when George surprised her with his gift. 'I know that you wish to come back and work in the firm after you're married, so I thought you ought to have your own time keeper.' The watch lay in a box lined with white satin. 'Ken isn't noted for his accuracy in maintaining the correct hours of work,' he joked, 'but I know you're a stickler for such things.' This compliment to his fiancée caused Kenneth to sulk for the rest of the evening. When they were alone he said, 'What have you been cooking up with my father? Working after we're married?'

'Only when you're away,' she hadn't thought he'd object. 'You said you'd be away quite a lot, didn't you?'

Kenneth immediately warned Elspeth as they walked through the front door into the hall of the house she would now be living in, 'This isn't going to be easy, here with my Dad, Elsy. It won't be for long though.' But she wasn't listening, the smell of Mansion polish a reminder of her old home, and then being offered tea and cake in the garden, she thought she might be very happy for quite a while. Ruby, who'd stayed behind to 'make sure the newlyweds are settled in,' lived up to her name; cheeks on fire with all the baking in preparation. 'It'll be nice for you to have the young persons living here for a bit, I was thinking, sir,' she'd said to George, who, in fact, was as nervous as his son.

Kenneth made this his excuse when Elspeth would try to coax him to be her lover that having his father in a bedroom further down the landing was the problem. The *'loving each other'* thing which her mother had referred to, she began to think was never going to happen. She tried to pretend that it didn't matter. After all her ambition for a 'good' marriage was fulfilled, and the job, to be admired for her work, was of equal value. And the house in Glebe Avenue was so elegant with countless rooms, and with Ruby in the kitchen providing all the meals and calling her 'Ma'am'. A beautiful garden too where she was free to stroll along the flower borders, play croquet on the lawn or sit with a book by the pond; it was all just lovely. Nothing needed to change.

The Home Front 1939

Elspeth worried about her first visit to Ma and Pa after the honeymoon. She didn't want to look as if she was showing off, with her new clothes and living where she was, when their two up, two down house had the privy out the back. For so long she'd wanted to be better than them but now it was their approval that was most important. Flaunting what she had wouldn't please either of them but who else was there to tell about what she'd seen, and done?

It was Saturday afternoon, Kenneth playing tennis with Jack and some other pals. And here she was walking down from the bus stop, the street seeming especially noisy and jolly, children playing out on the pavement, mothers sitting on their doorsteps, faces up to the sun. A sun which sparkled off the windows of the houses, beamed back an image of herself. She smoothed down the sateen skirt of her dress and knocked on the front door.

Ernest inched open the door but on seeing her flung it wide. 'Well, well, who's this fine lady? Come in, come in!' He took both of her hands. 'Oh, you look lovely, Elspeth! As you did on your wedding day. We were so proud.'

Elspeth leant forward to kiss him, to smell the fresh minty smell of toothpaste on his breath. Not stale tobacco. 'I like the book you gave me, Pa,' it was all she could think to say. 'I've finished it already.'

'That's good.'

They stood in the dim passageway, the light gone with the closing of the front door. The same polished fragrance as at Glebe Avenue encircled them.

'Your Ma's just gone out for some thread. She'll be so pleased to see you too.'

'Pa, I've not been gone as much as a fortnight!'

'Yes, but,' he looked at her straight on, no ducking from this, 'we did wonder whether you'd think we were a bit, well, dull to come back to.'

'Oh, don't say that!'

Ernest beamed as if to acknowledge her response. 'Ma'll be back any minute. But what are we standing here for?'

She followed on after him saying, 'I'd like to read more of Jane Austen's stories. It was such clever language, lots of words I didn't know, but you could get the sense of it.'

'Oh, yes! The library's full of them.'

Coming into the light streaming through the windows in the back parlour she warmed to the familiarity, the sewing machine up on the table, a pile of assorted clothes laid over the back of two of the chairs. 'Ma's busy, I see.'

'Yes, it's for Mrs Briggs Fanshawe.' Ernest cleared his throat as if to say something important. 'She's taken in some refugee children from Germany. A good woman, we've always known that. Ma's only too pleased to help out. Cutting down, making do. Poor little mites!'

'Really? That's good.' Elspeth paused. 'I don't think it was any of them we saw. But when we were on Waterloo station coming back, there was a line of children being taken off in a train. Got labels round their necks, I didn't like it.' She hadn't pointed them out to Kenneth and he hadn't said anything.

'They'd have been evacuees, sweetheart,' Ernest was saying, 'going to the safety of the countryside, out of London.' Elspeth's heart tugged, not for those children, but for him calling her 'sweetheart'. How special that sounded. Kenneth never used an endearing word, and calling her Elsy made it worse.

She said, 'Pa, I saw Buckingham Palace. There was the King's flag flying so he and the Queen must have been there. It was very exciting. And all sorts of other places too.'

'Well, that's good.' He moved towards the scullery. 'We could have a cup of tea while we're waiting, couldn't we?' he said.

'Yes, please. I want to know what you've been doing. I've all afternoon. Kenneth's busy.'

The sound of the water gushing into the kettle, the flair of the gas lit on the cooker, like back when she was living there, was reassuring. Tears pricked the back of her eyes. And then Pa was saying, 'Well, well this is like old times,' and he laughed, 'except it isn't. You'd never have been sitting all pretty like that. Up and off that was you, my girl.' He sat down beside her and she had to look back at him.

Madge came through the door at that moment, stopped on seeing Elspeth. 'Well, here she is.' And her face was a tonic too. A wide smile, her cheeks bunched up, pink and pretty. 'Well, well!'

'You're busy, Ma,' Elspeth could feel the flush on her own face, could feel another welling of tears. She bit down hard on her lip.

'Not too busy to stop for a chat with you.' Madge turned to Ernest. 'Well, is that kettle on or not?'

Pa bounced out of his chair as if on a spring but stopped to press a hand to Elspeth's shoulder, 'You're so welcome, sweetheart.'

'Yes, she is, love, but get a move on, and see if there's any of that fruit cake left I made for your meeting last night.'

Elspeth walked back down the road swinging her handbag. All that she'd seen and done in London had come tumbling out for they'd wanted to know it all. Although when she'd told how Kenneth loved to pick out clothes, was pleased to spend money, the look in Ma's eye she knew was questioning. Ma could see that it hadn't been quite the honeymoon she'd expected. 'He's a good husband, is he?' she'd said. To which Elspeth could only answer 'yes' though wanting to cry 'no'.

They too had so much to tell. 'There's terrible things going on in Germany,' Ma said, 'I was telling your Pa. Mrs Briggs Fanshawe's husband has a friend who was working out there before even Hitler started trying to take over other countries. It was going on then. Treating the Jewish people badly. That's why some of their children are coming over here. Their parents must be worried for their lives.' Ma had paused, and Elspeth could see how upset she was, an anger rising in her voice. 'She's opened her home to many of them. I always knew what a good woman she is. Proud to work for her I was, still am.' Madge picked up one of the garments, held it up as if to assess what she could do with it. 'Don't you ever let anyone say anything bad about the Jews. They've every right to live anywhere, believe what they want to believe.' Her hands were shaking and it was as if she was accusing Elspeth and Ernest.

Pa had said, 'Those disgusting Blackshirts promoting fascism when they should be supporting those that have escaped from Germany. But people listen to them, they're so fearful of the future they'll take on any stupid idea.'

Elspeth didn't know what to say. Hadn't Jack made some derogatory remark about men with hooked noses and too much money? Jews. Could she ask Kenneth what he thought about what her mother had said? 'If I can help, Ma. I'd like to do that.'

Madge had put a hand across to take hers, a gentle squeeze. 'There's going to be lots for all of us to do very soon.'

It had been strange leaving them after their spirited talk and interest in her, the pavement tripping along beneath her feet.

But by the time she reached Glebe Avenue her elation had dwindled. Did she really feel married? The sun was beginning to set, colours dimming to grey, loneliness creeping in with the dark.

Kenneth greeted her when she arrived back with, 'I have to go and meet Jack. He's in a tizz about joining up. Needs my support.'

'Jack? That doesn't sound like him.' She made it sound lighthearted, after all she'd known him for sometime, was part of their circle, wasn't she?

'Well, you're wrong, he wants my advice.'

'Shall I come too? It won't take me a jiffy to freshen up.'

'No,' he snapped, gathering up his keys from the hall table and swinging open the front door, 'Dad's home. He'll be pleased to have your company,' and blowing her a kiss as if to mollify her, he stepped out and closed the door in her face saying, 'Don't wait up. I'll sleep in the spare room so's not to disturb you.'

'He's gone out, hasn't he, Ma'am?' Ruby sang out from the kitchen.

'Didn't he tell you?' Elspeth hadn't worked out who should tell Ruby what with regard to menus or those wanting to eat. 'I'm sorry, I didn't know myself.'

'Not your mistake, Ma'am. He's a law until himself, that one.' The woman giggled. 'Sorry, Ma'am, shouldn't have said that. But I've known him since he was a babe. Looked after him all my working life, you see.'

How old was Ruby? Her plump, smooth skin belied how many years that might be.

'Thank you, Ruby. What time is Mr George expecting dinner?

'7 o'clock, if that's all right with you, Ma'am.'

'Of course. And I am hungry. I only had a piece of cake for my lunch.'

'That's not good enough, Ma'am. Can't have you wasting away. You're little enough as it is, if you don't mind my saying.'

'You're very kind, Ruby.'

Elspeth looked around at the bright yellow paintwork, the cupboards which stretched up from floor to ceiling, darkness clinging in corners where the light from the two pendant bulbs couldn't reach. Perhaps she'd ask Ruby how she ought to help, if that was appropriate. Of course, once she started back at work there wouldn't be time or need for her to know about cooking or cleaning. But she must find out how best to behave.

This was the first time she would eat alone with George - to call him by this name still felt uncomfortable. Meals with the three of them had been very awkward; Kenneth either sullen and monosyllabic or overbearing when he'd had too much to drink, which was usual. His boastful talk of what he was doing with the Observer Corps, his opinion on the state of the country was loud and embarrassing. 'You know, that chap, Winston Churchill? He's been warning about the Nazis, pressing for rearmament for ages. Jack and I were only talking about …' and he'd press on into a long lecture, and it was a lecture. Elspeth wanted to but couldn't intervene. She'd been pleased when George finally challenged Kenneth's statement that the general public would be too frightened or too stupid to use gas masks effectively.

'You have a very poor opinion of your fellow citizens, Ken. The response to setting up the Air Raid Wardens has been phenomenal.' He'd ignored Kenneth's rude response, 'Professionals are what we need, not any old Tom, Dick and Harry,' changing the subject to a topic which might interest Elspeth.

That evening after being with her parents she'd rather dwell on what they'd been telling her. Also she needed to muster the courage to ask George when and how she could return to her job.

The French windows were wide open letting the scent of the freshly mown grass filter through, allowing the garden to be part of the house. The table was covered in a thick white cloth, a pattern swirling in the sheen of the material, seeming to throw extra light up against the dark wood of the sideboard. Silver candlesticks held no candles but shone with their own bright polish. George sat at one end, Elspeth's place was to his right. She unwrapped her napkin and took a sip of water. Sitting here beside George on her own was nerve wracking. How was she going to eat and talk? And to ask him about coming back to work seemed an impossibility.

George could see her hesitancy, understood that it was up to him to make her feel at home in this odd situation. He said, 'How are your parents? I believe you went to see them today?' And he could hear relief in her quick response of, 'Very well, thank you,' her hands relaxing their grip on her knife and fork. Pleased with himself he continued, 'Tell me about your mother. I met her so briefly at your wedding; spoke mostly to your father, I'm afraid.'

Elspeth was thrilled; it was as if he'd read her mind, knew that this is what she wanted to talk about. She was easily able to tell him what Ma was doing, what she and Pa had told her, why they were angry. Finally she asked, 'Do you know anything more about what's going on in Germany with the Jews?'

George watched her with growing interest; her animation, her confidence to explain, and then this final question. Very different to the girl who'd sat silent and almost dejected when Ken was home. Her eyes, the amber brown of a newborn conker, sparkled with determination to say what she'd wanted to say.

He shook his head. 'No, only the rumours of atrocities. I'm afraid there's a lot of antisemitism in this country too. What your father says about Oswald Moseley's Blackshirts is spot on. Nasty crowd, they need to be opposed.' Then he put a hand across to hers, the one that still held her fork to say, 'I think I must give you a chance to eat though. Ruby won't appreciate a half full plate,' withdrawing it again quickly, but smiling to reassure her that he was joking.

Elspeth was overcome with his thoughtfulness, though to eat with his attention now on her plate would be even more of a struggle.

But he was already saying, 'Ruby's a treasure. Do you know that she's been with us since she was fifteen? Came as a scullery maid to help the cook.' He didn't tell her about Marjorie's attitude to her leaving to be with a husband, therefore not living in. There'd been a point when Ruby might have given her notice. Marjorie's intransigence causing George another period of grief. 'The woman's thirty, Marjorie,' he'd said, 'and with the shortage of men of eligible age after the war she's fortunate to have found a good man. You can't deprive her of that, the comfort of going home to the man she loves.' Marjorie had huffed and flounced and he'd gritted his teeth not to add, 'Isn't that what you ought to appreciate?' In the end it was the thought of having to train another woman to her exacting ways that caused Marjorie to concede.

'She's the mainstay of the household. Gentle and loyal, neither fussy nor slapdash.'

'Where does she live?' Elspeth was pleased to be able to ask.

'Out past the gas works. A good bicycle ride, but she comes whatever the weather. A treasure is our Ruby.'

Elspeth heard the 'our', as if she was now included, part of the household. She was emboldened. 'Can I ask you about me coming back to the office?'

A gardener 1940

It was on Tuesday the 2nd of July 1940 that the news came of a ship carrying German prisoners of war and Italian and German internees to Canada being sunk by a German U boat with the loss of 865 lives. George didn't mentioned it to Elspeth; it was Ernest who informed her, and Madge.

'There's an outcry already. There's a lot thought that locking up people for no reason except they're German or some such when it all started, even though they've been living and working here for years, was wrong. Old man Fischer, you know the optician on the corner of the high street? They took him as soon as war started, even though he's been in business here for decades. Wrong, all wrong!'

Madge was quick to add, 'And the German Jews who've come here for fear of what's happening in their own country, come here to escape persecution and what do we do?' She wielded the bread knife as if to bring in an imaginary orchestra or chop off someone's head, 'Brand them as aliens and lock them up!'

Elspeth sat with a bowl of water scrubbing new potatoes. 'How can I help, Ma? Perhaps you could teach me to knit?'

Ernest was right; a majority of people were outraged by the tragedy of that ship. Their opinion prevailed and camps were closed down with a limited number of internees being released.

Gustave Schmidt was one of those. At the end of August 1940, after eight months' internment, four weeks after the Smiths' furious condemnation, he was released and desperate to be reunited with his wife and two year old child, Ivan. As a German national he was no longer allowed to work as a journalist, although he'd written articles for several publications when he'd arrived in London in 1938. He'd had no choice but to flee his own country having publicly condemned the actions of the

German Reich after Kristallnacht. Apart from these expressed views, his ancestry, a Russian mother with Jewish antecedents, meant that his life was in danger.

At the time he fled to England, his Dutch wife, Mareke, who was pregnant, left Germany to stay with her parents in Holland hoping to join him when he'd found somewhere for them to live. The fear of Germany's advance into the Low Countries, though, meant that she, too, had to escape to England with their baby son, Ivan, in April 1940 where she found that Gustave was in prison.

Mareke's increasingly desperate letters were waiting for him when he picked up his belongings from the bedsit he'd occupied before his arrest. The room had been relet, but at last he learned that English friends had smuggled her to England and found her a position in a school in the South of England. The relief of knowing where she was, that he could contact her, was enormous, but he urgently needed to find work and a place to live.

None of this was known to George and Elspeth as they sat down to supper one Friday at the beginning of September; plaice with parsley sauce, new potatoes from the garden and runner beans followed by a large pink blancmange. Kenneth was in Stanmore, no longer a volunteer, but employed full-time; Observer Lieutenant Commander Kenneth Simms.

Ernest was gratified to find that his new son-in-law was taking a major part in defending the country. 'The RAF can't do it on their own,' he'd said. 'It's magnificent what our brave lads are achieving against the Luftwaffe but it's the Observer Corps that's just as important in keeping Britain safe. You've got a good man there, Elspeth,' he frequently told her. 'You must be proud of him.' She said nothing.

George never spoke of him to Elspeth, worried that the absence of her husband must cause her grief. Their talk was always of more immediate matters. An air raid shelter was built in the back garden, a cellar under the office in town made ready, blackout blinds hung. Ration books arrived and were handed over to Ruby, reassuring her that she had their trust in the difficult task of managing restricted food supplies. Gas masks were more of a problem; Ruby refused. 'I'm never wearing one of those things. I'd rather take what the Boche is dropping than put one of those over my face.' More cheerfully the garden was discussed; what was growing and what he intended to grow to help the war effort.

George filled Elspeth's glass with water. 'My father shared my love of gardens. He'd made his way up in the world, as they say. A clerk who trained in his spare time, rose to set up his own firm. To make a garden even on his small patch was the zenith of his achievement. I learnt about plants from him, the pleasure of taking a seed to growth, a cutting planted and coming into life. Nothing better!' He scraped up the last food on his plate. 'But I'm worried about how I'm going to keep it going.'

They might have been an old married couple for the ease with which this domesticity was now being shared.

'But you haven't time and we know that Mr Pearson …' she didn't finish her sentence.

'Yes, it's too much for him now that I've taken on one of the allotments.' The allotments which were conveniently at the bottom of the garden on land which filled the gap between the houses on the next parallel road, released for this purpose in 1938. 'He needs to retire, take a rest. And …'

'You haven't got time,' she finished for him. 'Could you get a new gardener?'

'It'll be difficult. Most men signed up.'

'And he won't want to give up, will he?'

'That's the worst of it.'

News of the first bombs falling on London and in the city only fifteen miles away couldn't dent Elspeth's happiness. Work in the office was constantly satisfying; she insisted on riding a bicycle to work, travelling separately from

George to maintain their different positions in the office. He was more frequently on duty with the ARP in the evenings, but she could read books borrowed from the library. Occasionally she heard him playing the piano which stood in the drawing room, sleek and grand, music which she'd never known before. He told her that he liked an audience as, 'it makes me try harder not to lose the skill I was fortunate enough to learn.' And as if to excuse himself. 'Music for me is like gardening, relaxation, a solace.' For her it was joy too.

Kenneth's infrequent appearances on weekend leave were an irritant rather than a pleasure. He was always tired, prattling on about the possibility that he might be chosen to go to sea, unable to settle. He forgot their first wedding anniversary saying when reminded, 'How can I be expected to remember! Dash it, there's a war on, my mates out fighting for our country, Jack, God knows where. You sitting here in the lap of luxury, when I'm …' but she didn't listen to him any more. A thread of steel wound its way through her.

Despite this, Elspeth often felt guilty for her privileged position. She listened patiently to Ernest's regular updates, learning of people in other places, other countries who were suffering horribly. The first air raid warning was almost a relief, going into the shelter until the All Clear.

Elspeth visited her parents most Sundays often bringing produce from Glebe Avenue garden. It was the end of September and the last of the runner beans. 'Where will you go if there's an air raid, Pa?' she asked.

Ernest brushed her remark aside. 'You don't need to worry about us, sweetheart.'

'No, but we should.' Madge shook her head at him, saying to Elspeth, 'He's been swept up in all the regulations, so fixed on his duty to the neighbours, and dog-tired most of the time.'

Her mother looked tired too. A big boned woman who'd previously carried her weight and height proudly, seemed to have shrunk.

'Eking out our rations isn't easy, and a lot more things'll be short soon,' Ernest pronounced, annoying both Elspeth and Madge with another dire prophecy.

Madge reassured Elspeth, 'Thanks for thinking of us, love. I didn't trouble about that last warning, but we've been told to use the crypt under the church whenever. I'll do that, I promise.'

The parlour was cosy with the smell of potatoes roasting in the oven, Madge singing scraps of songs to accompany Forces Favourites playing on the wireless and the click of Elspeth's knitting needles. It was difficult to see what the garment would become but this new skill her mother had taught her, was calming. 'Doing her bit' with a pullover for one of the children billeted with Mrs Briggs Fanshawe made her proud. Like Madge who helped in the new British Restaurant, the BR.

'Ruby says we're going to have a real glut of veg,' Elspeth said wanting to change the subject. 'But what's going to happen with all the work there is to do on the allotment is the worry. Mr Pearson's not up to it any more. Eighty, he is, but won't admit he's too old.'

'Never too old when you take pleasure in what you're doing,' Madge put in.

'Yes, Ma, but what if we found him dead down the garden; that's what Ruby's worried about.'

'I wish I could help,' Ernest sighed.

'And when, may I ask, would you have time, Ernest Smith?' Ma laid a hand on his shoulder and kissed the top of his head. 'He's all heart, your father, and it sounds like Mr Simms is too.'

Elspeth looked down at the thin linen cloth with drawn thread work round the edges covering the table. Hours of dedicated work had gone into making it, the tiny embroidered openings like a miniature train track, some worn away with all the years of use. But it was still precious, like they were to each other. Trying to keep her voice steady she said, 'Ruby says, "Mr George'll be growing Brussel sprouts in his best flower beds next!"

Gustave Schmidt 1940

Gustave Schmidt watched the woman scoop a portion of meat pie on to another man's plate. A big woman who exuded an authority which the others, spooning potatoes or carrots, didn't possess. She wore a bright red floral scarf to cover her hair which accentuated the heat in her cheeks. She looked practical, no nonsense. The line moved on and he was in front of her. She smiled at him briefly, passing him a plate with his portion and then looked to the next in the queue.

'Excuse me, I was wondering if you …'

Her smile disappeared. 'There's no choice, mister.'

'No, no, this is good,' and he could hear his abrupt German accent. 'I'm sorry I …'

She carried on spooning onto other plates, men and women overtaking him. 'Come and see me when we've finished serving. Half an hour,' she said

Why Madge recognised a genuine need she couldn't say. 'He'd a sort of air about him.' She later reported to Ernest. 'There are enough come in with a sorry tale, all true no doubt but you can't give them all the time of day.'

Gustave found a place at one of the trestle tables, the one occupied by men. Most of the other tables were occupied by women and children. Men alone were often marked out as skivers or aliens in some way. You could see the look passed on; why not at war or work?

A British Restaurant had sounded grand, but this was a parish hall as it said on the noticeboard outside. The small paned windows with blackout curtains pulled back were steamed up, but a stage at one end with golden drapes and an upright piano, showed that it was sometimes a place for entertainment; he yearned for the homeliness that the building exuded. He dug his fork into the food; whatever it was it smelt good.

It was longer than half an hour before she was ready, standing beside him, a coat and apron over her arm. 'What is it you wanted to ask?'

'I've come to look for my wife but I need work and somewhere to live.'

That was too much to say all at once but it was the truth.

Madge sniffed. 'Who are you?'

'I am Gustave Schmidt.' He bowed his head but looked up again quickly to engage her eyes. 'I came from Germany two years ago. I had to leave. My wife and child came from Holland this year, but I was not here to greet them.'

'Where are they?'

'Thirty miles from here, in the countryside. It is a school. She has found work there safely with my son. People have been very kind.'

'What is it you think that I can do?'

He showed her his papers. 'I do not want favours but I need to earn money.'

'Why ask me?' she said.

He shook his head, 'If I say you looked to be in charge and,' he clasped his cap, hoisted his bag further onto his shoulder, 'and a little like my mother, you will want me to leave. But I fear that is so.' He studied the scuffed floorboards, as used as the shoes he wore.

She followed his gaze, looking him up and down, a big dishevelled man. 'You're name again, Schmidt?'

'Yes,' he said.

'And you didn't know mine?'

'No.' What did she mean?

She turned away from him to survey the rest of the hall, all the diners gone, the helpers busy folding the tables, stacking the chairs.

'Okay,' she said. 'Come with me.'

Ernest said, 'You've shut him in the front room?'

'I thought it best while I pondered. And it gave me time to talk to you. I mean I don't want us to be seen as harbouring the enemy.'

'Madge, I can't believe you said, or even thought it.'

'Hang on! I pick up a strange man and bring him back to our own home and I'm not allowed a few niggles about what we should do?' Rissoles were spluttering in a pan on the stove. She flipped one over to cosy it back amongst the others.

Ernest took off his tie and undid the collar of his shirt, easing out his neck tortoise like. 'You're right, love.' He sat down to unlace his shoes. This wasn't what he wanted to come home to; not being on duty he'd planned an easy evening of sitting by the wireless, ITMA and Glen Miller maybe. 'What's he after?'

'It's a sorry tale.' which she told while finishing cooking tea.

'You were thinking of Mr Simms needing a gardener? Is that it?'

'Well, what do you think?'

'It's worth a try. But a place to live. I don't know about that.'

'But there's his wife and child to contact: without an address there's nowhere for her to write back.'

Gustave sat on. The room was cold, a cool otherworldly air hung around the cream walls, the faded pink and green floral fabric on two armchairs, a carpet worn by many years of many feet. He felt too large, even his own breathing was too loud. Dare he sit as she'd invited him to? A glass cabinet displaying two figurines, a shepherd and shepherdess and a bowl with images of a blue landscape reminded him of his parents-in-law in Holland. Precious items unused and rarely looked upon. The tea set on the shelf below would have been a wedding present, never taken out to fill and sip from, but greatly prized. It felt like a lost place and he forgotten. The woman had been understanding but what would her husband think?

'Good evening,' Ernest entered the room quietly causing Gustave to jump up, clutching his cap; submissive, fearful.

'Good evening,' he gave a small bow. 'I am sorry to have troubled your wife but ...'

'No, no,' Ernest grabbed his hand, shook it vigorously. This giant of a man towered over him. For a brief moment he wondered at the size of this race which the British Tommy, short and weedy, was trying to defeat. 'My wife has told me all about your troubles. I'm sorry that you've been treated so badly.'

Gustave blinked back tears, tried to smile, this warm greeting was overwhelming.

Ernest though was already saying, 'You're most welcome to have tea with us. My wife's the best of cooks but what with rationing ...' he didn't finish but indicated that Gustave should go first and lead the way back to the parlour.

Gustave wanted to say, 'Angels of mercy,' but he could tell that practicalities wouldn't allow for such extravagant expressions.

Later in bed, Ernest said, 'This is the right thing to do, Madge, I'm sure of that. But we can't have him for long. I was wondering ...'

But Madge interrupted, 'Will you ask Mr Simms?'

Ernest visited George in his office late the next evening knowing that he'd be there ready for a meeting of new recruits to the ARP; and it would be after Elspeth had left work. Madge had thought it might be awkward for her to be a go-between. 'I know she gets on well with her father-in-law but best not to trouble her.'

Elspeth, therefore, knew none of this as she looked from her bedroom window the following evening to see two figures standing beside the pond, their backs to her, appearing as dark intruders. Late September, dusk was beginning to shadow the whole garden as these men walked further on down to the gate at the bottom and into the allotments. A chill crept over her skin which was odd as it was a balmy night. Who could they be? The threatened invasion? She was half dressed having come up to change out of her work clothes before dinner. She pulled on a dressing gown and crept down to the kitchen. 'Ruby, where's Mr George?'

Ruby turned from stirring gravy on the stove, the circling of the spoon in the pan both comforting and sinister. 'I don't know, Ma'am. He came by earlier to say he needed another twenty minutes. That was quite some time ago'

Elspeth went out to stand on the veranda. The figures were walking back up the garden. Should she call out? As if to answer her, a streak of light from the setting sun spotlit George's half turned face. She drew back, her immediate fears allayed but who was he with? He'd said nothing of a guest for dinner. Unnerved by the encounter, feeling an outsider herself, she cautiously closed the French doors and went back to Ruby.

'Could I have something in my room, Ruby. I'm fearfully tired tonight.' And without waiting for a reply, she ran up the stairs to her room to see from the window George approaching the house deep in an animated conversation with the man beside him. Why hadn't she gone to say 'hello'? How stupid, what childish behaviour! She sat on her bed wishing she could go back downstairs.

George cut a hydrangea head on his way back into the house. Ruby would find him a small vase or glass to put it in. He was pleased to be employing Gustave; morally it was right, practically it was a godsend. Elspeth would surely agree. There'd be time to tell her even though supper would have to be rushed as he was on duty later. But as he went through to the kitchen with his floral offering he met Ruby crossing the hall with a tray carrying a plate of food and glass of water.

'Who's that for, Ruby?' he asked though, of course; it could only be for Elspeth. Something shrank inside him, elation dissolving unreasonably into a sense of loss.

Ruby's foot was on the first step of the stairs. 'Mrs Kenneth said she was very tired, sir.'

He forgot the hydrangea flower, left it on the hall table. He was not hungry, and going out on duty lacked the purpose he usually experienced.

It was midnight when he returned, found the forlorn flower, recut its stem before putting it into a vase. Taking a glass of water for himself he went up to bed but on the landing was surprised to see light showing under Elspeth's bedroom door. Had she fallen asleep with the lamp on, or was she still awake? He'd observed in the past that her room was in darkness by 10.30.

It was ridiculous to worry. She was a grown woman however physically fragile she appeared. On the other hand did she know how to get in touch with a doctor if she was poorly? She wouldn't have been able to contact her parents as they didn't have a telephone. And Ruby would have left by 7.30.

He tapped and spoke quietly, 'Elspeth, are you all right?'

There was no response but while he hovered, wondering whether to speak again, she opened the door. She was wearing a silky garment wrapped closely around her body, the sash tied tightly. Her hair was loose, a cascade of burnished copper, but she did look pale.

George drew back, 'I'm sorry if I disturbed you, it was just that I was concerned as you didn't come down for supper and then seeing that you hadn't perhaps been able to settle I ...' What a fool he was! What had it got to do with him? And he was about to retreat, when she smiled.

'You're very kind to worry but I'm fine really. I just felt in a bit of a muddle, my thoughts all jumbled up.' She looked down at her bare feet and despite himself he followed her gaze. 'It was stupid really.'

'No, no,' he said putting his hand out to take hers but then withdrawing as quickly. 'These are terrible times and trying to pretend they're not, takes its toll.'

'Thank you,' she saw his gesture and was immensely relieved at his words. 'I feel better now.'

'Good,' and he looked directly into her eyes. 'That's all right then. So I'll say goodnight.' And he turned to go but stopped. 'I'd wanted to share with you what occurred today. A man came to ask for work as a gardener and he appears to be highly suitable.'

'Oh?' the word was abrupt but at the same time she felt a long sigh ease out of her. 'That's good.'

'Yes, I'll tell you more in the morning. If you're well enough.'

'Oh, yes, I will be,' and it must have been a trick of the light for her cheeks regained their pink blush.

George drove Gustave out to the address Mareke had given. 'She has a room in the school in return for cleaning.'

The Downs rolled out around them, golden and green. Dark woods clustered in valleys or topped hills as gentle and unassuming as the sheep which grazed blissfully in unfenced fields, as in others stubble boasted stooks of straw.

'This is not possible,' Gustave said. 'This beautiful country. This beautiful day.'

George looked across to see the man wipe tears from his cheeks.

'If she is there, if she has our boy and I can see them both, I will be the happiest man alive.'

She was; a plump woman with short dark hair carrying a small child, who stared unflinching as his parents embraced. If I was a sculptor, George thought, this is what I would carve as it is for this that we fight, lay down our lives to protect. Human beings bound by love. He looked up at the Victorian turrets, the small mullioned windows, the pretence of a castle. If only he'd asked Elspeth to come with them, for her to see this reunion. He knew she'd felt excluded from the arrangements as well as her parents' attempts to find Gustave somewhere to live. It might explain her frosty approach when he'd come to work in the garden for the first time last week.

George waited on a bench while the couple walked around the gardens, Gustave carrying the child on his shoulders. He watched boys and girls coming back from the local church in two separate crocodiles. A sombre troupe, apparently not allowed to speak. It was a mournful scene.

Gustave returned to find George as if turned to stone, staring intently at nothing in particular. He was even more desperate to be reunited permanently with Mareke and his son. 'Ivan is named for my Russian great grandfather who I did not know. My grandmother spoke of him as if he was the Tsar himself.'

George smiled but an aching sensation weighed heavy on his shoulders which he couldn't shift.

Gustave said, 'It is most gratifying that my wife is able to keep Ivan with her while she works, with good lodgings too. But I need to be able to look after them myself.' The pride in his voice swelled as he spoke.

'I'm sure the time will come soon.' George glanced at his passenger. 'It's not easy to remain optimistic, I know, but it's the only way we'll survive.

To Elspeth George later said, 'How can I expect a man of his intellect to be taking my shilling for such menial work. He speaks three languages, talks of Shakespeare and Goethe as if family and is distraught that his country, which produced the musical genius of Bach, Beethoven, Mozart, Handel, and so many more, could succumb to the vile monster that is Hitler and his Nazi party.'

Elspeth shook her head, bewildered. Bewildered as much by the proposition as by the men of which he spoke. She knew of Shakespeare and Beethoven, even Mozart, but of the others she was ignorant. Should she say? To be less educated than the new gardener was an uncomfortable feeling. Would George want to talk to this man more than to her?

But George said, 'I wish you'd been there with me. I know you'd have felt the sorrow and joy as I did.'

'Yes,' she said. 'I'd have liked that. But you must teach me about those other composers, and that man, Gerter?'

George and Elspeth 1942

The phoney war was over. The Observer Corps having been key in winning the so-called Battle of Britain, had been given the title of Royal by the King in April 1941. No one could deny the essential work Kenneth has been doing, or criticise the fact that he rarely came home.

Heat lay like a blanket, the earth dusty beneath his feet as George staggered back from one of the butts by the greenhouse with a couple of cans to water the allotment plot. His shirt stuck to his back but it had to be done. Gustave couldn't do it during the day as the water would evaporate before getting to the roots. And it was relaxing to get out there, to breathe in the smell of the soil, the strange scents given off as dusk drew down.

Four trips, back and forth, were barely enough but it was all he could do. His shoulders ached, Ruby would be wanting to serve dinner and there was that army chap to entertain. No choice, it was the same for everyone; service personnel being billeted on those with a spare room. Ruby was the one who could complain but never did. She was living at Glebe Road while her husband, Ralph, was, 'I don't know where'.

They were chaperones, Ruby and the major. This thought had only recently come to mind with Ken never home, rarely in contact with Elspeth. But he couldn't criticise; the boy was brought up in a house where his parents had given a poor demonstration of compatibility, no affection outwardly expressed. No example to follow.

He set down the cans, stretched his back to look up at the cloudless sky, a sky free for a lone black bird to make a solitary flight.

Elspeth never complained either. 'I'm very lucky to live in such a beautiful house,' she often said. Sadly, though, over the last month or so she'd appeared more aloof.

Which was why the idea of an outing filled him with excitement.

He'd told her about the concerts suggested to Kenneth Clarke by Miss Myra Hess, the famous pianist, back in 1939; lunchtime concerts to raise the public's morale. He'd been delighted when Elspeth had asked, 'The National Gallery, what's that?' And he'd been able to ramble on about our heritage art collection, its importance, and how it was being squirrelled away to some secret locations for protection. Perhaps he'd been somewhat pedantic, but she'd immediately asked more questions as if she was truly interested. He'd been delighted that the girl who'd become vital in the office, possessed an inquiring mind.

How long was it since he'd heard live music, had been able to watch the skill of a musician, experience the pure sound? And it was such a coincidence that Myra Hess was herself to play Beethoven's Moonlight Sonata on August 3rd, a Bank Holiday, therefore he wouldn't need to account for their absence from the office. It was Fate's kind gift!

A trip up to London together, it filled him with joy.

Twenty minutes before there'd been several men and women making a last check on their crops before nightfall. One or two he was beginning to know by name, a community building up. This place, once an open field, occasionally homing horses, accommodated sixty different plots. Sharing progress and advice was gratifying, all absolutely necessary, no longer merely a hobby. And gardening was always a solace.

Wasn't that what he'd said to Elspeth soon after she came to live with him? Not with him, that's wrong, she's here as his son's wife. That she's such a delightful young woman, whose company he enjoys is neither here nor there, and he can admit to loving her. Everything about her is to love. Her rigour and tact; clients respecting her. She never appeared aware of her allure and he'd tried to keep any inappropriate thoughts at bay, scrupulous in resisting the urge to touch or offer any physical form of affection.

Heat rose to his cheeks, suffused the whole of his body. He took off his glasses, found a handkerchief to wipe away the sweat. He must remember his age.

He looked up at the sky, a disappearing blue with pink and orange strands vying for supremacy. There might not be a war for even the skies over London were clear again, Hitler having switched his attention to the Russian front. But that vile brutalities are being wrought everywhere else couldn't be forgotten. The world gone mad, again. He'd told her about being in the Army in the First World War. As a staff officer at the War Office - poor eyesight like his son - he'd been protected from the immediate danger and horror. Felt guilty because of it, he'd said. But he'd experienced enough, knew enough, in that war to be convinced that many men are fools, a few the devil, and that there was no God. It had been a winter evening back in '41 when news of the fall of Singapore had just been announced. He remembered saying to her, 'It seems wrong to be sitting here, relatively safe, a record playing exquisite music on the gramophone, a German composer to boot.'

'Except it's the Japanese in Singapore,' she'd corrected. 'Beethoven couldn't have wanted war, could he?'

His heart had swelled with pride, finding comfort in having a companion with whom to share intelligent ideas. He'd agreed with alacrity, told her that the composer had originally supported Napoleon, once our arch opponent too, but had become his most virulent critic. He'd also been able to tell her of his brother who was killed on the Somme, the grief of his parents who'd died soon after. He'd said, 'Do you think that people can die of a broken heart?'

To ask her such a question hadn't seemed foolish at the time. Wasn't it the release of emotions drawn out by the music, Beethoven's Moonlight Sonata? The very music to be played at the National Gallery, on the day he'd chosen.

He set the watering cans down beside the greenhouse. Images assailed him; her small bare feet, or a stray strand of hair loosed from her bun accentuating the curve of her neck, the sheen of her skin against the lustre of a pearl necklace. This was the problem, all these tiny fragments had been squirrelling away into his heart, just as those precious pictures were being rescued from possible destruction. What madness! His brain playing tricks. The ancient Egyptians believed that the heart controlled all thoughts, feelings and actions, that its weight on death would be assessed by the gods in order to grant a person's right of passage into the afterlife. What would they make of him?

Was it improper to ask her? Would such an action be misconstrued? By whom he wasn't sure.

Leaving the vents of the greenhouse open, he walked back towards the house. He has thought about this for long enough. A straightforward question for a simple proposal to ease the tension of day to day life. And here she was coming towards him, a shaft of sun spiralling low across the garden to gloss her red gold hair. She's wearing a cardigan around her shoulders, pink with pearl buttons. Ken bought it for her on their honeymoon; she'd told him that. He wished he'd managed to change out of his sweaty clothes before meeting her.

'Ruby asked me to tell you that dinner will be in half an hour, if that's all right?' She wasn't looking at him, as if embarrassed by his dishevelled state.

'Thank you. I'll go and change quickly.'

He could see her attention was drawn to the fiery sky beyond the garden. 'Elspeth,' he hoped she wouldn't notice the catch in his voice. 'I've had an idea. Myra Hess, you remember, the concerts at the National Gallery? I thought we could go up to London to hear her. The Moonlight Sonata. We wouldn't be away for long. Would you like to go?'

Elspeth stood in front of the mirror as if struck by a spell. A long oval mirror set in shiny dark wood. He'd told her which kind of wood, told her why different woods were used for different purposes, achieved different finishes.

The mirror was held by hinges so could be angled in whatever way she wished, tall enough for a full length view of herself, part of a dressing table with drawers on either side. It is hers and she loves it. She can sit close up to powder her face, paint her lips, dress her hair. To be glamorous, to attract a man, a man with more to offer than her Pa, was what she'd wanted. But that was more than three years ago. The woman perched on the end of the bed, looking back at herself, was no longer that naive girl.

The room was stifling. Her bones felt brittle, her skin stretched and shivery. She'd have to go down to join him soon. She said, 'yes', she wanted to say 'yes'. It's a wonderful offer. A concert up in London at the National Gallery, the place he'd told her about, the pianist he'd spoken of, the piece of music he's played to her, music she loves. But that's the problem she didn't want to think about, love. That was what she was afraid of, of herself, what she feels, not him. He's all kindness, teaching her, his knowledge extraordinary, and the way he explains, so casually, never making her feel foolish.

Exotic and pungent scents floated up to her window from the flowerbed below. Marigolds, bright orange and yellow, growing between the leeks; an odd combination but part of the war effort. Going to tell him about dinner, she'd been amazed by the sunset vividly replicating those colours, and then hearing him ask gently, shyly, 'would you like to go', she was overcome.

She could hear George talking to Major Grayson on the veranda. How can she go down when he's there too? It ought to be easier with this other man in the house and then Ruby living-in as she used to years ago. *Before I was married to Ralph,*' she'd told Elspeth. The house being full of other people, it should have stopped all the silly thoughts. She no longer sits alone with him, talking to each other so easily, like he's her husband, as they used to; which was all wrong.

In the office she has always been a different person and now that she's in sole charge and so busy, Miss Bowker having left the firm over a year ago to take care of her sister's children, there's been no time for such silliness. Routine's the only thing that has stopped her going mad.

She sat on the edge of the bed, scratched her nails along the embroidered pattern on the bedspread, tracing the patterns. Pink with blue and green threads, little loops like chains, circles and swirls not going anywhere, that never join up. A beautiful thing made for his wife, George's dead wife, not for her.

She reached forward to take a handkerchief from one of the drawers in the dressing table. The smell of lavender from the little bag that Ma made, wafted out, fresh and soothing. She dabbed the corner of her eyes with the clean folded hankie that's been washed and ironed by Ruby. Ruby is a treasure, as George says. And this is the trouble, everything he says is right. But is it wrong to feel like this?

Desire is a terrible affliction. Stupid emotions come upon her, as if to smother especially at night. It's like a fever. The craving to stroke his face, trace the lines on his cheeks, to kiss his lips? Or worse wanting so desperately for him to hold her. She mustn't think any more, foolishly imagine. Her cheeks are aflame.

To be asked to go with him, the two of them, as if on a date, is impossible. Except it isn't like that, is it? He's offering a treat, to share something that he wants to do, thought her a suitable companion. It's frightening and too good to be true.

What must he have thought of her, rushing away as soon as he'd asked and she'd said, yes? She must go down. Ruby said, '7 o'clock, if that's all right with you, Ma'am.' She must go, sit politely as if nothing's new, all the same as ever. Eat when her throat is blocked by the thumping of her heart. She must go down.

If only Kenneth, not Kenny, or Ken as his father calls him, if only he … But what was the point of finishing the thought. Three years of marriage and he's never even wanted to share a bed, apart from that one night on their honeymoon. 'I need my sleep, Elsy. It's all too much.

There's a war on!' Yes, she knows a war's on, everyone knows there's a war on, even if they're not fighting or bombed out or in prison.

Has their marriage been consummated? A wretched unease often makes her sharp or too glib when she's asked, 'How's Kenneth?' People noticing, making odd remarks. Maxi, who's in the ATS, said only last week, 'Where's lover boy?' Pa often says, 'We haven't seen Kenneth lately,' and she's seen the warning look Madge gives him. Can Ma see what's happening? That she's in love with the wrong man.

She got up quickly, smoothed the bedspread, the patterns of crewel work dizzy before her. Underneath were the crisp white bedsheets, changed and laundered every week by Ruby. Dear Ruby who's without her husband, not even knowing where he is, but never grumbling. What does Ruby think? Ruby who goes to the pictures every Tuesday afternoon with her sisters and mother, 'Thick as thieves we are, Ma'am. Have a good laugh together or a good cry. Does us the world of good.'

Would this concert do her the world of good?

There was a knock on her door. 'Mrs Kenneth, dinner's ready and Mr George was wondering if you're able to come down.'

The Moonlight Sonata 1942

They went by train, second class. George apologised. 'I thought it would be appropriate to our day out, not business. I ought to have realised that being a Bank Holiday many other people would be doing exactly the same.' To be truthful, he preferred to be anonymous rather than meet his contemporaries in first class.

Elspeth was pleased that they would be two people amongst many. His regret though made her feel special.

It was a muggy day with drizzle draining down the windows of the carriage. One was open which meant that as they went round corners, rain and smuts blew in.

'You can't, the straps broken. Have to put up with the filth,' George was informed when he tried to close it.

George looked askance at his informant. 'Is that really so?'

'Try it, mate. You'll not have any joy,'

Elspeth was smiling. 'It doesn't matter, does it, we need the air.'

Nothing mattered. She'd put aside all fears of feelings which are out of bounds. They're friends united by a love of music. It was all quite proper.

As the train shunted out of another station, a spray of smoke and soot overcame the open window again. Raising his hands as if to fend it off, George said, 'I think we ought to have worn boiler suits, don't you.'

'At least I'm wearing grey,' she giggled, 'it won't show.'

Her laughter was a release. Close to him, her stocking clad knees impossible to ignore, nothing else counted but to make her happy. For a few hours nothing else signified.

They fell to watching their journey pass in silence letting the hubbub of other passengers swirl around them. Cattle huddled under trees, and sheep bobbed like blobs of cotton wool over fields beside the track. 'It's hard to believe the awful things that are happening everywhere else,' she said.

'Yes,' he replied. 'But I'm afraid we'll encounter the worst soon.'

He was right. It was as much of a shock to see people walking along the streets in London as if oblivious to the half bombed buildings and rubble, making their way through doors into offices with glassless windows, as it was to see the damage itself. He wanted to take her hand for reassurance. Instead asked, 'Are you all right?'

It wasn't the cyclist's fault. The holes weren't like those in the roads at home, caused mostly by wear tear with no chance of repair which she, as a cyclist, knew how to avoid. Here they were bomb craters hurriedly filled and patched with broken masonry. The man with his bicycle was thrown directly into George's path. Elspeth instinctively responded as if she'd seen it about to happen. She grabbed George's arm to pull him close to her, pressing them both up against a shop window. He faced her, her arm still crooked around his, his body strong and safe up against hers. And he didn't pull away, the shock had to be absorbed. Her heart raced as if she'd run all the way down The Strand. Was he hurt? Their eyes met, a look neither has experienced before. A split second of recognition, but of what?

'Oh my goodness!' he said stepping back. 'Thank you.'

He turned to look at what had hit him. The man was struggling to his feet, untangling his bicycle. 'Sorry, sir!'

George raised a hand to show that the incident was of no concern, saying. 'Are you all right?' but the man was off. He turned to Elspeth, 'I think we need a cup of tea, don't you?'

He took her to the Lyons Corner House on Coventry Street to recover. Packed with people, the noise of talk and laughter rose from floor to ceiling. 'What a beautiful place!' she said. 'All the flouncy patterns, sort of old fashioned and new.' She marvelled at the cheeriness around them, men in uniform, hands held across tables, the caps of the waitresses - 'like cake frills my Ma once put round our Christmas cake,' she said. And that made him laugh.

They forgot Ruby's picnic. With the hubbub around them, they were merely another couple sharing toasted teacakes and a cup of tea, out in the world for all to see.

Music is a solitary experience. That is what George has held to be true. But there, with the crush of people in the gallery, he was conscious of hearing it as fellowship, and she was part of it. With her straight back, the sober grey office skirt, her hair catching brightly in a beam of light despite her hat, she was beside him, her face lit with attention, her hands, gloveless, neatly folded in her lap.

The music was magical; the sonorous bass line repeating the same pattern of notes, the right hand rising up the scale tentatively, to fall back and then rise again, each time as if with more hope, more courage. His whole body was consumed, the minor key filling him with both joy and despair. Tears trickled down his cheeks and he made no move to wipe them away. It was inevitable, the release of feelings drawn out by the glorious sound which filled the gallery, the sole performer evoking such a spellbinding moment. He dared not look at Elspeth.

When the sonata ended, the audience rose to applaud, an instant ovation. He turned then to see Elspeth dabbing at the tears on her cheeks. She gave him a weak smile and continued to clutch her balled up handkerchief.

'I'm sorry,' she whispered, 'I don't know what's the matter with me. It's just so very lovely that I can't stop crying.'

He took her hand. 'You are not alone,' he said. 'I think more than half the audience will have been moved to tears too. I was.'

And so for the remainder of the concert, he continued to hold her hand, a way of warding off the power of the music to overcome.

He looked up at the ceiling, the ornate moulding miraculously in place. Dust hung as a reminder of another night's random raid but he knew this to be one of the happiest times in his life. The Moonlight Sonata with Myra Hess, as well as two cello and piano sonatas, neither of which he knew. A perfect programme.

On the train home they were forced to stand, strap hanging. He said that he felt like the onions strung up in his shed. She laughed. 'Or a trapeze artist at a circus.' Their bodies were close, swinging together with the rhythm of the train. 'That was bliss,' she said again. He agreed. 'The best performance I've ever heard.' 'How lucky we were,' she said. And he agreed again. 'I'm not sure that I can bear to listen to my record after that though.' 'Oh, yes, we must,' she assured him. Exhilaration ran between the two of them, Elspeth thinking that she was like soda pop, fizzing with excitement.

It was 5 o'clock. There was a note on the hall table. Folded paper addressed to Mr George; Ruby apologising that she had gone to her mother for the night but will be back in the morning and has left yesterday's pie and prepared some salad. 'There's a tin of peaches for afters,' she'd written, and, 'Major Grayson told me he won't be back till Wednesday.'

Elspeth hovered while he read. 'Is it bad news?'

George looked at her, shadowed in the darkened hall, her reflection in the mirror brighter than the woman who stood before him. 'We seem to have been deserted.'

'Oh?'

'It seems we are alone.'

'Oh!'

He explained.

'I see,' she said.

Neither of them moved. Was their day to be ruined? The euphoria lost. The clock chimed the quarter and they stood as if waiting for the upbeat half-hour notes. She took off her hat. 'I think I ought to change.'

'That clock is always fast, I must …' but he didn't finish. He can't let her go. Not let the day be frittered away. 'I can make us supper,' he said. 'Scrambled eggs on toast?'

'Oh, yes, please,' and he heard the uplift in her voice and he saw, his eyes more used to the lack of light, that she was smiling. 'Thank you,' she said.

He stood at the kitchen table with a tin of powdered egg. He'd washed and wore an open necked shirt. She came up behind him, seeing the breadth of his shoulders, the stretch of the blue checked cotton over his back. She'd washed too and put on a floral frock, her hair tied back with a satin ribbon. He turned, saw her bare arms, her expectant smile. 'I'm reading how to cook this stuff,' Is all he could think to say.

He takes off his glasses. A gesture that renders him young and vulnerable. And handsome. Unlike Kenneth whose face becomes unframed without his glasses, the contours as if eroded.

She looked away, nodding to the tin he was holding. 'Can I help?'

'Please.'

'I think it's like with real eggs.

'That's what I was hoping, only how much should I use?'

She stood beside him to study the label on the tin. 'You know I can't cook. But I can read.'

He laughed, it was obvious that's what she wanted. He could smell her perfume, lily of the valley; was she wearing it for him? Their eyes met, a look which was too much for both of them. He replaced his glasses. 'I'll guess.'

'No!' She snatched the tin from him. 'One tablespoon equals one egg, it says. And then the amount of water. See?' But as she handed it back, the tin slipped, fell to the floor bouncing off his leg.

'Ouch!' He winced, not attempting to pick it up.

'Oh no,' Elspeth was on her knees retrieving the tin, 'I'm so sorry.' But he was gripping the table, pulling out a kitchen chair to sit down.

'No, not your fault,' he was saying, his head bent, a hand bracing his knee. 'It's that cyclist, where he crashed into my leg.'

'What? You didn't tell me.' She was still on her knees, looking at his trousered legs. 'Show me.'

Reluctantly he revealed the purple bruise, his shin livid and swollen. She tentatively laid her hand on his leg. He didn't draw back. 'That's bad,' she said. 'Shouldn't you see a doctor.'

'No, your touch is enough,' which he didn't mean to say but too quickly it was out there for her to hear. There was no going back. He leant his forehead to hers. Her cool hand easing out the heat, she stroked his leg, as if to soothe the hurt. 'Why didn't you say?' But neither wished for his reply. It was surplus to the time that passed and rested between them.

'Elspeth,' he said, and lifted her face to his. 'What do we do?'

His hands were rough against her cheeks, holding her face as if it was precious porcelain. But she wasn't. She was wild with want, rough with desire. A desire she'd tamped down, denied. But here they were, the scene was set. She knew what to do, for so long she'd known, and too well. Wasn't this what her mother tried to tell her? How could they resist? He kissed her, carefully, fearful of retreat. But she responded, kissing him again and again, his leg forgotten, her arms around his neck, her eyes bright with longing, not afraid to show passion. There was no escape. He lifted her onto his lap, cradled her to him.

The tin of powdered egg waiting on the floor.

'What do we do, Elspeth?' he said again as her body pressed against his chest, the silk of her hair folding into his neck. She felt the pulse of his heartbeat, breathed in the earthy smell of soap and man. And she looked up into his eyes, saw herself reflected. 'I love you,' she said.

'Oh, Elspeth, Elspeth!'

'Yes, yes!' And she kissed his cheeks, his eyelids, his mouth to stop any questions. This was the ecstasy her mother had spoken of. It wasn't wrong. It was their due. She felt the fervour in his response and flicked her tongue between his lips. Where had she learnt this? She took his hand and placed it on her breasts.

'Oh, Elspeth, dearest, I love you so much, but …' conscience pricked but what for? Who were they hurting?

There was no 'but' for Elspeth who put her hand over his mouth. Her voice full of tenderness. 'There is no going back, is there?' Her body was alive; "*Women don't need to be shy, to hold back*," was what her mother had said, "*we are made for the pleasure too.*" 'I love you, George,' she repeated. 'This is all I've wanted. And you?' She guided his hand to the buttons on her dress.

'Yes, yes, but no! This is wrong.' he pushed her gently away, to sit her upright, a child on his lap. 'You're married.'

Elspeth stared at him. 'No! I'm not.' Her cheeks burned. 'No, no!' What must he think of her? She pushed away from him, stood up, smoothing her skirt. Her breathing coming fast and deep, to recover, pull back from what she'd thought … But no, she was not going to be humiliated. 'I am not married,' the words pronounced defiantly. 'Didn't you know? He doesn't want me. Kenneth doesn't want me as a wife ought to be wanted.'

George looked at her pitifully, the pain in his leg magnified by the remorse he felt for what he's just done. 'I'm sorry …' he began.

But she hadn't finished. 'To say he has a wife, that's all he wants, an excuse.' Her voice rose to the ceiling, a ceiling where the distemper's grey rather than white. It was a release to share the shame. 'You know, he didn't want to touch me on our honeymoon. He was drunk, made himself ill. Three nights I waited before he shared the bed and then he could barely … I don't need to explain. I don't want to explain.' She stared at him with narrowed eyes. 'Don't you see? There is something wrong with him and I thought it was my fault. I didn't know what it was to love someone. I married him thinking I knew.' She shook her head slowly, 'I'm nobody's wife.'

George was appalled. It's what he knew, had known for too long. 'Oh, Elspeth, I'm so sorry.'

'Are you? Sorry for what? That my marriage is a sham or that I love you?'

'Sorry that I've been blind.'

'Blind to what?'

'Oh Elspeth, my dear!'

'Stop saying that!' She stepped right back. The cupboards loomed out of the half light. Somewhere inside one of them she could find a saucepan and cook the eggs. How foolish to let her heart be known. How utterly foolish.

He could still feel the featherweight of her resting on his thighs. 'I've been such an idiot,' she heard him say. But it was too late; she'd turned away assessing the possibilities of where to look, for what Ruby might keep where. She'd cook supper. 'Yes, Ma'am,' she hears how Ruby speaks to her. Mistress of the house. She'll not run away.

And she couldn't for he caught hold of her arm to pull her round. 'I am the biggest fool, Elspeth. I knew, I worried for you but put that aside because …' He didn't finish for she was above him, looking down on him. He saw the tilt of her chin, the condescension. He almost wanted to laugh. 'It could be because I began to love you as I shouldn't, kept telling myself I was wrong!'

'Maybe you are?'

'No.' He reached out with his other hand to pull another chair beside his. 'Please, sit down.' Reluctantly she did so. How could they go back to where they were? The hurt was setting in; her fierce anger depleted. 'You're right.'

She shrugged. 'Am I?'

'Elspeth,' he took hold of both her hands. 'My marriage was a failure too. I am not betraying Marjorie if I tell you that she was unable to respond to my physical advances. I believed it my fault. Ken was a one honeymoon night miracle.' He held her gaze. 'To say that I've longed to love and be loved is an understatement, but I'd never thought possible.'

Elspeth held her breath, returning his gaze boldly.

'How can I believe that I'm allowed to love and be loved?' He took her hands to his lips. 'That you might want me is a fabulous dream. But what a sissy I sound.' He kissed her fingers. 'How can I impose myself on you? Usurping my son's rights?'

'Stop! Didn't you hear me? Rights he doesn't want?' she flashed back. 'And what about mine?'.

He reached forward to kiss her mouth. 'If we, and I mean we, allow ourselves this chance for one night, how will we manage all the others?'

She shrugged again. 'I don't know. Who knows?' She didn't return his kiss. 'Is it worth the risk? I thought so, but you don't.'

'Oh my darling woman! Yes, yes. You're right, we've been given this night. A gift. Please, Elspeth, let me love you.'

'Before or after the scrambled eggs?' she said.

Ruby was surprised that the blackout curtains were drawn back. She wondered if they'd been closed at all. It was 7.30, the time she usually started breakfast on a working day. She hadn't knocked or rung the bell. She had a key to let herself in as it was her home after all, as well as her place of work.

There was not a sound in the house, as if no one was there. Where were Mr George and Mrs Kenneth? Hadn't they returned last night? Then she saw the tin of powdered egg on the table, a washed saucepan and two plates in the draining rack. She found the pie and salad untouched in the fridge. Later she told her sister. 'It was real odd, Molly. Why he'd seen fit to cook something when I'd left them provided. And he come in the kitchen right then, gay as you may, said he'd been up early, to let in the summer day. Not what I'd have called it, rain coming down in sheets.'

'Tried out my culinary skills,' George said. 'But thank you for leaving supper, Ruby. We can have that tonight.' He picked up the tin from the table, turned it in his hand and put it down and without looking at her said, 'Wouldn't you like another evening off. Major Grayson won't be here, I believe.'

'Thank you, sir. That's most kind. Me and my sister could go to the pictures, if that's all right with you.' And again later, she tells Molly, 'If I didn't know him better I'd think like he was wanting me out the house.'

George went back to his bedroom, smoothed the bed sheets and plumped up the pillow where Elspeth's head had lain. He picked off three bright strands of hair as if they were precious as gold. He took off his dressing gown, caught sight of his half-naked torso in the mirror. The memory of what has occurred fills him with awe. That she kissed and caressed his body with such passion, bringing them both to the heights of what? Sexual satisfaction? Such a prosaic expression for something beyond wonder. A wild rampage of desire would better express what they'd experienced. His heart might burst with joy; all his nerves alive as if with their own electricity. He shook himself for this wouldn't do. There was a normal day to start and proceed. He sluiced his face at the washbasin, foamed with soap and shaved.

Rain fell fast and straight outside, drops slithering down the window pane, merging into trails of water to wash down the brickwork. He towelled his face feeling its rough exhilaration. Had there ever been rain like this before, sluicing from the guttering, drumming on the top panes of the greenhouse, droplets bouncing up from the pond? Alive and refreshing, the allotment was having a good soak. He wanted to shout through the rain, the rain which echoed their triumph; look what we can do too!

Elspeth was also wondering at the pattering of rain on her windowsill. It sounded like applause; applause for all that her mother had promised. Nothing else mattered. She studied her face in the mirror. Did she look different for she felt different? There was a distinct redness around her mouth and chin. The result of his whiskers, their passion. It must be covered as their love must be concealed. They will live with their secret as best they can. When he said something similar last night, she'd wanted to cry. She hasn't wept for a husband who doesn't want to love her but she could weep for what she now knows and possesses. Will she always have to fight away tears of joy with sorrow?

Elspeth drew back the sheets and pressed a head shaped dent into her pillow to leave nothing suspicious for Ruby to query. Subterfuge, the constant vigilance for maintaining this subterfuge will have to become second nature.

August turned to September and into October with apples falling rather than rain.

'I thought she looked peaky, didn't you?' Madge sifted flour and lard through her fingertips, lightly binding to breadcrumbs. 'That husband of hers hasn't been home in months.'

'Not his fault,' Ernest gouged a maggot from an apple. 'The war …'

But Madge was there with, 'Don't give me that damned excuse again! He's not away at the Front, he's less than a hundred miles down the road. And he has a car.'

'Petrol, sweetheart, it can't be wasted.'

Madge gave him a glance as cutting as the knife that teased cold water into the pastry crumbs. 'She said he's coming home this weekend. Though I can't say she sounded excited.'

Ernest picked up another cooking apple and carefully pared the skin. His ambition to keep a complete coil of peel had been eclipsed by Madge's anger.

'Not much chat either. No straight answers. And what of her appetite?'

Ernest looked up. 'Yes, that wasn't like her. Picked at the cottage pie.'

'The best mince I'd saved from our rations too.'

'No, that's one thing about our girl, slim as she is, she could always finish a good plate, and second helpings. Remember how I sang that song to her when she was little about the goat; "His tummy was lined with zinc".'

Madge was binding the crumbs to a ball. 'She talked about work. A safe topic, you might say.'

'Oh yes, she's really taken on running the office.' All the apples were peeled, waiting in a saucepan of cold water so they wouldn't brown. 'These windfalls are a boon; she said Ruby had more than enough.'

'Hmm! She doesn't mention Mr George any more.'

'Oh, Madge, you're not to worry. It's probably a cold she's got.'

Madge plomped her pastry ball onto the floured board. 'I can't make out this change in her. I mean when she'd been on that trip to London back in August it seemed to really revive her. She was full of it. How music was this, that and the other. It was lovely to see her all chirpy.

Perked her up.' She drew in a deep breath and let it out as if to rid her irritation.

'Don't fret, Madge. I mean, I could say the same of you. Tired out with all the extra work you're doing. Sit for a minute.' He pulled her down onto his lap. She didn't resist. 'You can't live her life for her. She certainly wouldn't want you worrying.'

The greenhouse was warm, away from the wind, the sun glazing the glass. Elspeth breathed in the scent of the geraniums, astringent and alluring. George had his back to her, engrossed in breaking off the last blooms, saving some to a jar of water. Her desire to stand close at his back, the heat of him absorbed into her, was all consuming. A fortnight ago this was what she would have done. This was where they've been coming since that day in August.

Her footsteps were too soft to register that she was there at the door. Her presence, though, must have brought a change to the air for George swung round, a smile and a blossom held out to her. 'Are you all right, dearest?' he said;

Elspeth wished she hadn't come, didn't dare look at him. 'Yes and no.' How can she tell him? This thing that'd happened when everything was so lovely. But, of course, it had. All precautions thrown to the wind for that first unexpected thrill of insatiable love. Love that still fires through her.

His contrite face was too sad to see. She looked past him to the rows of flower pots, zinging with red and pink flowers. 'I've missed a period, two actually,' she said. Must she spell it out? A baby growing inside her. A child that she doesn't want. Except it's his child. And then what must be said, 'Kenneth is coming home tomorrow.'

George stood still clutching the flowers. Her two statements were at odds with one another. He moved towards her, but she backed away. And then he grasped what she'd said. 'Elspeth! Do you mean that …?' But she'd gone, up past the rose trellis, the wind catching the whippy shoots, and on up to the house. Was she expecting a baby, their baby? For surely it must be his. Elation and uncertainty ran in parallel. What was he meant to think? Did this explain how quiet and withdrawn she'd been the last week or so? Why couldn't she have talked to him? Is he being foolish to think it isn't a problem? He looked down at the flower in his hand. Perfect petals, silky soft, a vibrant colour. These were his loved ones before Elspeth came.

He closed the greenhouse door, took the jar of flowers to Ruby in the kitchen.

She greeted him with, 'Mrs Kenneth's not feeling too good tonight, sir. Says she'll have a tray in her room if that's all right.' Ruby's statement sounded like a question. Did Ruby know? 'Major Grayson is coming down at 7.'

George was overcome with weariness. How could he make polite conversation when this enormity has been presented to him? He must talk to her, surely this is theirs to share. All the loving, the openness, the delight of the last two months was shadowed. He climbed the stairs, knocked on her door. 'Elspeth,' he called, quietly, 'Are you all right?'

She opened the door. 'I'm sorry.' Her face was blotchy, her eyes red. She shook her head. 'We can't talk. I'll be better soon.'

She closed the door and he stood with a stone in his stomach. What can he do?

'Oh good, Mr Simms,' it was Major Grayson further down the landing. 'I was wanting to thank you. You've all been most accommodating, such hospitality.' He closed in, stretching out his hand. 'I'm off at the end of the week. Being moved.'

'Oh, right,' George steered him down the stairs and into the dining room. It was a wooden soldiers' dance for the rest of the evening.

Elspeth stared up at the ceiling, at the intricate rose around the central light, willing the nausea away. The weak morning light traced the crack which wiggled down one wall, a rare blemish in this perfect house. Last night she'd asked Ruby for cream crackers which she'd saved to nibble as soon as she had the strength to get out of bed. Will she feel better once the pretence is over? She'll have to tell before long, soon it will show. If only she'd stayed with him last evening, let him reassure her. Except would that have been right? Would he have wanted her to? It was their problem. It wasn't her fault but it was she who must find a solution. A child was inevitable; the consequences terrifying. Its parentage must never be known. Over and over she played through all the possibilities. Kenneth was coming. She's written to say she's ill. A half lie with the big lie. His presence and what she must coax him to do, disgusts her..

She thought of Maxi playing her way through a pack of men, blithe in the knowledge that she's been cute enough to avoid any complications. At least that's the line she shoots whenever they meet. 'You're not going to catch me at some man's beck and call, a bun in the oven.' But it's not like that for her, Elspeth reminds herself; it's the power of love to eclipse all common sense.

'Where is everyone?' Kenneth pushed past Ruby who'd opened the front door.

'It's good to see you, Mr Kenneth,' she said. 'Can I bring in your case?'

'What?'

'Your luggage?'

He was looking past her without acknowledging her presence.

'A whisky is what I need. I'm whacked out,' he said, as if to the mirror in which he preened his appearance.

'Right you are, sir, and I'll tell your wife you're here.' Ruby was piqued. She'd tell Molly, 'There's no call for him to treat me like that. And whisky at that time of day!'

He wandered through into the drawing room, slumped in an armchair. Ruby came back with a bottle and glass on a tray but still wanted to offer something better. 'I'm afraid they've had lunch,' she said, 'but I could make up a plate, warm it up quick.'

'Don't fuss, Ruby. Just the whisky. And there's my attaché case in the car.'

The alcohol stung the back of his throat, an instant warmth, stilled the jumpiness of his nerves. By choice he wouldn't be here. Jack's whereabouts are troubling. He hasn't heard in weeks how he's faring. The North Africa campaign isn't going as well as they hoped, that's clear; Jack's unit being out there is a constant worry. In the mess it's easier; a bit of loose talk acceptable.

The hall clock chimed 3.00; he poured himself another whisky. He heard footsteps coming down the stairs, or were they going up? A few more minutes on his own was what he wanted. He needed time to adjust. Elspeth's letter struck an odd note, the tone between pleading and peremptory. She'd never been like that before. A good wife, no pressure on him to explain what he's doing, his job being top secret. Dad used to nag him to come home, but that's stopped, thank goodness. Must have realised that he's too tired between duties. Much better to relax in the mess.

'Kenny, you're here!'

He dragged himself out of the chair. And then was surprised by how pretty she looked, instantly, proud of his choice of wife. But she flung herself at him, hung on his neck. 'Hey, steady, Babe! Give a bloke a bit of space.'

Elspeth, only too pleased to back away, shrugged coquettishly. 'I've missed you, that's all. Can't a wife …' but they were interrupted by George who poked his head round the door.

'Hello, son.' He stretched out his arm and the two men shook hands. 'Ruby fetched me from the allotment.'

'Digging for Victory, eh?' though his tone and expression sneered rather than praised.

Kenneth munched morosely over dinner and then played his jazz records at full volume all evening. George was on air raid duty, Elspeth exhausted. How she was going to entice her so-called husband to sleep with her, didn't bear contemplation. It was a battle she had to win, a vital victory.

The silkiest nightdress, her hair brushed to a sheen, perfume flooding the room, she climbed on to the bed. Kenneth came from the bathroom yawning.

'I hope you're not expecting any high jinks tonight, Elsy,' he said. He tried to make it sound jokey but she could identify an underlying note of terror. How truly laughable; this was one time they were in accord! Laughable too as there had never been any 'high jinks' in the marriage. But she crushed her anger.

'Just a cuddle,' and she mimicked Greta Garbo's sultry tones.

Reluctantly he climbed in beside her, pulled the covers up to his neck. She snuggled up and quickly rolled over to lie on top of him. With the nausea of pregnancy this action doubly sickened her. She kissed him and at the same time undid his pyjama cord, slid up her nightdress. She found his flaccid penis, clasped hold and gentle pumped the sheath up and down, up and down, murmuring, 'Oh, oh, oh!'

'My God!' Kenneth began but she blotted his mouth with hers. He couldn't struggle, it was as if she'd the strength of a mad woman. And, of course, that was exactly her role. Unwillingly his cock strengthened, was stiff enough for her to force it between her legs. He was merely a rag doll with whom she had to make some sort of congress.

For barely two minutes they were clasped in this undignified embrace until she felt the trickle of a meagre ejaculation run down her legs. That he had entered her was doubtful but she hoped not important. To deny that he'd been part of the act, the production of a child, would make him look foolish. She's sure that's how his mind will work.

She rolled back to the edge of the bed, stumbled to the bathroom where she scrubbed herself clean. Never again, never again.

A first victory 1943

In February the Germans surrendered to the Russians at Stalingrad. By the end of May the Germans and Italians had capitulated to the Allies in North Africa and the Battle of the Atlantic was effectively over. Ernest says, 'The tide is turning. We can but hope.'

Georgina Margaret Everley Simms was born on the 21st of May 1943. The labour was long and gruelling, a nurse and doctor in attendance for forty eight hours. Kenneth was unable to come home therefore didn't experience any of the horror or concern. George paced and sat the nights out, tormented by each anguished cry of the woman he loves. Ruby bustled back and forth with hot water, cups of tea, and soothing words. The baby was swaddled and taken to show to her grandfather, as they believe. He looked down at the tiny crumpled face, felt the featherweight of his daughter in his arms and was doubly in love. A love he has no need to conceal.

Ruby was entranced. She's not been 'blessed' - as she tells those that ask - with children of her own. There's never rancour. 'I've enough nieces and nephews to give love to,' she's often said. Now here was another child for her to love. Her sister, Molly said, 'That's a bit early, isn't it? I mean, didn't we wonder right at the start that she was sick before Mr Kenneth ever come home? You remember?' Ruby doesn't.

Elspeth was aghast. Having opened her body to bring forth this child, wracked by pulsing pains, ablaze with sore stitches, she's trapped, sunk in an abyss of fear and self-loathing. Imprisoned with the overpowering smell of baby powder, stale blood and sweat, she thinks she'll go mad. This creature who sucks savagely at her breast is unlawful, evidence of adultery.

It didn't help when George commented on the beauty of the child for it is there that the terror lies. This baby is too big, too brown and, to the outside world if they knew, a bastard.

George's sympathy for what she'd suffered was not enough. Everything he says sounds flat and trite as he misunderstands the horror of the situation. That she looked ghastly, unwholesome in a nasty cotton nightdress, bound up with a nursing bra, the paraphernalia of this new thing, motherhood, he ignored. Through the fast shut window she saw the clearest blue sky, the tips of the trees which were the freshest green. In the flowerbeds below the wallflowers were in bloom, rich reds and gold, the tulips unfurling their petals under the sun. She had to escape.

Where was their easy camaraderie of less than a fortnight ago? She longed for his touch, his rough cheeks on hers, to snuggle into the nape of his neck. But their words are banal, stock phrases of pity or frustration.

George was bewitched by the little creature lying in her cradle, his daughter blissfully storing sleep. 'I'm so proud of you both,' he kept saying. 'Georgina you've called her. I am thrilled and honoured.'

'Was that a good idea?' Elspeth asked. 'Doesn't it make it more difficult?'

'Difficult for what?' But his question was automatic, forgotten as soon as uttered.

Elspeth followed his gaze, his attention drawn from her to the cradle. Finally she pulled him down close, kissed him fully, lulled by his eager response. Resting her forehead on his she said, 'What are we going to do?'

'What about?'

'Her,' Elspeth could hear the whine in her voice, 'the baby.'

'What? What's wrong?' He looked across at the cradle again, happiness changed to alarm. He wanted to get up and go to see for himself, but Elspeth kept him held, her hand firmly in his, clasped in her lap.

'It's the size of her, George, her colouring.' As the words come out of her mouth, 'She looks like you.' she knew they were wrong.

He was baffled. 'Georgina? You mean the baby?' He stared at Elspeth. He was tired too, disorientated. Sleep had long since ceased to restore him; the office was in chaos, evenings taken up with Air Raid Warden duties, his home housing strangers, another officer billeted, a nurse coming and going. Each visit to Elspeth and the baby, he thought perhaps selfishly, would revive his spirits. But this?

'Look at her,' Elspeth said. 'All her features are yours. It's plain to see.'

She released his hand, let him go. Tentatively he lifted the blanket that half covers his daughter's face. 'Really?' he said.

'Don't you see? She should be tiny, blonde, pale. People will know.'

The child transfixed his gaze. The plump pink cheeks, the minute fingers which seem to play a tune on an instrument, making music as she sleeps. She's a picture of perfection, an innocent scrap of humanity that he'll defend with his dying breath.

'George,' Elspeth begged. 'I'm so frightened.'

'Really? My dearest, is that all?' He looked down at the infant and back to Elspeth, relief flooding through him. 'You don't need to be. People accept differences, we aren't all like our parents.' He gently stroked his daughter's forehead. 'She's beautiful, everyone will see that.'

Elspeth stared at him. The man was oblivious, couldn't see what exposure would mean for her. Why didn't he understand? Defiant, she said, 'You have to let me out of here, otherwise I'll go mad.'

'Patience, dearest.'

'I need to get back to work.'

'The nurse and doctor will know best.'

'Don't! I've had enough of them. I'll be the judge of when I'm ready.'

He ignored her, was about to go.

Elspeth quelled her anger, scared that a rift had come between them. It was all such a mess, everything tipped upside down, never to be right again. But, poor man, he looked desperate. 'You look tired,' she said. 'What's the woman like who's come to help in the office? I didn't think much to her when I handed over.'

George appeared not to hear as he leant over to kiss her forehead. 'We'll be all right,' he said as if to the air. 'I held Georgina briefly on the night she was born, you know. It was wonderful. Dawn it was. The sky blushed pink before the sun was above the horizon.' He pressed her hands to his lips. 'It was a good omen.'

Ruby came up with a cup of tea, gentle footsteps and tap on the door. Elspeth left the tears on her cheeks; what does it matter? No one cares. Even he isn't willing to understand the intricacies of timing, the number of weeks to a pregnancy, what she had to do that night with his son? She cannot speak of it.

'Being stuck up here must get you down, while all the world is clumping past your door.' Ruby's cheeks glowed with righteous indignation. She rivalled the flaming tulips that Elspeth imagines in the garden below. 'You'll be out and about in a trice, though, I'm sure.'

Elspeth fought back more tears.

'Can I have a little peek at her ladyship, Ma'am? You know I've a real soft spot for babies.'

Elspeth nodded not daring to speak.

'My, you're a little charmer,' Ruby gazed as if at a magical creature. 'You'll not be giving us any grief, will you little one,' she said to the baby. 'So dark, just like your grandfather. A little throwback, isn't that lovely? It's what he deserves, if you don't mind me saying, Ma'am, and his name too. Just right.'

'You think so, Ruby?' Elspeth dared to say.

'Oh, yes!' and she leant in closer. Shook her head in wonder. 'Perfect, she is. A Thursday child with far to go. Gemini too.' She laughed. 'That might be a bit trickier!'

George knew nothing of star signs or fortune-telling nursery songs that Sunday morning. He knew less how to deal with what Elspeth said. It was a shock. He stood below her window. The bees were circling the tulips, zoning in on the black and yellow centres, focused as if on the sights of a gun. He expected that she'd be feeling out of sorts, having gone through such a dreadful experience. He'd been heartened as the days went by to hear and see how well she and the baby were progressing. But this? To speak of Georgina so disparagingly? Her size and colour are wrong, 'like you', she'd said. It hurt.

For a year, less than a year, they've both lived with such joy, never displaying their feelings openly, never scurrying into corners, only taking the rare opportunities when truly alone for any physical love. Even her unhappiness, when she found she was expecting this miracle, eased. He didn't want to think that it might all have to end. It is too precious.

Having an affair with his own son's wife would be abhorrent to anyone. But who might suspect? Ruby? No, not her. Kenneth? He's never at home. But what will they do when he is? Yes, he didn't want to think too hard about the future. Perhaps this was the cause of Elspeth's unhappiness?

Ruby kept her counsel. She hadn't told Molly of any likeness, merely dwelt on the little one's beauty. Molly kept her suspicions to herself. But she'll say to Millie, her youngest, many years later, 'I'd have chosen Mr George over Mr Kenneth any day.'

Elspeth was in the drawing room fully dressed when Madge and Ernest visited. 'Open the French doors, Pa. I'm suffocating in here.'

'I don't know about that,' Ernest said. This house made him nervous. How could he sit down on the blue brocade chair covers which looked far too fragile?

'Do as she asks, dear,' Madge said for she was uneasy too. Shouldn't she, as Elspeth's mother, have been here to help? Her daughter moving up in the world, employing a nurse, was one thing, but how not be peeved was another. But she said, 'Georgina Margaret, they're good names, Elspeth. Yours and Kenneth's choice?'

'No, mine. They're for her grandfather and grandmother, you. Ma'

'Oh! I hadn't thought.' Madge looked over to Ernest. 'Well, that's really nice, isn't it? Did you hear that, Ernest? I sometimes forget my full name.'

Elspeth sat pale and prim in a floral dress, thinner than you'd expect. Madge saw no sign of contentment; it was as if a dark cloud circled her. All through pregnancy Elspeth had been reclusive, rarely visiting them and even then being quite off-hand. Madge hoped the baby's arrival would change all that, bring back the daughter who'd begun to feel close and happy in their company.

Ernest while trying to work out which bolt to undo and how to secure the wide open doors was drawn to look out at the garden. He could see Gustave doing something at the far end. He wanted to make an excuse to go to say 'hello', discuss the latest news of the allied forces closing in on the Germans in Tunisia.

'The nurse leaves tomorrow,' Elspeth was saying. 'I'm fed up being ordered around.'

'But it must be helpful …' Madge began despite herself, at the same time as Ruby came in with a tray of tea.

'Shall I tell the nurse to bring her ladyship down?' she said.

'Don't worry, Ruby, she'll come when it's good for her and the baby.' They exchanged the look of conspirators.

And as if on cue, the nurse knocked on the door and entered with Georgina. She stood over Elspeth. 'Would you like to take her, Madam?'

'No, give her to my mother. And thank you, that will be all. Ruby will bring her back to the nursery shortly.'

Madge was impressed with the deference of the woman, her immaculate uniform. She was startled, too, by her daughter's abrupt instructions. But then there was the baby in her arms, a little dark stranger who fluttered her eyelids, peered and blinked, sucked and settled to sleep. Ernest stood above them. Tears welling, he swallowed.

'What a healthy baby,' he said. 'She's a lovely size. You'd never think her only two weeks old.'

'Nearly three,' was Elspeth's swift reply.

'Who do you take after?' Madge questioned the baby. 'Not your mother, I think, or your father.'

'She looks like George,' Elspeth was even quicker to say. 'Ruby says she's a throwback. Taking after a previous generation.' It all came out pat as if she believed it herself. 'That happens sometimes.'

Neither Madge nor Ernest seemed troubled by this explanation. And when Ernest said, 'You're a clever girl,' the room settled and a stirring of fresh air circled the room.

Elspeth didn't offer to take a turn holding her child, why should she? Watching her parents cooing and cuddling was enough to ease some of her fears.

Ruby, too, reinforced the admiration when she came to fetch the baby saying to Madge, 'She's beautiful, isn't she, Ma'am?' And seeing Ruby's pride in being in charge, the look of devotion in her gathering up and cradling of the precious burden, Madge was relieved. Later she said, 'She'd make a perfect nursemaid.'

Elspeth was surprised and delighted by her mother's words.

After they'd gone Elspeth stepped into the garden, breathed in the scent of the wallflowers. Ruby to look after the baby? What a thought, and such a good one. She sat on the seat under the sycamore tree to absorb what had just taken place. It was as if the world had turned back or maybe gone forward. A beam of sun spiralled through the poplar trees as if to agree.

She felt the brass plaque on the back of the seat slippery against her dress. She knows that it says. *'In memory of my dear wife, Marjorie.'* A photo of that wife is hanging in the dining room showing a severe young woman, thin and upright, hair tightly framing her face. It's not a heart-warming likeness; it appears as if the 'sitter', who is in fact standing, disapproves of those who admire her countenance. What she was really like, Elspeth often wonders? Adored by her son, though that's easier to protest in hindsight. George out of loyalty makes few references after that initial revelation of her rejection of the sexual aspect of their marriage. Ruby, too, has let slip that 'she was a stickler for everything being just so', joking 'and that was all of us, Mr George included.'

Poor George! Her lovely man who she adores above all. How stupid she's been to quarrel, to be so nasty about the child, his child. That he loves her, and she him, is all that matters.

Kenneth arrived that evening, meeting George in the hall as he returned from the office. 'Can't stay long,' he said. 'It's a frightful mess out there, though that's not what gets in the news. Hush. hush, of course.' George can't help but think Kenneth relishes his role as holder of inside knowledge, carrier of bad tidings. He showed no interest in what dangers and tribulations they were suffering in his own home town.

'The house is somewhat full, you know,' he said. 'The nurse is still living with us; you realise Georgina's birth was not easy?'

'Yes, Elsy told me but she's all right now.' And without waiting for a reply, 'I'm only here for a couple of nights at most. See her and the babe.'

George regarded him with contempt. How can he be so casual? It's three weeks since Georgina was born. He should've requested leave long ago. Is he fit to be thought the father? But that this should enter his head, is wrong. He tried a conciliatory tone. 'Ruby lives-in again as her husband is fighting in North Africa, you know, and we have another officer billeted with us …' but he was unable to finish as Kenneth chips in with, 'Dash it all! No room at the inn, eh?'

George again swallowed his dislike of his son's pose, for that was what it must be. 'He's from the United States,' he added, 'but fortunately he's away for the weekend.'

'An American, eh?' Kenneth was impressed. 'Mind you, they took long enough coming into the fight.'

Kenneth found Elspeth resting in her bedroom. 'Sorry I couldn't make it earlier, Elsy' The breeziness of his manner was annoying but his, 'My God, you look all in, old girl,' was laughable.

'Hi, Kenny, good to see you,' she said, patting the side of the bed.

His eyes circled the room, he sniffed the air. 'It's a bit stuffy in here isn't it?'

Elspeth said nothing. Does the new moustache suit him, so fair and sparse? It's as if he's drunk a mug of Ovaltine and failed to wipe the remains from his upper lip.

'Not much room in here either,' he observed approaching the bed and kissing her cheek. 'Where's the baby?'

All these comments were as Elspeth expected. Ma and Pa's visit earlier has braced her.

'Georgina Margaret will be brought in shortly to be fed. I hope you like the names, Kenny.'

'Right, okay, fine.' He was dithering, still trying to identify the smell, wondering whether to light a cigarette.

'You'll have to let me know when you can get leave so that we can arrange her christening,' she said.

'What?'

'And we're calling her Gina.'

Any response he might have made was overtaken by the entrance of the nurse.

'Oh! You have visitors, Mrs Simms. I didn't realise. It's time for baby's feed.'

'This is my husband, Nurse. He'd like to see Gina first.'

'Oh!' Her disapproval was evident as she looked Kenneth up and down. 'Well, briefly.' There was a moment of doubt as to whether she would hand over the child. She was taller than Kenneth and he reckoned several pounds heavier.

'Sit on the bed,' Elspeth said, 'She won't break.' But Kenneth was still unsure as grudgingly the baby was laid in his arms.

This transaction amused Elspeth, her mood again lifted.

'Gee! She's quite a weight,' he said as he stared down at the tightly wrapped bundle. Gina squinted up at him, puckered her mouth as if to introduce herself. 'Gee!' he said again, 'How fearfully exciting! She's quite something.'

'She is, isn't she.' Elspeth agreed with immense relief.

Kenneth was relieved too. He'd done his duty and could withdraw.

Alone, Elspeth took her daughter to her breast. The baby's eyes were wide open, misty with the pleasure of the nipple. Her dark lashes fluttered with the rhythmic sucking. Elspeth looked down on her, this strange being. 'What can we do? Your father and I,' Elspeth whispered. 'One day you'll know how hard it is to walk this tightrope. Tied into secrecy as tightly as you're wrapped in this shawl.' Weariness washed over a feeling of reprieve. More than one hurdle has been jumped. It's clear that Kenneth will be able to boast. His lack of virility never called into question. He'll never wish to query the child's parentage.

Kenneth decided to sleep in the lodger's bedroom. 'You said he's away, didn't you?' he demanded of his father. 'I mean I can't sleep with Elspeth. The room's full of baby stuff.'

George didn't argue. It was probably better that way. Elspeth's fragile temper mustn't be disturbed. Since that awful outburst a fortnight ago, he'd avoided any reference to Georgina. He liked the shortening of her name, visited the baby without fuss.

Elspeth had tried to heal the wound she'd inflicted with, 'She's very sweet, I know. It's just that I'm feeling so trapped, like a caged bird.' Her apology after that awful accusation was as a petulant child, grumbling again about his complacency. He hadn't been able to ask about her parents' visit.

Ruby came up trumps as always. 'You don't need to worry, sir. There are clean sheets on the other bed in that room. I'll check it's tidy enough.' She'd have liked to give Mr George a hug, cheer him up. She said, 'What excitement! Mr Kenneth seeing the baby at last.'

George didn't notice her reference to 'the baby'. No one notices that Ruby never honours Mr Kenneth as Georgina's father.

Kenneth toasted the baby's arrival several times that evening with his father's whisky, talked of his bonny daughter. George was sickened to listen to Kenneth's new enthusiasm for the child, his child. He ought to have been delighted, instead was angry and ashamed.

After breakfast the next day Kenneth visited Elspeth. 'I think I'll go for a spin. Might meet up with Jack. He's on leave, bit of a surprise, back from Africa.'

Elspeth couldn't care less.

'I'll be off tomorrow, if Dad doesn't drive me out sooner. He's being positively gruesome. Is he always like that these days?'

This was too much. Elspeth could no longer hold back. 'Have you thought of the upheaval you've caused? Ruby is half out of her wits managing the rations and you just swan up as if we're a hotel. Don't you know there's a war on.'

'Hey, steady on, old girl. You've no need to tell me …'

'Oh shut up, Kenneth! Do you know anything of what's happening here? What your father is coping with? Have you asked?'

Kenneth shrugged. 'There's no need to give me a lecture.' It wasn't worth arguing; women were supposed go a bit funny after childbirth. One of the chaps in the mess had warned him. He took out his cigarette case, selected and tapped a cigarette on its silver surface. The cigarette dangled from his mouth as he rummaged for his lighter. 'You think I'm having an easy time?'

Elspeth flared as hot as that wretched lighter. To tell him that Gina is not his child, that he's a useless husband, that their marriage has never been consummated, was her most desperate desire. Instead she shook her head. 'Get out then and take that damned cigarette with you.'

He put up his hands in mock defence moving towards the door.

Fury overtook her again and she was up and out of bed, seizing her housecoat, coming towards him while pushing her arms through the sleeves, wrapping round and tying the sash tight. What joy it would be to let rip, to push him out and down the stairs, never to see him again. But she had no intention of touching him.

'It's three weeks since Gina's birth when I almost died, and where were you?'

Kenneth mouthed, 'Shh!' his finger to his lips.

But she was shouting back, 'Don't kid me that you're irreplaceable. I'm not that much of a fool. Go! I need to feed the baby. And give some thought for your father.'

Her voice carried out of those four walls, all the pent up anger flaring, a grenade about to be thrown. But it didn't matter. Everyone needed to know if they didn't know already. Their marriage is a sham.

How was she going to live the whole of her life with him? She must get back to the office, outside in the world, be the one who makes the decisions. It's the battle she has to win and soon.

Fighting back 1943

In September 1943 Gustave rejoiced with George at news that Italian forces had surrendered to General Eisenhower. Hope rising for a change in the tide of the war.

Gina was three months old, sleeping in her pram parked under the sycamore tree on the terrace. All was quiet except for a thrush battering a snail on the paving stones. Elspeth was sitting in a deckchair not far away, reading a book. Discarded on the stone slabs at her side, a ball of wool with knitting needles stuck through as evidence of the beginning of some sort of garment. A casual onlooker would have judged this to be a scene of perfect motherhood. That, of course, was not the case. She still chafes against the restrictions that this child imposes.

She looked up at the sound of Gustave wheeling a barrow full of potatoes up the garden path. He nodded to Elspeth and she called out, 'Hello, how are you, Gustave?'

'Good morning, Ma'm.'

'And your wife and child?' She was anxious to talk to him. A thought had occurred to her a few days ago when talking to her mother about who will care for Gina while she goes back to work full time. Already Madge looks after the baby for two days a week but she can't do more. Ruby was too busy, and most other women have gone off to work in factories or on farms.

'Well, thank you Ma'm,' Gustave called back. This woman rarely speaks to him. It has struck him as strange that she's the daughter of Mr and Mrs Smith who are so open and friendly. Mr Simms treats him as an equal too, despite his inferior knowledge of gardening.

'Where are you living now?' Elspeth asked knowing perfectly well.

Gustave rested the barrow on the path. 'Mrs Pearson, the wife of your previous gardener, who is widowed and … but of course you know.'

'Yes, we were so sorry. Mr Simms worries that Mr Pearson should have stopped working earlier, it being too much for a man of his age.' Though privately she thinks that when he gave up his job nothing else mattered, that he perhaps died of boredom.

'We are very lucky to have rooms with Mrs Pearson. And I think we are company for her.'

'I'm sure you're right.'

Elspeth remained seated, hoping that he might come to sit beside her. He was uncertain as to whether to stay. And she wasn't sure how to propose her offer. He bent to take hold of the handles of the barrow, was about to move on when she said, 'How old is your son?'

'Ivan is five.'

'He'll be starting school soon then?'

'Yes, Ma'm. We hope he will start in the autumn.'

'That's good. I know there's a problem with schools having closed or being too full of evacuees.'

'He enjoys learning. Thank you for asking, Ma'm.' He began to move on.

'I'm pleased. I look forward to Gina going to school.' And she laughed. 'I've a long time to wait for that.'

'It will come round soon enough,' Gustave waited for her to finish the conversation. In front of her, his foreignness weighing as heavily as do the potatoes in the barrow.

'I'm sorry, I shouldn't have stopped you.' Elspeth stood up. 'Those potatoes need to go somewhere.'

'They're for the British Restaurant. Mr Simms is making a contribution.'

'That's good. Do you take them along yourself?'

'No, they're collected. For now I put them in bags from the shed.'

Elspeth came to where he was standing. 'I think I need a glass of water. What about you? Can I make you a cup of tea? Ruby's gone to the shops.' She laughed. 'We might be able to steal one of her rock cakes.'

Gustave made way for her to go first. She was not as before. Such a change, the aloof air gone.

'Your wife is Dutch, I believe,' she said as they walked up to the kitchen together. 'And you are German so will Ivan be trilingual? Can I say that?'

'I hope so. My wife, Mareke, wishes that I teach him Russian too.'

'Heavens! That means …' she knows this man is clever, George has told her many times of his learning but it still surprised her. 'You speak Russian?'

'Yes, my grandmother came from the Ukraine so …'

'I'm sorry,' Elspeth realised that there may be horrible implications to this conversation. 'I hope that … well this is such a terrible world just now it is hard to comprehend what other people are suffering.'

Did she want him to explain?

'It must be dreadful to be away from your own country when …' She looked at his face as if for the first time. His hair is quite long, cut as if with scissors not a razor. He's a good looking man even so. His eyebrows are very bushy and dark and at the same time he looks so young. 'I don't mean to intrude.'

'No. Thank you for your concern.'

And strangely there was Ruby coming through from the hall carrying the carpet sweeper. 'There's been a wretched bird in the dining room, Ma'm. Got in the window, I suppose, couldn't get out, silly sparrow! And what a mess!' She then saw Gustave. 'Oh, the potatoes for the BR. Thank you, Gusto. I'm expecting the man to collect them any minute.'

Elspeth looked from one to the other, feeling excluded. 'Has it gone now? The bird?'

'Yes, but it led me a right dance to catch and let it out. Can't bear to see the fright on it.'

'You're a marvel, Ruby,' Elspeth hoped that Gustave had noticed their friendly relationship. 'I thought you were out shopping. I've just come in for a glass of water and I was going to make Gustave a cup of tea.'

Ruby beamed from one to the other. 'I'll do the tea, Ma'm, and bring yours out to you.'

What could she do now? With Ruby there it was impossible to talk to Gustave. She turned to him. 'Please give my best wishes to your wife, Gustave, and to Mrs Pearson.'

When George came home she said, 'I hadn't realised that Gustave spoke so many languages. German, Russian and his English is perfect. And his wife being Dutch I wonder how they communicate. Which language I mean? You've always said that he's a clever man.'

George wanted to say, at least we speak the same language, but he didn't want to risk any possible offence. It wasn't her fault that motherhood didn't suit, thrust upon her as it was and in such a tangled situation. Her insistence on coming back to work, part-time, had eased things greatly in the office, but Kenneth was cross. The arrival of Gina seemed to have alerted him in some way to an interest in controlling what happened at home. 'It's quite wrong, Dad. Can't you at least see? I mean, the child needs its mother, not being handed hither and thither.' That those taking care of his child are eminently qualified, her mother and occasionally Ruby, made this assertion both rude and ridiculous. But George was wary. Despite what Elspeth said and what he plainly saw for himself, he still worried that he'd driven a wedge between husband and wife. Nothing made much sense any more. He's achingly tired. Sleep fails him. ARP duties mean that there is little pattern to when he gets to bed. The baby cries at cock crow, of course, and Elspeth rarely hears her. Ruby is the one who trots along the corridor, shushes the baby, takes her down to the kitchen to make up a bottle of milk, and tend to the feeding. But he's woken, his head crowding with nightmare images, a jumble of guilt, the burden of work and the strain of keeping his emotions boxed up, except for his little daughter who grows more adorable each day. He feels that his heart will burst each time she smiles at him. The toothless expression of excitement and joy that she offers whenever she sees him, soothes much of the tribulation. And Elspeth allows this love, no longer chides him. 'You're both dotty,' she says. 'A pair of Cheshire cats.' But it's said gently with a sense of wonder, perhaps even pride.

Elspeth wheeled Gina across town to her mother. The great chariot of a pram gleamed in the early morning sun. Gina was fast asleep, bottles, milk powder and nappies in the pannier under the handle. This pretty woman, neatly dressed, hair of such a glorious colour tamed to a neat bun, was the embodiment of maternal perfection. They, the powers that be, might have used this as a propaganda poster; *The war does not ruffle the mothers of England.*

Elspeth, with quite different views, hoped to stop and chat with her mother even though she'd be late into the office. If Ma approves, it will help to put the plan into action; the perfect solution.

Madge was on her hands and knees scrubbing the scullery floor. 'You're very prompt, love,' she said. 'Give me a few minutes and then I'll put little precious in the garden. It's a lovely day, thank goodness, and she can watch the washing on the line when she wakes. She loves that you know. I heard her cooing to a row of your Pa's socks the other day.'

'Can I put the kettle on, Ma? I was hoping for a chat.'

'Yes, but I've no milk I'm afraid. I let your Pa have a mug of Ovaltine last night when he got back as he looked all in.'

There were tea leaves left in the pot which Elspeth didn't rinse out. They'd been left to be used again she knows that. Weak tea didn't matter if her mother accepted her plan.

'Ma,' Elspeth began. 'I'm ever so grateful to you for looking after Gina. You know that don't you? I'm so happy to be back at work even …'

'I know, and you look so much better for it.' Madge thought she knew what was coming; more days and she'll be paid for it. But that wasn't right. To be given money for looking after her own granddaughter, would be wrong. And it wasn't as if she didn't want to help for she knows so well the satisfaction of earning your own wage, being valued for a job well done. Motherhood gives that to nobody. There isn't anyone in the world that thinks it's not your duty, nothing special, something that comes naturally. The announcement that having babies contributed to the war effort was the last straw; she'd told Ernest, 'More canon fodder, that's what they want.'

'Look, Ma,' Elspeth broke into her reverie. 'I know it's difficult for you; I mean if you didn't have Gina these two days you could be doing something more worthwhile. I mean earning a bit extra.' Madge didn't say anything. It was best to let it come, the whole bit of asking. 'It's just that I had an idea from something you said the other day. You know, about Gustave's wife?'

'Did I?'

'Yes, you said what a sweet person she is, and how sad that she can't work.'

Elspeth found Gustave sheltering in the greenhouse. Sheets of water slapped down the panes of glass so that from inside he couldn't see out. Her entrance was a surprise. She furled her umbrella. 'Such dismal weather, what can be done?'

'I'm afraid that I've done very little today, Ma'm.' She still scared him. Twice since her friendliness a few days ago she'd called out to say, 'hello'. Was she checking up on his work?

'Gustave, I want to ask you something outright,' she said. 'There's no point in beating about the bush - you know that English expression?'

'Yes, it means that you will be straightforward.'

'Just so.' The cold outside, the chill water on the glass and the warmth from a paraffin heater was causing a mist to rise. It was as if they were in a cocoon. 'I want to go back to work full time,' she said. 'My mother looks after Gina for two days a week but can do no more. Ruby, who would love to help, has too many other duties.' This was much easier than she'd expected. 'Your wife, I believe, is looking for employment although I know that this was not necessarily what she is trained for. I mean, all women are supposed to be good at motherhood … no, what I mean is … I'm sorry, what is the work she is seeking?'

He looked at her directly. 'Mareke is a translator. Those skills ought to be used but we foreigners …' he shrugged. He didn't mean to be rude but to be grateful and grovelling is infuriating. His talents are being wasted, hers too. Hers especially. Her country overrun, a victim not an enemy alien.

'I'm sorry,' Elspeth said. And she was truly sorry. Her imprisonment, as she saw it, made her feel that she understood more than most. 'Everything is so topsy turvy, though that's a silly expression to use, I know. Hideous, dreadful, cruel, and that we go on day by day as if it's normal seems worse sometimes.'

He could see that he'd unsettled her. 'Tell me then this bush which is not to be beaten around? Are you asking if my wife would look after your daughter?'

Madge and Elspeth visited Mareke leaving Gina with Ruby. Ivan, the four-year-old boy, opened the door, a replica of his father. Behind him stood Mrs Pearson and Mareke. 'You are welcome,' he said. There were smiles all round. 'He's a fine lad,' Mrs Pearson purred as proud as if he were her own child.

Elspeth didn't need to be cowed by Mareke's scholarship. This woman was as plain and capable as anyone you could meet. Her cheeks were round and pink and she smiled so readily you expected her to break into song. Elspeth visualised the bonnet and clogs with a windmill in the background.

'Gina wasn't planned was she?' Ma said as they walked home.

'No.'

'You forgot the contraceptive cap, an accident?'

'Yes.'

'Well, you've paid for it, love. Always the woman who has to pay.

Nothing more was said. Nothing more will ever be said.

'You don't think it matters?' Kenneth lounged in the armchair that belongs to George. 'My child being brought up by a foreigner. The wife of Dad's gardener.' They were statements intended to provoke.

Elspeth ignored him. All's right in her world. On Saturday afternoons she and George are often alone. Ruby, as puffed out as a peacock, is always pleased to take 'her ladyship for my sister and her girls to see.'

Kenneth stared across at his wife. 'I don't know what's got into you, Elsy.' He ground his cigarette stub into the ashtray. 'Scuttling back to work as if you have to.'

She ignored him her concentration on the knitting pattern open on the arm of the sofa, the sound of Glenn Miller swinging along on the gramophone. The room chilly with no fire in the grate.

'Don't I give you enough money?'

She didn't look up.

'I mean this woman's not trained to be a nanny, is she?'

Elspeth counted the stitches on her knitting needles.

Kenneth sat forward, 'Elsy!' but he hesitated to get up and come across to where she was ensconced on the sofa. It was plain to see that this was where she always sat, comfortably at home in this room, without him. 'Damn it! Are you listening to me?'

'Yes, I heard what you said.' Her voice as smooth as the background music.

'And?'

'You're talking rubbish, but I didn't want to say.'

'Rubbish! That's a nice way to talk to your husband!'

'Stop shouting, Ken, you'll wake Gina. And your new friend? Bob, isn't it, what's he going to think?' She looked up. 'Where is he anyway?'

Kenneth picked up his glass, swirled and gulped the last of the whisky, turned to see that the door was closed.

'He'll not think anything. He knows what's what with wives going astray. We've talked about it.'

'Astray!' Fear caught her for a second but seeing him, clutching his empty glass, she knew it was bluster. He'd thought to cow her, waiting for her submission, '*Oh, Kenny!*' But no more. She's been through all this. He's already claimed the baby as his offspring, boasted the fact, Gina is accepted unquestioningly. Laying the knitting in her lap, she said, 'Who is this Bob person anyway? This man to whom you've talked about our marriage?'

'Well, no, it wasn't like that.'

'Like what?'

He got up, the empty glass dangling as if an extension of his arm, the other hand jingling the loose change in his pocket. 'This isn't about us, it's about you.'

'Me?' She laughed. 'I'm the one here, keeping the home fires burning, as they say.'

'You're not getting my point.' He looked again to the door, hoped Ruby couldn't hear. He's seen how she dotes on Elspeth.

'Really?' Elspeth examined her knitting keenly. 'Why did you need to bring him here anyway, this Bob? To check on me? Make life difficult for Ruby, catering, clean sheets, without warning?' She'd regained the high ground and was determined to hold it.

'You know why, I told Dad. Bob needs a break, like me.'

Elspeth looked up at him again, 'How often have you needed this break, then?' holding his gaze until he had to turn away, 'if you're going to question my wifely duties - if that's how you put it?'

'I didn't say …'

'No? Well I think a lot of people would be amazed at your lack of interest in your husbandly duties.'

'There's a war on, Elsy! I'm involved in vital work.' He flounced over to the wall cabinet, opened it to peer inside, pulled out a bottle of whisky. 'Why doesn't Dad keep the stuff on a tray anymore? It used to be set out with glasses. Not hidden away in here.'

'There's a war on!' Elspeth mimicked, raising her voice. She knew that Ruby wouldn't be surprised. She understands Kenneth. *'He was a lad for tantrums,'* she'd once said. *'But you could always nudge him back into being a nice boy.'* She would think nothing of it. And the American lodger might enjoy a bit of domestic drama. But Elspeth had lost her nonchalant bravado. 'Do you believe that I'd let my daughter be taken into the home of an unsuitable person. Do you consider me so irresponsible?'

It was his turn to ignore her as he checked the level of liquor in the bottle, filled his glass, found another and filled that too.

'Have you met Mareke?' she persisted.

'Who?'

'The wife of Gustave who is taking care of Gina.'

'Of course I haven't,' he snapped back. He'd rather lost the gist of what he was saying.

'Well then, you can't criticise.'

'No, I wasn't saying that.' He regretted that he'd started this. *'Never stir up a hornet's nest, old chap,'* was one of Jack's sayings. He ducked away from her straight stare. 'You're not the girl I married, Elspeth,' he said as if to himself.

She laughed. 'You're right, and is that surprising?'

'Well, I don't know.' The record had finished, the needle scratching round in the centre of the disc. He went to lift it off. 'I mean,' he turned back to her, 'I suppose it's the War.'

'Always the excuse.' But her anger was spent. He looked foolish and vulnerable; the moustache hardly suited him. 'Perhaps we didn't really know each other well enough before.'

But that was dangerous talk. There was no way out of it. She'd checked grounds for divorce with Jim Furland; an easy question in the office where her desire to understand what clients want or need was considered essential. *'You're a clever woman, Mrs Kenneth,'* Jim had said on many occasions.

Kenneth lifted the played record from the turntable, slid it into its paper sleeve. He rifled through his case of discs to find something cheery. Bob might come down at any minute, he was only having a nap, said something about letting Kenneth '*have time alone with your missus*'. He took out another record, checked the title.

'You'd better come and meet Mareke, Ken.' Elspeth said. 'I thought you of all people would be pleased, a person of such learning. She speaks three languages, you know?'

'Stop going on, Elsy,' he glanced round briefly, 'you know I can't take more time off.'

A tentative tap on the door saved him from further ridicule, a head peering round. 'Oh, you're in here. I thought I'd …'

'Come in, old chap!' Kenneth thrust the glass of whisky at him. 'I'm just about to put on one of my favourites, Duke Ellington, 'Riding on a Blue Note'. You like jazz, don't you?'

'You don't have to say 'yes'.' Elspeth smiled sweetly, though bitterness was what she felt, and dread of the future; the day when the War is over, for it will one day be over. It doesn't bear thinking about, living in another house without George.

A month later there's a tea party in the garden for Gina's first birthday. Mareke, Gustave with Ivan as well as Madge and Ernest were invited. Ruby had saved real eggs specially to make a cake; the icing spare and pink. One candle flickered and died before Gina could blow it out. 'Dratted wind,' Ruby muttered as she placed the cake on the tea trolley. George laughed, 'It's a miracle that we still have candles. Left over from when Ken was a child, I guess?' 'Yes, well,' Ruby said, handing Elspeth a knife. She was definitely out of sorts. The news from Italy, what there was, ought to reassure, as well as the bombing of Berlin. But, '*It's hard to keep your pecker up, Ralph being out there still,*' she kept saying. Her pride in '*he's one of them fighting to save us,'* has frayed. Fear for him, fear for what her sister kept calling his 'charmed life', seemed to have aged her. Elspeth said, 'Please, Ruby, come and sit down, Gustave will find another deckchair from the shed.' And as Gustave strode off George called after him, 'I think there's still an old scooter of Ken's in there. Bring it for Ivan, please.'

Ruby sank into the seat offered, worried she'd never get out. And despite being able to watch her 'little treasure' crawling after the boy, it wasn't right. To be waited on was all wrong though it's kindness that's offered. It was Mareke who saw her discomfort, knows her well as every morning she comes to collect Gina, is fond of her too. 'How do you cut the bread so thinly, Ruby?' she said referring to the paste sandwiches. Ruby's reply was sharp. 'I've always done it like that. It's what my ma and grandma did. It's just what I do.' Mareke could see that it's more than embarrassment that distresses Ruby. Five years of privation and bottled terror; it's remarkable and troubling that more people haven't gone mad. She has said to Gustave, 'Are we becoming less human?'

The cake was cut, happy birthday sung, Gina clapped her hands, George blinked back tears. Elspeth congratulated Ivan who passed everyone a piece of cake. Ivan is obedient and intelligent. A perfect little friend for Gina. Ken's attitude, his demeaning of Gustave and Mareke was ludicrous and nasty.

And as if on cue there he was, calling out: 'What's going on here?'

No one had heard the crunch of gravel as his car swerved into the drive. They were all enjoying Ivan's attempts to push off on the scooter while Gina shouted furiously for his attention.

Elspeth lazily turned, 'Oh, you've come. Gina's birthday party.'

'I know.'

'You didn't say you were coming. We'd have …'

'I'm here aren't I?'

It was a sour exchange followed by silence. Even the children paused, Ivan putting down the scooter and scurrying up close to Gina on the grass.

'Well, good,' George got up, 'come and join us. The cake's cut; Ruby's performed another miracle.'

Kenneth didn't move, frowning down at those still seated. 'I don't know these people.'

'Oh,' George looked back as if he'd forgotten too. 'But you know Elspeth's parents. And Gustave I'm sure you've met. The man who's another wonder, making my garden grow.' His smile was a little too wide, he sounded a little too jolly. 'I didn't realise that you haven't met Mareke. Mareke, this is my son, and Elspeth's husband.' Mareke was already on her feet, nodding a greeting. How could anyone not be charmed by her sweet open face?

But Kenneth didn't come forward to shake their hands. 'I'm Gina's father,' he declared.

Meanwhile Ruby was struggling to get out of the deckchair which seemed to push her back down every time she shoved herself up. Mareke went to help. 'Dratted thing,' Ruby muttered, 'and thank you, dear.' She was close to tears. 'If you'll excuse me, I'll just be putting that kettle on.'

'Thank you,' Elspeth nodded her gratitude, and then to Kenneth. 'Do you want a piece of cake?'

Ivan had crawled over to be with his parents, Gina following to sit at Mareke's feet.

Kenneth surveyed the scene again. 'Gina!' he called out. She looked up, turned to the voice, but put her arms out to clutch Mareke's legs. Mareke picked her up, was about to take her to Kenneth but the child screamed and hid her face in the woman's shoulder.

Kenneth shrugged morosely, and turning to Elspeth, who was offering him a slice with cake, 'I need to speak to you, Elsy. Privately.'

How many seconds they stood in this ominous tableau, nobody will remember. The gardener with his arm around his wife, who carries a child on her hip, another hiding behind her legs; George with his false smile waiting for his son to acknowledge his introduction, and Elspeth ramrod straight, her arm stretched out with that plate of cake.

'Now,' Kenneth said, though it was hardly an order as his voice cracked.

Elspeth looked back at George who saw the question in her eyes, before she turned to Gustave and Mareke, Ma and Pa. 'Will you excuse me?'

Kenneth was already in the drawing room staring into the mirror over the fireplace. Driving here, his shoulders stretched taut gripping the steering wheel, the speed of the car, concentration on the road, had held him together. In this room, the familiar blue, the polished furniture picking up any light, it was all dissolving. The shaking came as a relief. He put an arm out to the mantelpiece to steady himself. How could he say it out loud, to admit that it is true?

'Ken?' Elspeth closed the door. 'That was rude. I can't think …' But then she saw him crumple, bent forward, emitting snorts of sound. She stared at his stooped body, the trembling that forced him to kneel on the floor. She went over to him, 'What is it?'

It was that, her words, which caused the flood of weeping. She knelt to put her arms around him. She cradled him to her; what else could she do? 'What's happened, Ken?'

'Jack, it's Jack!' He howled. 'I've lost him.'

Demobilisation 1945

Gina was two when Madge collapsed and died on VJ Day, August 14th 1945. The post-mortem revealed ovarian cancer.

Elspeth stood beside her father at the funeral, rigid with remorse. Her mother worked tirelessly during the war, scrimping and sewing, serving at the British Restaurant, making-do and mending for refugees, as Mrs Briggs Fanshawe, standing at a lectern, was saying to the small congregation. 'My right hand woman when I wanted anything done.'

Elspeth heard these words and hated herself. Hated that she'd never known her mother, not truly. She'd wanted to be better than her which was stupid and wrong. Why had she never recognised who Ma was as well as what she gave her? The clothes she'd run up out of nothing, letting her take that shorthand and typing course which cost more than they could afford. She'd never thanked her properly.

The columns of the church loomed gaunt and grim as if to emphasise her paltry self. The organ plodded out hymns which made no sense in such a cold dank place. Had Ma believed in all this? Had she ever said? *'I want you to be happy, Elspeth,'* was what she had said. Ma, who knew about love, who'd given her the advice which was right. *'Women don't need to be shy, to hold back, we are made for the pleasure too.'* The words came as comfort and gall. She couldn't hold back her tears. There was so much to cry for. If only she'd told her about George. Ma might have understood. Perhaps she had anyway?

Kenneth stood at her other side. Disconcerted by her grief, he tried to put his arm around her. He hadn't thought she cared much for Madge. He'd never taken to her. She'd always appeared quite sniffy towards him. It was a surprise, too, to hear that other woman praising her.

Elspeth felt his touch and shrank back. She turned to find George in the pew behind her. His head bowed, his eyes shut. Why wasn't he beside her, his arm around her? Ernest was there though. She took hold of his hand, gripped it tightly. He turned to her, shaking his head at the same time as offering a reassuring smile and whispered, 'It'll be all right, sweetheart.'

Bomber command no longer needed the services of the Royal Observer Corps. Kenneth was demobbed. Another day of tragedy. 'You don't understand, do you, Elsy?' he said, though the accusation was unfair. Elspeth did understand. Hadn't she pressed hard to carry on with the job she loves? But it was better to accept and ignore as he repeated this accusation again and again as if to bolster his self-esteem. 'That was a real job, worth doing. People looked up to me. It was the RAF and ROC that won the War.'

George didn't want to have a row but the obvious needed to be stated. 'You're lucky to have a job to come back to, Ken, hundreds don't.' This had to be made clear. But guilt and sadness at his own conflicted situation made him try for a more conciliatory tone. 'You'll want to brush up on what you already know, of course. You can be very proud of what you've done these last few years, but now you can be proud of being back with the firm.'

'Proud?' Ken snorted. 'Sorry, Dad, but you know it's drudgery.'

'If I thought that I wouldn't be doing it. This is your grandfather's firm, started with Jim Furland's father.'

'What's that got to do with me?' The dining room was cold; drizzle drumming on the windows. Corned beef and salad on their plates. Kenneth reached for the salad cream, banged the bottom of the bottle repeatedly until a tongue of mayonnaise emerged. 'Christ! Can't even get a decent meal in this house.'

'That's enough!' George slammed down his own knife and fork. 'Don't you understand about rationing? Ruby works very hard to give us decent food; we're lucky enough to be able to grow most of what you're eating. Be thankful.'

'Well isn't that …' but he didn't finish for George had raised a hand to stop him.

'You may have eaten better in your mess, but that's over. And you'd better get used to what's on offer here because you'll find nothing better anywhere else.' He wiped his mouth on his napkin, folded and placed it with exaggerated precision on the table. 'I seem to have lost my appetite.' He pushed back his chair. 'Look, Ken, I have sympathy for the change in your life, but I don't wish to hear anything else on the subject.'

The hall was dark and chill. George found that he was shaking, his legs gone to jelly. He grabbed hold of the banisters, sank down onto the stairs. What will become of us, his abiding thoughts. Nothing can be denied, or explained. Merely endured. He climbed the stairs, as if each tread was steeper than the last. He peered into Gina's bedroom, the crease of landing light into the open door enough to see the child's sleeping form. He tip-toed thief-like to her bed, the snug body turned into the pillow, dark hair plastered to her cheek. He bent to hear her breathe, smell the sweet odour, kissed her forehead. Her beauty is astounding, the miracle of this little being is overwhelming. If nothing else, she will always be his to cherish.

Elspeth was with her father sorting out what should be done with her mother's remains, her clothes and all 'her bits and pieces'.

'You don't have to do it all now, Pa,' she said. The casket of ashes sat in the middle of the table where there once had been a vase of flowers. It was shocking to look at it. How could such a small container hold all of her mother's body?

Ernest took the bag of produce she'd brought. He peered inside the bag. 'Runners, you know I'm partial to runner beans. Ma used to make white sauce to go with them. A meal in itself.' He headed for the scullery. 'It's lovely to see you, sweetheart. Let's have a cup of tea. No, don't you get up, I'll make it.'

He was too calm, she thought. How can she tackle the subject of where he'll live? How can he afford to keep this house without Ma's earnings?

Clouds skimmed across the sky, rain came in squalls, rat-tatting on the window. The parlour was cold and gloomy, the red embroidered table cover barely showing any colour. There was no other sign of her.

'Where's her sewing, Pa?' The machine taking its place on the table with garments strewn on chairs were all gone. Gathered up and stowed under the stairs as they would have been when a meal was made ready. 'Did she put it all away?'

He brought through the tea appearing not to have heard.

'How's our little Gina. Do you know what she said to me last week? "You're a ickle pickle, Gramps." Made me laugh.' He poured the tea smiling to himself.

Elspeth didn't smile. 'It's an expression Ruby uses to her. You little pickle. I'm sorry she said it to you.'

'No, no! It was lovely. I am in a bit of a pickle without my Madge.' He looked at her with a gentle shrug.

'Oh, Pa! It's not fair.'

'No, but that can be said for thousands who've died in this last five years. Has to be faced.'

Elspeth shook her head, looking back at him as if pleading for something, she knew not what. To tell him, as she wished to tell Ma? But no, this wasn't why she was here, it was for him. 'Pa, I have to ask. How will you live here? The rent? Do we need to look for less expensive accommodation?' She'd rehearsed these words; not 'cheaper' for that would have devalued what they already had. She might have wished for better when she was a child, but it had always been home, a home that they were proud of, a well-kept home as she's learned to see it.

'You didn't really know your Ma, did you, Elspeth?' Using her proper name struck as a reprimand. He stirred sugar into his tea, circling round and round. 'She was clever with money. Made it and put it aside.' There was no hurry for he knew the main subject of her visit had been broached. 'You've no need to worry for me. There is enough put away that I can live on here, in this house, for a very long time.' The stirring went on and on and she knew not to interrupt. But his hand was shaking and as he took out the spoon, it clattered into the saucer.

'Oh, Pa! What do we do?'

Tears that were hardly tears wetted his cheeks. Hers fell fast even as she wiped them away with a handkerchief pulled from her purse.

'Nothing,' and he put a hand across to stroke her cheek. 'Having you come here is enough.'

'Oh, Pa, anything!'

For a moment they sat in silence while he watched her attempt to staunch the tears. Finally he said, 'Well,' and sniffing, his mouth pursing and pouting, trying to hold the words intact, 'it's not something I want to do yet, But …' He placed his hands tenderly on the casket, 'And it isn't as if I can't …'

'What, Pa?' And then she knew. Putting her own hands over his she said, 'Is it where to put this, her, Ma?'

He nodded.

'Did she say anything about it? I mean, I know she chose the cremation.'

'Always practical, my Madge!' And he managed the wisp of a smile. 'It's the park, she said. Remembering that lovely day we all had there on VE Day, all of us together, even your … Mr Simms.'

It was too much. 'Your Mr Simms'. It wasn't meant to sound like that, he'd wanted to say 'your father-in-law', of course, but that was it. George is hers and there's no one to tell, no one to share that the world is upside down, hemmed in, wrong. 'Oh, Pa!' Sobbing, her head bent over, pressing his hands, tightly held around the casket. 'I can't bear it,' she cried.

'Now, now,' his voice not much more than a croak. 'It'll be all right. If we could do this together, sweetheart, I know she'd like that.' He cleared his throat. 'Not yet, when we're stronger. It would mean the world to me, if you'd come with me.' Again an upward lift to his voice. 'I'm not sure what's allowed so we might have to do it surreptitious like. Not that we'd be doing any harm. Up by those big chestnut trees, with the candles and then the conkers. Could we manage that do you think?'

She released her hands and he his. 'Of course, Pa. Yes, you just let me know when's the right time.' She blotted her eyes, blew her nose and gathered in her breath.

'That's good, that's my girl.'

Sun streaked through the rain, glinted off the glass, sharp, eye piercing. He blinked, put the cosy back on the teapot, and took a sip of tea. She leant forward to kiss his cheek.

'I wish …' she began, the handkerchief scrunched in her lap..

'I know,' he shook his head wearily, 'wishes are all very well but it's deeds that matter. And I know your Ma's peering down at me, making sure I keep up standards.' He gave a little chuckle. 'That's what I'll have to do. Keep up standards. That's what we do, isn't it, sweetheart?'

Elspeth and Gina would always remember that day, the last day in the house that was their home. A day of the bluest sky above the greenest lawn where handkerchiefs lay to dry like an invasion of waterlilies. A day when everyone, except Kenneth, was unhappy.

Gina sat on the steps close by the pond, watching for the goldfish which have swum to the bottom mud, away from the heat. She was four years old and hot; the cotton hat she wore wet with perspiration. She would have liked to throw a stone into the water. To disturb those fish, to hurt them as much as she was being hurt. But that would upset Grandpa and she loves Grandpa more than anyone in the world.

George was either in the greenhouse or on the allotment though never in a place where he could be found. He thought it best to keep out of the way, get used to being alone. For it needed to be faced. They were going. Elspeth was his son's wife and he needed her. Except he didn't. It was painful to allow, to accept. As Elspeth kept saying. 'I'm a trinket, a useful cover.' Though no one delved too deeply into the implications.

The soft thrum of bees on the lavender bushes beside the greenhouse was blotted out by the sound of Ralph, Ruby's husband, dismantling the Anderson shelter. The shelter which had for the last seven years conveniently blocked the view of the greenhouse from the kitchen windows or from anyone coming from that direction. The greenhouse,' our secret haunt', where they'd escaped to be alone. And for months inside the fug and earthy smells the abomination of her leaving had driven every conversation. 'I won't even be able to sit with you in the evening. I'll be alone with him,' she cried. George tried to console with, 'You'll come back to visit, there'll be reasons.' He didn't know what these would be. Like her he was sinking under what was inevitable. And here was the day and there was nothing to be done but remove himself.

The shed at the bottom of the garden was hot, the sun bearing down on the wooden rafters, a strong smell of creosote familiar and comforting. He lifted the shears from their hook. Cutting the privet hedge required enough energy to exhaust, might distract from the gloom that shrouded everything. It was useless, of course, for back came her voice. 'I belong here, I belong with you.' He'd said nothing. How could he? What did belonging mean when there'd been a contract signed between Kenneth and Elspeth? That was the reality.

He can't counter with how much he'll lose. To be alone with the knowledge of what love really means. She's taught him that. To be the lover he wanted to be. To lie naked together on his bed, the sheet pulled up as a shield against the chilly room, their bodies glowing, the fire of love making over, wallowing in the sweet glory of giving and receiving. 'Why should we feel guilty?' she'd said. 'It's not what Kenneth wants, none of it.' And she'd smoothed her hand down the length of his body to rest on his buttocks. No shame. It was what they can do, want to do. 'Why should we deny ourselves? Who are we hurting?

That was the last time, a Sunday afternoon months ago, frost covering the lawn where the sun couldn't reach. Condensation dribbling down the inside of the windows, languid pools settling on the sills; the old blackout curtains sucking up the wet, leaving a white tidemark.

There has been little privacy for months, few chances even to sit alone, to talk, to listen to music. Beethoven and Mozart no longer grace the air waves. Jazz rules. Kenneth is lost without Jack, has found that other returnees from the War are settling down to married life. Going 'out on the town' is no longer in fashion.

George felt sympathy for his son that this was the case, but his lack of effort in the office was an intense irritation, a near scandal.

To add to his grief was the prospect of his precious daughter no longer living with him. The pain of it was as sharp as if he'd sliced through his arm. His daughter, Gina, who was sitting beside the pond with her white hat and floral frock. 'Grandpa, do you like the flowers on my dress,' she'd said many times splaying out the skirt for his approval. Above the snip and snap of his hedge cutting and between the hammer blows on metal, he could hear her singing, 'Half a pound of tuppenny rice,' a song Ruby has taught her, the words of no consequence except for the explosive ending to each verse. He could picture the performance that he's witnessed many times, as she flings her rag doll into the air with each 'pop' of the weasel.

Ruby took up another of Gina's frocks. Slowly she folded and smoothed and placed into a suitcase as if ministering at some ritual, a rite of passage, which it was to some extent. 'It's a house fit for royalty, Ma'am,' she said to Elspeth to brighten the mood. She isn't going with them, her place is with Mr George; this has been her home for more than thirty years. Another young woman had been found to 'do' for them. 'A lucky girl to be keeping that house up to scratch with all its mod cons.' Ruby repeated this and her previous observation until Elspeth finally pleaded, 'Lets not talk about it.'

Elspeth hadn't slept last night or the one before that. The vista of Kenneth, Gina and herself stuck together in a structure which was entirely of his making, sickens her. Hadn't she been patient enough in fending off Kenneth's misery on returning to civilian life? He'd bleated on about, 'the conspiracy between you and Dad,' when he realised that he was expected to work on Saturdays. He'd complained that, 'I don't know what's got into him letting you take over what should be a manager's job.' He'd snorted sarcastically to his father, 'What's this thing with Elspeth running around the office as if she's queen bee?' He continued to mutter about the food. 'What's the point of having money if you can't get people to do what you want?' Elspeth didn't argue. Her defence was not to react to his taunts, to ignore them. Rows required effort; she needs to preserve her sanity to cope with this terrible state of affairs.

Kenneth was putting the finishing touches to his house, a child with its new toy. His best buddy, Frank, a young architect, helped him design the new build on a piece of land acquired before the War. Land in Hinton Road, a road running parallel to Glebe Avenue. The track further down leading to the allotments backing onto his father's garden, which will become a favourite route, a life line, for Elspeth and Gina.

Elspeth had purposely ignored the prospect of this day. She'd focused on keeping Kenneth occupied, encouraged his love of sport, desperate for him to find young unmarried men who needed to let off steam playing squash, tennis, golf. And afterwards, or when the golf course was too wet or frosty, to while away time in the clubhouse bar; members only. Anything to keep him out, not to have to suffer his company.

Did it matter that he drank a lot, or that he was grumpy when sober? Or that he frequently wore a V necked khaki pullover which belonged to an army officer, part of his uniform, possibly Jack's? She pitied him, tried to appear interested in discussions on this new house. He'd spread the plans out on the dining room table. 'What do you think, Elspeth?' He began but doesn't wait for her opinion. 'You see the L shape, the bow windows on the downstairs front rooms. And there's the sundial over the main door.' His finger has pointed out this feature many times before. 'Jolly touch that.'

It could be an elephant enclosure for all she cares.

Gina took off her sandals and contemplated her doll's lack of shoes, lack of toes. She moved to the edge of the pond where it's possible to lean over and dip both their feet into the water. The cold was a shock but soothing. Clouds of weed swirled and tickled. Were the fishes nibbling? If she climbed in she might reach the muddy bottom.

The greenhouse was full of flowers. Through the anti-shatter tape which still criss-crossed all the panes of glass, the pink and white and green became a jigsaw pattern. Her footstool was in there. The place where she stands to help Grandpa fill up flowerpots. He dibs a hole in the earth, hands her a tiny seedling to plop in place. She's learnt how to press her fingers gently around that delicate green shoot to settle it in. '*Like when I tuck you up in bed at night,*' he's said. He's told her that she can come again after they've moved to the new house. He'll need her help. But Mummy may not let her, or come too and spoil it.

The noise of demolition continued behind her. Upstairs Elspeth sat down on the bed and wept. The screech of nuts and bolts being prised apart, metal on metal, the clank, clank as each piece fell away echoed what was happening to her heart, her life.

George stepped back from the hedge. He needed the ladder to reach the top, also the wheelbarrow and rake to clear away the clippings. A bonfire would be in order as there was no wind; after dinner when Gina was in bed. Though she'd been enthralled when he burnt the old rose bushes, '*Is it magic, Grandpa?*' she'd said, holding his hand tightly, drawn to watch the flames, transfixed. '*Are those fairies in there?*' Maybe she'd like to help him now.

She twirled the water with her feet, saw the mud churn, the lily pads glide to and fro. She stepped over the edge to find her feet on a ledge, the water up to her shins, no further. And she held her doll close to her shoulder as it was too deep for its short body and legs, it would spoil its dress. She hitched her own dress into her knickers like Ruby had done for her when they went to the seaside once. But it was difficult while keeping her doll safely held. And then it happened, the silly doll jumped out of her arms, flew up and over to land right in the middle of the pond. The foolish creature lay on her back, its raggy hair soaking up the water. Gina knew it was her fault and she didn't want to lose her doll, not now when it's the only friend she has to take to this new strange place. Fish know how to swim, it looked easy, she's sure that's what she can do. She jumped right in and to begin with the water fills out her dress to float around her, like a ballet dancer, but then she's pulled down and down with no breath only water to breathe. She wanted Grandpa but she couldn't shout for him to help.

Gina didn't drown, though many times after she wished she had. George pulled her from the water, muddy and wet, with weed as a drab crown. Hugging her to his chest he said the words that either she didn't hear or understand, 'My darling child, my precious daughter.'

Gina sat beside Ivan on his bed. She wanted to put her arm round his shoulders hunched as he was, staring at his hands. To put both arms around him in a big hug would be even better. She liked how he smelt of soap and pencils, warm and woolly. She hated that he was so unhappy and she couldn't make it better. It was three weeks since his mother died, killed in a road accident, knocked off her bicycle by a speeding car. Mareke, who Gina loved too, not her mother but the best sort of mother, and now she's gone. Yesterday there was her funeral. Gina hadn't attended which wasn't right. She'd been to a funeral. She knew how to behave.

Grandad, Ernest Smith, had 'passed away' in February, two months before. 'Do you mean he's dead?' Gina had said. 'Yes, we won't be seeing him again.' Elspeth had explained. 'He was tired. He'd led a full life; ambulance driver in the 1st World War, Air Raid Warden in the 2nd, worked all hours when he married my mother, loved us both, more than I deserved.' She had sounded sorry and proud all at once when she said, 'He missed her after she died. He was just worn out with it. A clever man, he was, read and thought deeply, an honourable man, Gina. He'd want us to be brave, not sad.'

    Elspeth had allowed Gina to attend that funeral, to see the coffin ablaze with flowers, to stand beside the deep dug grave and throw a scattering of pebbles into the hole. That was all. Then no more visits to the house in Mill Lane. No more butterballs offered from an old golden syrup tin. No more jigsaws spread out on the parlour table and being allowed to find the lost piece to fill in a boat or plane. No home for him any more, merely a grave.

This day in April there could be no bravery, only terrible sadness. Not only has she lost another person she loves but she's also going to lose Ivan too who she loves more than all of them. For Ivan is going to London to live with his father, Gustave.

'It makes sense,' Elspeth had told Kenneth at breakfast. 'Gustave's been living up there for years and Ivan is clever enough for an easy transfer to a new school.' She hadn't looked at Gina. And Kenneth wasn't looking at Elspeth who continued with, 'Ruby's taken it very badly, George says. I think she thought of her, Mareke I mean, as a younger sister. Wanted to cosset her. Always Ruby's role.' And then she'd smiled at Gina, 'I know you'll miss her too,' as if that concluded their involvement with the Schmidts.

Gina had wanted to scream, Ivan, Ivan, he's my only friend and he can't leave me. Her throat clamped shut, she couldn't eat, perhaps wouldn't eat ever again. She'd escaped to the kitchen where she'd emptied her cornflakes into the boiler. Ruby wouldn't have wanted her to prise off the hot silver lid, but Ruby wasn't there. The flame had flashed and hissed as the soggy mess landed on the seething orange fire. Gina had stared into the inferno, tempted to thrust in her whole hand to see how much that would hurt.

'Ivan,' she said, 'I can come and visit you, can't I?'

Ivan nodded, his big hands clasped tight together.

'It isn't far, is it? I could come on the train.' Whether she'd be allowed to go alone needn't be thought about. She could take her pocket money and walk out of the house. She knew how to get a bus to the station, she knew how to buy tickets, it would be like running away. That has been one of her recurring dreams, to escape.

But what can he dream of? How can he escape from such a calamity? Nothing is going to bring her back. Gina hadn't seen what Mareke looked like after she was run over. Had Ivan? That would be terrible to see your mother squashed and bloody. That couldn't have happened.

'I love you, Ivan,' she said.

He looked up at her. There were huge teardrops swelling in his eyes, like frogspawn, they looked like frogspawn. And then a tear fell, plop, right down his cheek onto his hands. His lips were pressed together, his eyebrows - she loves his bushy black eyebrows - squished together, hooding his eyes, as if to protect them, trying to cover up the hurt.

'Oh, Ivan! I am so so sorry. I wish ...' and then she stopped for she knows that there is nothing to wish for. 'Will it ever get better?' said as much for herself as to him.

Ivan leant forward to rest his head on her shoulder, his big head on her small shoulder. He was older than her but she's the one who felt grown up, as if she must be able to soothe him. Almost joyfully she put her arms tight round him, cradled him as Grandpa sometimes cradled her. His body was solid against hers, weighty and cushioned. Her bones felt like sticks, no softness to enfold him. '*She's a skinny one,*' she'd heard Ruby say. '*Needs feeding up.*' But no one was going to 'feed her up' now. She couldn't eat as she was full of all this aching agony.

George too was weighed down with sorrow. He'd brought them together, Gustave, Mareke and Ivan, when war thrust them apart. He'd seen the love, the close comradeship, two people who were confident, matching each other, a perfect pair. And George was worried that Ruby cried whenever Ivan's name was mentioned, especially when he told her that going up to London was the best option for both Gustave and Ivan.

'I had to tell her,' he'd said to Elspeth, 'a complete change may seem drastic now but will be better in the long run.'

He was cradling Elspeth in the greenhouse, had licked the tears from her cheeks. 'It makes me realise how fortunate we are despite ...' but he didn't finish. 'How is Gina?' he said instead. Elspeth didn't reply.

She'd told Gina to treat Ivan with kindness. 'He doesn't need you crowding him and asking silly questions,' she'd said. She herself was baffled to think how Ivan must feel, a boy who was so quiet and polite, whose mother was always his mouthpiece. *'Speak up, Ivan,'* she'd say, in her precise foreign way.

'It will be devastating for her,' George said. 'Her childhood companion, a big brother, cut out of her life. We must be gentle with her.'

Gina felt Ivan shaking. His heaviness might push her over, to lie together on his bed which would be rather nice except that it wasn't something to think of at this time because nothing could be nice.

'There, there,' she said. And then she heard a little gulping noise, the kind of sound that fish might make, if fish could speak. It came again only this time it was more like the hoot of an owl. She hugged him tighter, wanting all her loving to go into his body, swirl around and fight off the stabbing pain. 'It'll be all right, ' she said, though she doubted it was true but that's what Ruby always said when everything was horrid for her. And this was a truly horrid thing.

Outside she could hear people on the street, someone laughing, someone else shouting back. There was the sound of a bus slowing down for someone else waiting at the bus stop, the grind of its brakes, the call of the bus conductor. She'd come on a bus, that's allowed. The 106 which passes Hinton Road to stop at the top of Glebe Avenue and make its way across town to Mill Lane. Not far. It's the bus she takes to school but going a bit further on.

'Have a good cry, Ivan. It's what you deserve,' which was what Grandpa said to her when she cut her heel badly on the boot scraper. 'I think it's right and proper.' She nearly said that it's what Mareke would have suggested, Mareke who advised singing songs to help a hurt knee or a nice piece of plaster. 'Your mother, Mareke, was such a special person, I loved her too,' which made her want to cry though she had to hold it in. 'Not as much as you, of course. You were so lucky to have her as your moeder. And I like that you called her mummy too. That's not what I call my mother.' Talking rather than silence seemed better. 'Do you remember when Mareke took us to the funfair and how much she screamed on the dodgems? You were driving the car and everyone bumped into us and you were bumping them back and she wasn't cross but laughing. I'm going to remember that for all of my life.'

Ivan unwound himself from her and sat back upright. He sniffed and wiped his eyes and nose on his pullover sleeve. Gina watched with horror; it was a good thing Mareke couldn't see because she'd always been very strict about being clean, not getting snot on your clothes. Gina pulled a handkerchief from her sleeve. 'You can have this,' she said.

Ivan took it and blew his nose several times. He handed it back to her. 'No,' she said, 'you keep it and I'll collect it when I come and visit you in London.'

'You'll be most welcome,' Ivan said and smiled.

The greenhouse 1955

Gina was eleven when she found her grandfather dead on the greenhouse floor, her mother's hands swathed in blood. The floor was carpeted in glass, a sparkling mass of slivers and shards on a sunny Sunday at the end of March. The sound of her mother wailing was as dreadful as the sight of her body rocking back and forth, but the thought that she was mad, had killed Grandpa, was terrifying.

Primula shivered in the breeze wafting in through the glassless frames, her beloved grandfather's favourite plants. That was why she knew the name. But what to do? Those delicate flowers would be ruined by such cool air. Which was a stupid thought when he was there on the floor, dead.

She stood in the doorway, still holding the brass knob that would have opened the door if it hadn't already been wide open. She looked back from whence she'd come, back down the garden from the gate that leads to the allotment; the allotment path that was a link to the road where she lives. Maybe if she didn't look again it would all be different. Like in a nightmare when it all changed in a flash and you couldn't remember what happened before. If she returned home and came back a bit later it would be all right. Her mother and the blood gone, the greenhouse whole, and Grandpa smiling and busy, asking her to help him with whatever he was doing, like he always did.

Nobody had followed her. Nobody would know that she'd come and seen what she's seen. Her mother sitting with arms outstretched as if to parade the red oozing from her arms, didn't see her, no one did.

There was a box inside her chest, hard and hollow, which made it difficult to breathe. Made it impossible to think what to do.

A robin sang its syrupy song above her head. It made her want to cry and crying never helped anyone she's been told many times. It's her mother, Elspeth's, favourite phrase, it's what she'd be saying to her at this moment if she hadn't been sobbing herself.

Ruby might have been in the kitchen. But was it right for her to see this? Ruby loved her mother, and she loved Grandpa. She wouldn't understand. She'd say 'Oh my goodness!'. She might have even fallen down in a flat faint. It'd happened once before with the news of Mareke's death.

And she loves Ruby. Ruby's like her other mother, better than the real one. The real one whose lovely amber hair hid her face, hid from her what she'd done, the shattered glass, the trembling flowers, Grandpa dead.

Gina let go of the door handle, backed out and turned to make her way up to the house. Was it the shock or the fright that stopped her breath coming? It was as if she'd run a race, a race that she'd never win. Ivan always wanted to run races with her when they were little. And he would always win. Why not? He was four years older but it never mattered. Ivan her best friend, she loves Ivan. Ivan who would have known what was the right thing to do. But Ivan was in London, clever Ivan who could speak every language under the sun. He had said, 'Phone me if you want.' It would mean a trunk call, cost a lot of money.

The goldfish no longer hiding in the bottom mud, circled the pond, sunlight catching the dark water. Slow and untroubled their bright orange bodies swam round and around. There was a telephone in the hall. If she'd been able to avoid Ruby, there was a chance that she could have rung Ivan. It would mean that she'd have to ask an operator to dial the number which was in her diary. Anyway that was no use. Her diary was at home under her bed; and Daddy might have come back from playing golf. She wasn't going to tell him. He didn't like her mother or Grandpa.

She backed away from the awful scene, went to sit on the top step of the path that led up to the terrace and the French windows. There was no movement in the house, it looked to be empty, like her body was empty. Perhaps she should call the police? Go inside and call the police. If she dials 999 the police will come and they'll see what she's seen, know that she hadn't touched any thing. Isn't that the right thing to do? Not to touch any thing? They might ask her why, why has her mother killed him, for Gina knows that Elspeth loves Grandpa.

The robin's call came again. The bird sat a few feet away as if to offer an answer. What would Grandpa have wanted her to do? Which was such a wrong question, a question that filled her with fear, the box in her chest no longer empty but filled with gulping sorrow. As the goldfish gulp air, she gulped back howling grief. Her hand clutched her mouth to hold back the noise, the same noise her mother was making. She stood up to look back down to the greenhouse, down over the lawn and vegetable garden to the gate through to the allotment path. And she ran as fast as she'd ever run in a race with Ivan, not looking back, past the dug earth, the rickety and upright sheds, a man who called out, 'Lovely day, isn't it?', to find the key she'd left under the doormat, up the stairs to her room to find the diary under her bed. There was the address, the telephone number but she could no longer speak. No words were possible as she lay on her bed and wept and wept.

It was six o'clock in the evening when Kenneth came to tell her the news, the news that her grandfather was dead and her mother in hospital. He didn't ask why her face was blotched, her eyes swollen and red. He didn't ask where she'd been, what she might have seen, what she thought or felt.

No one ever explained, if they could have explained. She told no one. Not even Ivan, not until she was seventy and there was no choice.

Letter to Ivan March 1955

Dear Ivan

I'm sorry to tell you that my grandfather is dead - George Everley Simms died of a heart attack two days ago. Anyway that's what they've told me. He was in the greenhouse with his plants, you know the ones with the fragile pink flower, Primula Rosea. If you remember he keeps one on the desk in his office. I don't know what will happen now.

Elspeth is in hospital. She hurt herself on the broken glass, they say. She was with him when he died. Daddy is in a frightful state, as you can imagine. Far too much whisky being drunk.

I haven't seen Ruby since this happened. She will be devastated.

So am I.

With lots and lots of love from your best friend

Gina

Letter to Ivan April 1955

Dear Ivan

Thank you for telephoning. It was lovely to hear your voice and I'm sorry that I cried. It is hard to be brave. I loved him very much and I know he loved me very much too. I know this even more now that the will has been found, his will I mean, and he has left the whole of his house and garden to me. Isn't that extraordinary? Daddy read it to me, 'For my granddaughter, Georgina Margaret Everley Simms, my house and the land upon which it stands,' it said, or something like that. Of course I won't have it until I'm 21. Ruby and Ralph are to live there to look after it until then. That's if they want to, which I hope they do.

This doesn't make it any better that he's not here any more. Though I do feel proud that he wanted me to own it like he did. He was so wise and sympathetic. I know more through talking to him than going to school. I suppose I'll have to work even harder in future to find out things for myself.

Elspeth is still in the nursing home. I haven't been allowed to see her yet. Daddy says that the cuts have healed but she's very tired and they are trying to make her stronger. They'll be going mad in the office without her. Even Daddy said that he was desperate for her to come back, which is interesting. He told me that he can't sleep. I didn't know what to say as I don't want to sleep because of nightmares.

Ruby sends you her love. She says that she'll bear up for his sake. By 'his' she means Grandpa, of course. Ralph is going to repair the greenhouse quickly to save his plants. They took most of them into the house so that they wouldn't catch cold. And I have three here in my bedroom which I like.

That's all for now, Ivan. I don't know when the funeral will be but I don't expect you and Gustave will be able to come as I know you are very busy at school and at work.

But you will be able to come and live in the house with me when I am of age.

With lots of love

Gina

Walking back from the post box at the top of the road she paused outside the house where she lives. She would have liked to walk down further to the allotment path, through past the tidy and the ramshackle, on to the gate which would unlatch and take her through up into his garden. But she knew that she can never take that route again.

White cherry trees 1955

'You have to help me, Gina.'

'What do you want?' Gina was expecting to be asked to
fetch a book or make a cup of tea. It was Millie's day off.
Elspeth had come down from her bedroom dressed as for
the office. She looked as lovely as before, sitting on the
window seat, her hair shining in the sunlight from the bay
window. She wore a navy skirt, a short sleeved pink blouse,
the colour of those flowers in the greenhouse.

She'd been home for two days. Kenneth had opened the
front door to allow her entrance with, 'She's back, your
mother's back but you mustn't make a fuss.' As if Gina was
the sort of child to make a fuss, not the one who'd been
schooled in the art of emotional reticence. Elspeth had
said, 'Don't worry, Gina. I'm quite better,' kissed her
briefly and disappeared upstairs. Her appearances at
mealtimes had given no clue as to her state of mind. She'd
asked the usual questions of Gina, grumbled about the
condition of her hair. 'Why hasn't it been cut?' The
accusation directed at Kenneth. It seemed nothing had
changed, the hostility between her parents chilling the
already bleak dining room. The last month had been wiped
from memory and it was as if they would chug on after a
small unexplained hitch.

Was this what Kenneth hoped for? Surely he must have
thought differently, that he would now be in charge. He
had, after all, seen to his father's funeral, returned to work
after a suitable pause to find that Jim Furland was greatly
stressed. Jim had mentioned that soon they must think of
how to replace George, but he'd realised that Kenneth
couldn't be rushed into decisions. Apart from concern for
her health, no one had asked what Elspeth wished for the
future.

'Where's Kenneth?' Elspeth said.

'Playing golf, I think.'

'Good.'

The scars looked like caterpillar tracks or even slug trails running up her arms, straight and purposeful. Both arms were the same though the lines were less pronounced on the right. Slash, slash would have been her action. She seemed content for Gina to stare at those disfigured arms.

'I wanted you to see,' she said. 'I don't want you to be disturbed by keeping this hidden.'

Gina couldn't take her eyes from the pale runnels displayed before her. Should she say that she'd seen how they bled when she saw the whole scene in the greenhouse? But that would open up the box of terror which she'd been fighting to keep closed.

'Do they hurt?'

'No, not any more. And I don't want you to hurt either. George wouldn't have wanted either of us to suffer.' She reached out to Gina. 'Come, you can touch them.'

It'd been difficult for Gina to reconcile her opinion of her mother as the person who'd killed her grandfather with the fragile woman she'd visited in the nursing home. The woman with the face of a ghost, whose arms had been swathed in bandages, who'd wept at the sight of her daughter. It'd been even harder to think how to respond now that she'd come back home. There'd been no mention of what happened in the greenhouse in Glebe Avenue. Ruby, who'd found Elspeth, bandaged her arms and called a doctor, had talked to Gina of 'your grandfather's sad death', saying of course 'he worked too hard'. Of Elspeth she'd said, 'It must have been such a shock, finding him', and 'all that dangerous glass'. How it got like that hadn't been revealed. Kenneth had said nothing other than, 'Your mother's had to go away for a while, a bit of a holiday.' No one had suggested attempted suicide, though that's what Gina had heard Ruby's sister say.

Gina took a step towards those outstretched arms, let her finger draw gingerly along one of the tracks. 'Who did this?' It had to be said.

'I did.'

'Why?'

Elspeth stroked Gina's cheek, gently as if mimicking her daughter's touch. 'I can't explain. I'm sorry. Perhaps when you're grown up.'

'They told me that Grandpa had a heart attack.'

Elspeth leant forward. 'Come sit down, give me a hug.' Gina put her arms around her mother and Elspeth did the same to her. 'I'm sorry,' she said again. 'This is our tragedy, yours and mine.'

It felt very odd, it sounded odd, one of the oddest things Gina could remember. There had been few times when Elspeth had paired herself with her daughter, or asked outright to be held by her or vice versa. And neither was plump enough to make the embrace consoling.

'Gina, we have to look after his legacy.' Elspeth pulled away but still held Gina's hand. 'No more weeping, we have work to do.'

Gina said nothing.

'You were told about George's will, weren't you?'

'Yes.' Gina wished she'd say 'Grandpa'.

'Good, so you know that you will inherit his house and garden when you're twenty-one. A wonderful gift from a wonderful man. You know that don't you?'

Gina nodded.

'And did you know that he also requested that you and I have an equal stake in the firm, with Kenneth? A division of his shares.' Elspeth had let go of Gina's hand but held her eyes, willing her not to look away. 'Jim Furland holds the other fifty percent.'

'Oh!' Was all Gina could say, for what did it mean? And why talk of Kenneth instead of Daddy? Was this change of relationship with names in order to be business-like? A phrase she'd heard her mother use a trillion times.

Elspeth pressed on. 'I'm worried that during the last month things will have been falling apart. I need to go and talk to Jim.'

'Oh,' again was the only response. But Jim, not Uncle Jim.

'We need the car.' The woman who seconds ago had wanted to reassure Gina, show affection, had been briskly replaced by the mother of old, the one anxious to get out of the house, '*get back to work*', another favourite phrase.

'But Daddy sold your car, he said you wouldn't be needing it.'

'I know. I mean George's car. We need to find the keys.' Elspeth was on her feet. 'Fetch my jacket, Gina, the one that matches this skirt. In my wardrobe.'

'Where are you going?' Gina thought she'd better ask as Daddy was sure to want to know when he got back.

'We're going to Jim's house. It's Sunday, the office won't be open,' she said as if Gina was foolish enough not to know that. 'Come on hurry up.'

'We? You mean I have to come?'

'Yes. I'm not allowed to drive on my own for a few days.'

'But I …'

'What?' Elspeth suddenly smiled as if she was having fun, that this was going to be a huge treat. Had she forgotten that Gina is a child, eleven years old? Was she still confused, not right in the head? But she looked as pretty as always, pink lipstick, blushed cheeks, her hair swooshed into a sort of pleat at the back of her head, a tortoiseshell comb to keep it in place.

The car snarled and coughed before the engine fired, the big green Wolseley with shiny seats and polished dashboard. Gina pressed her palms onto the cool leather. This was Grandpa's car, the car in which he drove her to piano lessons, when it had been too wet for her to cycle. He'd always asked about what she was playing, and sometimes she was able to go back to his house to practice the music, so he could hear her play. He played for her too.

Elspeth adjusted her seat, checked the rear view mirror, smoothed the gears and accelerator to glide out of the drive as if nothing had altered, the power under the bonnet hers. The windscreen wipers rhythmic motion back and forth echoed the air of control and normality. The April rain, little more than a wet mist, cleared as they moved out onto the main road, the screen burnished by a burst of sun. Despite all this serenity there were subtleties to the scene that no one, least of all Gina, could have observed or understood; Elspeth's hands gripped the steering wheel, her teeth clenched, her heart pumping misery with each beat. This was their car, that's what he'd said. George who'd urged her to learn to drive after Mareke's death. It was he who'd taught her. It was he who'd put his arm around her shoulders when they'd circuited a deserted aerodrome many times and said, *'Enough. You're good enough, you're more than good enough.'* It was he who'd found those secret places on the way there or back, to be themselves. It was he who had in the last five years accepted that they weren't committing a crime, had tossed away all guilt, revelled in their covert liaison. *This is our pumpkin, Elspeth darling, may it never change into an ordinary carriage,'* he'd said. But that was all gone, forever. This, now, had to be her mission, to carry on as he'd have wished, to think that he would be proud of her.

'You do realise that this might be a struggle,' she said.

Gina didn't reply.

'Kenneth never liked my role as manager and he'll like it less now.'

Silence.

'Jim will see it my way though. The firm needs building up. Replacements and additions will be necessary. And I'm thinking of another branch, expanding. There is so much work out there, plenty of young people trained, we need to take advantage of this country's advance.' To keep talking was the answer. 'Simms and Furland'.

Gina pulled down the sun visor, the glare blinding. The words, too, needed to be shut out.

'You'll be part of this, Gina. It's your legacy, a career ahead of you, the future opening out. It would be a betrayal of George if we don't take this forward.'

Gina heard gibberish. Career? The future? Wouldn't Grandpa rather she just played the piano? Maybe that's what she'd like to do. Her stomach screwed up tight, a lead ball. Ivan, if only he were here. But even Ivan talked of a career, his future, a linguist, top universities.

'Gina, you need to be determined,' Elspeth glanced at her briefly, 'this has been given to us and we mustn't let it slip through our fingers.'

Gina looked down at her own fingers splayed and digging into her seat. Slipping away was what she wanted to do, to be rid of all this talk. To be at home doing her hateful homework would have been preferable, to be playing the piano as if for him which made her want to cry. But there was no escape for they were there, the car sliding into a snug space outside a large house, three storeys, dark fir trees guarding each side of the gateway. Elspeth turned off the engine, looked across to Gina with a triumphant smile. 'We did it, didn't we? Okay? You and me, we'll make his wishes come true.'

What they talked about Gina had no idea. Jim Furland had opened the door, visibly startled, kissed Elspeth's cheek and ruffled Gina's hair. Tea had been served with biscuits. There was a dog to play with so that she could ignore what was discussed and decided. All she knew was that her mother sounded as if she was in control and Uncle Jim agreed with her.

Elspeth started the engine, smiled and waved back at Jim and drove around the corner to a road lined with cherry trees. Gina looked up at this canopy of blossom, white petals shivering in the soft breeze. The branches swayed gently, frilly flowers dancing above them, an archway for a bride. The car, as if mesmerised like Gina, slowed and stopped, the engine still running. It was such an exquisite show, such a surprise of loveliness that sitting in the middle of a road in a stationary car went unnoticed for a few minutes. 'Isn't it beautiful,' Gina said looking across to find Elspeth draped over the steering wheel, shaking violently. Faint noises came from her, mewling noises that a kitten might make.

'Mummy, are you all right?' A stupid question because she clearly wasn't.

The reply was a long wail, as if the sound would overtake them both.

'Mummy, don't,' Gina said. She patted her mother's shoulders. 'What's the matter?'

Elspeth's feet abandoned the pedals and the engine jolted to a complete stop. Her head was thrown back, her eyes closed, tears running down her cheeks. She sobbed, a fearful sound, a fearful sight. There, in the middle of the road, above them the best that spring could offer, they blocked anyone else's entry.

'Mummy! What if a car comes? Hadn't you better park properly?'

Elspeth looked dreadful, eyes smudged black, trails running down her cheeks.

'Mummy, please!' and quite sharply, even though she wanted to cry too, she said, 'Mummy, what's the matter?'

Elspeth's voice was a hoarse whisper. 'George, he's gone, he's dead. What choice do I have? How do I live?'

Gina stared. It was horrible, like in the greenhouse. 'Mummy, you'll be all right, we'll be all right.' What else could she say? 'I'll look after you. You said, you and me, we'll make his wishes come true. You said that Grandpa wouldn't want us to suffer.' She tried to sound certain, as her mother had sounded but tears ran down her cheeks too. She took her mother's hands in hers; the damaged arms were covered up. 'Mummy, Mummy, look at the blossom. It's like the tree in Grandpa's garden, my garden.' What else could she do? She had to take charge; she could do it all, she had to do it all.

No car came, no one saw these two women weeping, no one saw Elspeth finally take up her daughter's hands to kiss, no one saw or heard the great sigh, the shudder of 'pulling herself together'. 'You're a clever girl, Gina,' Elspeth offered with a pathetic smile.

Back on the main road, Elspeth suggested, 'That went well. Jim understood.'

Gina's hands were stuck to her seat, the shiny leather wet with sweat.

'Ruby too. She understands. It was Ruby who saved my life,' Elspeth cleared her throat, her voice assuming its normal tone was quite steady as if nothing discomforting had only recently occurred. 'She thought that she saw you in the garden and came out to see why you hadn't come in to say 'hello'.'

Gina's cheeks stung with dried tears. All the bravery of 'me and my' gone.

Elspeth's eyes were on the road, the car, once again, under her command. Lightly she said, as if an answer was of no consequence, 'Were you there?'

Gina looked away as if she hadn't heard; it could have been construed as a shake of the head. Not a lie, merely an evasion of the truth.

Gina was eighteen, living in London, 'proper grown up' as Ruby liked to say. The arguments over whether she needed to attend a posh secretarial college in Kensington rather than go to somewhere local had been won. Those battles took place over meals in the dining room where the decor suggested neutral ground. The mushroom coloured carpet matching the mushroom coloured walls where hung black framed etchings, supposedly a valuable wedding gift, as uninspiring as most of the discussions. Except Gina's parents didn't have discussions, for when a point of disagreement occurred, and those occasions were frequent, they spat at each other like terrorist snipers. Never outright shouting matches or storming out, it was always sotto voce. Without the animosity it might have been a kind of ping pong.

Kenneth had opposed any idea that 'going all that way, entailing all the expense of living up there,' was necessary. It struck Gina as bizarre that Kenneth, who spent a lot of time 'popping up' to London for odd bits of entertainment, should think the city an unsuitable home for his daughter. Elspeth always countered with, 'Don't you want the best for her? For the firm. The family firm in which she has a stake, as do I.' Always the reminder, a bitter twist for Kenneth who, if the truth be told, was becoming more of a cypher in the business due to his lack of interest in what he called, 'the whole caboodle'.

When Gustave invited Gina to live in his flat with Ivan, the argument was won. That he was often away on assignments in Germany, might have caused Elspeth certain qualms, but somehow nobody bothered to say.

Ivan was an angel, loved and trusted. He helped Gina find her way round London when she arrived, had taken her to a few bars to meet friends, and cooked supper most nights. Gina was in her best dream; living with the man she loved.

Then there was the party.

'What's a pretty girl like you doing here?' The man dived towards her, having manoeuvred his way through the other bodies leaning, lounging or lying on chairs and floor. She was one of the few standing, her back against the door through from living room to kitchen.

'I live here.'

'Oh, you're the one from down south. The family friend.'

Gina wasn't prepared to deny or confirm any of this man's speculations. Even the 'pretty' sounded like an insult. He was an overgrown schoolboy wearing a ridiculous blazer. 'And you?'

'What can I say? A mate from university?'

The room was choked with smoke, the walls swelling with the heat, everyone outdoing the other in a desire to be heard.

'And do you work as hard as Ivan, then?' Gina looked round to see where he might be.

'Oh, that reputation of his. I reckon it's a myth.' Blazer man tossed back the last dregs from his glass, swayed slightly before righting himself on the door frame. 'Many things are myths, you know.'

'So I believe.'

'Such as that boy meets girl, falls in love, gets married and has kids, you know. That kind of tripe.'

'Oh, really? But aren't you mixing metaphors. Isn't it either myth or meat?'

'Ah, I see. Brains and beauty.'

Gina was exhausted. The party, if that's what you could have called it, had been going on since early evening. The flat was trampled

'Would you like a glass of water?' she said, ducking under his arm. 'It's too hot in here and I've had enough alcohol. Same for you?' He could take that whichever way he wished as she was already in the kitchen pushing her way through to the sink. She flushed out her glass, refilled and drained it. Empty bottles of wine and beer stood sentinel on top surfaces and floor, or overflowed from the waste bin. The pan in which Ivan had cooked bolognese was crusted dry, a few strands of spaghetti dangled from another saucepan. If only they'd all leave so that she could do the washing up. It was going to take ages to get rid of the smell of cigarette smoke and stale ash trays.

'Water? That's a novel idea.' Her pursuer was addressing the other people in the kitchen none of whom took any notice. He held out his glass. 'Are you like a sister to Ivan, taking care of him?' he said.

'Why do you ask, whatever your name is?'

'Well, Ivan isn't into girls, is he?' He smirked and held out his hand. 'Of course we haven't been introduced. I'm Roland Hughes, of Welsh origin by the way, so how do you do.' He mocked shaking a hand as she didn't offer hers.

All those wretched cocktail parties at home when her parents had entertained, Kenneth inviting his 'chums' and Elspeth people who 'are good for business,' had trained her to respond with polite answers as she passed around plates of vol-au-vents and things on sticks. Tonight, and all the other nights of her life, wouldn't be like that, she'd decided. She was a free spirit which Ivan had told her she should be. 'Don't follow the crowd, Gina. You're an individual, not fake. Stay like that.'

'Here's your water, Roland, and goodnight. I'm off to bed.'

'What so soon?'

'I heard the cock crow, didn't you?'

'Well, make sure there's no one in your bed, won't you?'

'My door's locked.'

A last thud of the front door was a signal to say that Ivan was alone, the party dispersed. Gina had been lying on her bed for the past hour, fully clothed, trying to read, words and sentences blurring and shifting on the page. She held her breath and waited, the air above hanging heavy, weighting her body down. She must talk to him. Her mind was scrabbling to make sense of that one remark, '*Ivan isn't into girls*'. Though posed as a question it was more of a statement, the man hadn't needed her to agree.

A clink of glasses, music abruptly changed, Helen Shapiro silenced, a Schubert lieder soothing its way under her door. She sat up, shuffled into her shoes and smoothed her skirt. The creases were horrendous, scrunched up taffeta, her best frock, royal blue. At the beginning of the party, before everyone had arrived, she'd been pleased that she'd dressed up, the full skirt swirling around her knees, the boat neckline emphasising her bare shoulders, the diamanté necklace that had once belonged to Kenneth's mother, a grandmother she'd never known. But then as everyone arrived wearing odd assortments of sports jackets, shirts without ties, one girl in an ordinary skirt and blouse and the other in sort of cut off trousers, she'd wanted to hide. It was Ivan though who had said she looked lovely, 'dazzling' was what he'd said. He was wearing his old cords and pullover but then that's what he always wore, she'd not expected anything different.

Thinking back to all the people she'd met with Ivan over the past two months, most of them were men. But then those were the people he'd met at university; he'd said that there were too few women studying. He'd even chided her for not going to university. 'You've got the brains, Gina. The world could be your oyster.' He hadn't said, directly, for he was far too kind and polite, that studying to be a secretary and then going back to work with her parents was throwing her life away. But what else? Nothing much had had any focus since Grandpa died. Elspeth was blindly convinced of the merits of work, and, in particular, for 'our business'. Kenneth had no opinion. No one ever asked what she, Gina, wanted, and she'd never known. Only this, to be with Ivan.

Opening the door a crack, she was sure no one else was in the flat. She must catch him before he went to bed. She crept along the corridor cat like, whiskers twitching, ready to pounce or retreat. But she wasn't a cat, that man Roland had made her feel more like a mouse.

'Ivan?' He was sitting on the sofa, head back and eyes closed. The music played prettily in a room where the air was stilled, almost holy. 'Ivan, have they all gone?'

Ivan sat up and swung round. 'Gina, I thought you were asleep.' It was he who looked tired, perhaps he'd been trying to sleep on the sofa.

'There were a lot of people,' she stated the obvious. 'Are they all from college?'

He yawned. 'Mostly.'

'I knew some of them from when we've been to the pub. But I hadn't met the girls before.'

'No? They're reading languages too but they don't often socialise. Too much work their excuse.'

'I met Roland Hughes. Is he a particular friend?'

'Ah, Roland, of Welsh origin.' Ivan laughed. 'I hope he was on his best behaviour.'

'What do you mean?'

'Well, we call him the Welsh wasp, buzzing around making stinging remarks.' Ivan leant back to take her hand. 'Come and sit down. I'm sorry, you look troubled. It was all a bit out of hand, wasn't it?'

'No, I enjoyed myself. Felt a bit overdressed though. And there's a frightful mess in the kitchen.'

'Forget that. Come on, give me a hug.'

She sat beside him, nestled her head into his neck. He kissed her hair. 'I'll worry about the kitchen and the rest of the flat tomorrow morning,' he said.

'Oh no,' she pulled away. 'Lets do it together now.'

'No, you've got college in a few hours,' he checked his watch. 'Bloody hell, it's 4.30 already. Come on, off to bed.'

She unfurled herself from his shoulder to sit upright, her hands clasped in her lap. 'No, not yet. I need to ask you something.' Except she didn't for every nerve and muscle wanted just to go with him to his bed. To lie and do whatever it was lovers did. That would sort it out. Years ago she'd believed that that was what they were going to do. She was fifteen and had come up to be with Gustave and Ivan for a weekend when they'd whirled her around London, taken her to see 'My Fair Lady'. Driving back in a taxi after the show, Gustave in the front with the driver, she and Ivan together in the back, she had taken his hand, snuggled up to him, and he'd looked at her in a way that meant more than 'you're my friend'. It'd been a long look into her eyes, serious, the glint of streetlights reflected, and then he'd smiled and kissed her cheek. For one glorious moment she'd thought that he was going to kiss her offered lips but he hadn't because after all Gustave was in the front and might have seen them in the rear view mirror. Since she'd come to live with him and his father, it seemed that nothing had changed though. They were as they'd always been, like brother and sister, friends.

He wrested his arm which had lain along the sofa behind her to hold himself in a similar prim pose. 'Oh dear, what have I done wrong?'

'Well, it's something Roland said which I didn't understand. It might mean nothing but …'

'I'm sorry, what was it?'

'Ivan isn't into girls, is he? And I thought I ought to know what he meant, if he was right.' She was relieved to have said it, and desperately hoped that he'd deny the implication.

Ivan said nothing but gave her that long look again, the gentle stare, focusing on her eyes, his eyes in her eyes. The singer on the record player continued to yearn, as she was yearning, for love that was romantic and passionate. 'Gina, I thought you knew. You, my best friend, I didn't think I needed to explain.'

'Explain?' This was worse because she didn't know. If what he meant was true, it was something nobody talked about, or if they did, the subject was ridiculed. Worse was that her blissful belief, her childish certainty, that he was hers and would be for ever was shattered. 'Am I so foolish, Ivan?'

'No, of course not.' He didn't look away as he might have done in embarrassment or disappointment. 'Does it make a difference to what you think of me?'

'No, oh no! But we've always told each other everything and this seems such a huge thing not to have admitted.'

'Admitted? Is that really how it has to be?'

'Oh no! It's just …'

'Gina, please, I love you as my dearest friend. You were my first companion, we share the people closest to us, your grandfather, my mother, Gustave, your mother, the list goes on. You're like the sister I never had.' He brushed his hand through his hair, looked down at her, frowning. 'We know, always knew, that we could tell each other everything. But this, I thought that …' He paused, as if waiting to find the right words. 'Gina, I'm homosexual, or prefer to say gay. That men attract me, that's just who I am.'

A bottle from somewhere in the flat rolled and dropped with an ominous thump, but there was no shattering of glass, merely a movement to some lower space where it settled.

'Does that mean we can't be married?' It was such an idiotic question but it came out before she could stop it.

'Gina, I couldn't marry you even if …' the sentence hung but was quickly justified with, 'It'd be wrong, the worst sort of cheating.' He wanted her to look back at him but she'd turned away. 'That's what a lot of men have done in the past, you know, married and not only been unhappy but made life hell for their wives.' Doesn't she know, what Gustave and he had discussed, that her father is queer too, which is the cause of his bleak marriage? Obviously not.

She stared down at her hands and his hands which both appeared alien. And her silly dress, the bright flouncy dress, that was part of the charade. How naive she'd been! The assumption of her destiny had been merely a myth. Roland's point.

The LP finished with a final lament and the record player's automatic arm lifted and came to rest in its holder. Their silence as a milk float trundled past below was vast. The words, *'tell each other everything'* hung like a banner above them. That was what she'd said and he'd repeated. But, of course, like him she hadn't. That terrible thing that had happened when she was eleven. What she understood at the time of that scene in the greenhouse had been blocked, for didn't secrets let out become worse in the telling? Hasn't his?

'Gina, I'll always love you.' His gentle voice was pleading. 'I need you. Please don't love me less.' She didn't look up for those big hands clasped in his lap brought her back to that day soon after his mother died, a pain as sharp as a shard of glass stabbed at her heart. He, solid and warm, needed her.

'You chump,' she said. 'of course, as if you have to ask.' To say more, to sit on as if nothing had changed, was impossible. Her throat was clenched tight as if she might choke. She hoisted herself up and out of the sofa, making it as if a comedy act. 'You're right, I ought to go to bed. At least get a couple of hours sleep. You won't touch all this tonight, will you? It can wait till the morning, surely.'

In her room nothing had changed, her book lay open, abandoned, the eiderdown holding the imprint of her body shape. She unzipped and stepped out of her frock to let it lie as a deflated pouffe on the floor. It was no part of her any more. Tomorrow it would go into a litter bin. She wrapped her old wool dressing gown over her petticoat and prised off her silver strapped sandals. If it had been possible to open the window, sealed as it was with an age of accumulated paint, she'd have flung them out onto the street. The necklace could go to a junk shop. The girl who wore such frippery no longer existed. She sat on the bed, her body suddenly immensely cold. A groan from the radiator signalled the coming to life of another day. And she had to live in that day and the day after that, on and on. But how? It was as if she'd turned the page of a novel to find a different plot, characters taking different roles. Where did she fit in?

Ivan, though, was exactly as he'd always been, certain and brave, proclaiming honestly who he is, even though he'd be ostracised or worse if people knew.

Tomorrow, or today as it was, she'd have to work out who she was going to be, what her life was for. Nobody else must know the lie she'd been living. No hysterics, slashed wrists, crumpling like the frock on the floor; like Ivan she'd be brave.

Decriminalisation 1967

'I hope you're impressed,' Gina said.

The greenhouse was clammy and crowded. Cucumbers dangled from fragile stems, tomatoes in pots vied for space. There was hardly room for the three of them. 'I wanted you to see this, my pride and joy,' she said. 'It's the first thing I tackled.' The sharp tang of leaves and ripe fruit was overpowering. An August day when Ivan had brought his new boyfriend for Gina's approval; not that he'd said that exactly. And she was relieved to find it wasn't the Roland who'd taunted her at that party. This man, Rodney, appeared quite different, quiet and well-dressed.

'It's a miracle!' Ivan was already backing out taking Rodney with him. The wet heat was suffocating.

'Yes, it feels like that a lot of the time.' Gina dived down amongst the laden trusses to pick the ripest fruits, lobbed them to Ivan calling out, 'Catch!'

They'd only arrived an hour before.

To Rodney she said, 'It's eleven years since Grandpa died. It was the most important thing in his life, gardening, so I'm walking in his footsteps.' She wouldn't have admitted that it had been therapeutic, banishing ghosts, recovering from disillusionment. If anyone had proposed that idea, she'd have denied 'their cod psychology'. It was what she'd said of Ivan's argument that she was running back to the childhood she'd never had when he'd tried to dissuade her from leaving London.

Rodney looked quite wan. 'I'm amazed but I'm afraid I know nothing about plants. Not had the chance. Town boy, I fear.'

Ivan had already told Rodney that the house and garden were left to Gina in her grandfather's will, therefore someone snooty in twinsets and jodhpurs, with a horsey accent was what he'd expected. Not this child-like girl, whose skinny figure and cropped hair reflected the latest fashion. He was hoping though that they'd soon find some shade. Midday, the sun was relentless, especially for a man in a suit.

'Well, I mustn't bore you then,' Gina batted away one of the many tendrils and fluffed a little laugh. 'Come on, let's go. I thought we could eat out in the garden.' She leapt ahead up the crazy paving steps. 'You can find the table in the shed, Ivan, and the deckchairs, Rodney and I can bring out the stuff.'

Ivan wondered whether he should have left Rodney with Gina. It wasn't like her to keep up this running commentary. A kind of nervous defence? Living in this place, he'd predicted, wouldn't be good for her. 'Burying yourself in a backwater, at the beck and call of your parents?'

'What?' she'd said, 'With my own estate? A job, a salary? That seems like independence to me.'

The shed was a stifling cavern, old wood and creosote soaking up the heat. Tools ranked military fashion on hooks, were polished clean. Cobwebs looped along the ceiling, cradled the corners; startled spiders shot out of nooks and cracks. He found the table, disentangled the chairs whose joints were decidedly rickety, their canvas faded and torn. When was the last time these had been used? Years ago, this was where they'd found his scooter.

'You obviously like cooking too,' Rodney was saying to Gina

'Not really, but you can't go wrong with a salad, can you? And Ruby - Ivan will have told you about Ruby, I'm sure. She was the maid from the age of 15, lived in, and … it's a great saga. But…' she whipped away a tea towel to reveal a plate of sliced ham. 'She cooked this for us. It's Ruby who does most of that sort of thing.'

'My mother was a maid straight out of school,' Rodney said. 'Proud to be so.'

'Oh, that's like my mother's mother. Though I hardly knew her.' Gina pulled a tray of ice cubes from the fridge.

'You work for your mother, Ivan says.'

'Really? Well, he's wrong.' She sluiced the ice tray under the tap, the force of the water drenching her dungarees. 'I've shares in the firm so really I'm working for myself you could say. Ivan's just miffed because I left his beloved London. '*A capital city of such history, yet open to change, so much beauty, so cosmopolitan. It's all happening here.*' Her arms flung wide as she delivered her mimicry and the ice cubes flew, plink plunk on to the floor. 'That's his mantra. On and on.' She bent to retrieve the ice from the floor, rinsing it under that full force tap. 'For me it's all noise, dirt, not a breath of fresh air. I stuck it out to get my qualifications, even spent another year learning French and German at night school, just to please his lordship. Pulled pints, had the obligatory sex which was always on offer, went to France for another year as au pair to spoilt children and a lecherous husband. The French monsieur, par for the course!' The ice cubes dissolved in a jug of water. 'Hang on, we need glasses.'

As she knelt and burrowed in one of the cupboards, Rodney looked up to the cupboards above, which reached up to meet the high ceiling, cupboards where might still lodge sugar in a blue paper bag, jelly cubes or a tin of dried egg powder. The smell of Vim challenged old fat and the dirt of generations, all embedded in the paintwork, pressed into and under the linoleum-covered floor.

'You're right,' Gina said straightening up and following his gaze. 'This whole place needs a facelift. And I'm not frightened to do it. It's essentially Edwardian and disintegrating. I won't have it becoming a mausoleum.'

'A brave undertaking. Sounds fun.'

Head cocked to one side, she said, 'What do you do for a living?'

Elspeth said to Rodney, 'What do you do? Something to do with languages like Ivan?'

'I'm more hands-on, Mrs Simms. Tailoring is my trade, dressing men to look their finest.'

'Oh?' The dark glasses which swamped her face, made it impossible to judge her true level of interest. Except her glance from Rodney dressed in a suit, open necked shirt with spotted blue scarf and matching socks to Ivan in crumpled shirt and the ubiquitous corduroys, summed up exactly what she was thinking. 'How do you come to know each other?' But she didn't wait for an answer. More urgent it seemed was to say, 'My mother was a wonderful seamstress. Sadly she died at the end of the war.'

Gina's quick, 'I told him already, Granny Madge,' was followed by an awkward silence where they all looked to the far distance, beyond the geraniums on the terrace to the sprawling herbaceous border, where a riot of overgrown roses, giant yellow heleniums, and michaelmas daisies competed for light. And further on to where brambles, bindweed and nettles marked the boundary to the vegetable garden.

Gina put an arm on each of their shoulders, Ivan and Rodney, 'You can see there's still lots to be done. I feel like the prince fighting through the undergrowth to find Sleeping Beauty.'

Elspeth laughed, a short disdainful snort. 'I'm worried that it's you who's the lost child needing to find a prince.' She looked despairingly across to Ivan. 'How do I dig my daughter out of this gardening rut? Apart from the office she won't go anywhere.'.

Gina closed her eyes. There was no point in defending herself. This was playing entirely into Ivan's argument; it was insufferable.

But Rodney intervened with, 'I don't think we can say that creating such loveliness is being stuck in a rut.'

'The perfect diplomat!' Elspeth nodded to Rodney with a beaming smile, 'But I must be off. I just had to pop in to see you,' and taking hold of Ivan's hand, 'It's such a long time since you visited us, Gina's eighteenth birthday party with dear Gustave? Please send your father my best wishes.'

Ivan and Rodney stood on either side of Gina waving as Elspeth drove away in her green Morris Minor.

'Smart little car,' Rodney said.

'Smart woman,' Ivan added.

'Grandpa had a green Wolseley, a darker colour, with leather seats.' Gina looked across to the garage, empty apart from her bike. 'I don't know where that went. I thought she'd keep it forever.'

Ivan put his arm round Gina's waist. 'A really decent man, your grandfather. Gustave always says that we owe our lives to him, and your grandmother, the one Elspeth spoke of.'

Gina sniffed. 'Well, that's that then. I'm going to make another pot of tea and we can enjoy Ruby's cake. Come.'

The back garden was still awash with light, the glass of the greenhouse shimmering, the scent of the geraniums sharper and stranger.

'Why don't we sit here.' Ivan indicated the seat on the terrace, 'A bit of shade under the tree?'

'The sycamore, you mean?'

Ivan shrugged. 'Still pedantic about names?'

'Of course, essential. And haven't you any shorts to change into? And, Rodney dear, you really ought to take off your jacket.' She smiled as if at errant children. 'Haven't you told him my plan, Ivan?'

Ivan brushed seed heads and feathers from the seat. 'No, I didn't think you were serious,' and looking up at Rodney, 'you can see what she's like, I did warn you.'

'Warned him of what?'.

'My bossy friend.'

'Huh! I thought I was the one doing the judging this weekend.'

Rodney holding his jacket, looked askance at Ivan's efforts. 'I believe it's mutual, Gina. And I don't take his opinions for granted, like to form my own.' Undoing his scarf, 'And you must have already observed, we don't share the same taste in our apparel.'

'In that case I might be beginning to like you,' and she took his jacket from him. 'Do you play the piano?'

Ivan rolled his eyes. 'Is this another test? I thought you were after brawn not brain.'

Gina ignored him. 'It's my other passion, Rodney. The garden and the piano brought me back here, this backwater!'

'A perfect combination, I'd say. And, what Ivan doesn't know is that I can rattle out a near professional Chopsticks with the right partner. Or a one fingered solo of 'Blue Moon.'

'Fabulous!' Gina looked Rodney up and down again. 'That's settled what we do this evening then.' And taking his arm, 'Come, you can carry the jam sponge.'

'A tragedy losing the allotments,' Ivan said. 'Was there no opposition?'

The sun was dipping below the line of poplars which screened off the new housing estate.

'No, I'm afraid. Kenneth was spineless and Elspeth didn't seem to care.'

'So there's no route through from your parents' house?'

'No.'

Gina and Ivan sat alone on the garden seat; Rodney had gone to change 'into more appropriate attire.'

'I wanted to ask you,' she spoke as if to the garden. 'The Sexual Offences Act, I've been following its progress through parliament. Is that an advance?' Are you safe was really what she was thinking.

'You mean decriminalisation? "Allowing" me in private, and, again, I emphasise "private", to love another man? A mere crack in the door of civilisation.'

'Oh! I hadn't seen it like that. I'd thought you were out of danger.' It was her turn to look distressed. 'I thought we might celebrate. I've a bottle of champagne on ice.'

He leant into her, 'That's lovely! Can the celebration be for Rodney and me?'

'You love him?'

And as if on cue there was Rodney stepping out through the French windows resplendent in cream cotton slacks and short sleeved pink checked shirt. 'What have you been saying behind my back?'

'That you look lovely!' Gina sprang up to greet him. 'I'm off to make myself ready for our party, find the fizz, before we plot our strategy for tomorrow's exertions.'

As soon as she was out of earshot Rodney said, 'Do you think she likes me?'

'Yes, and the champagne is for us.' Ivan stood to seal his words with a kiss.

And as if on cue, so many actors, it seemed, wanting to get in on the act, 'What ho!' could be heard making its way round the side of the house. 'Anyone around? Gina?'

Springing apart the lovers turned to see Kenneth ducking beneath the last archway of overgrowth. 'Ah! Spiffing!' Kenneth brushed down his blazer and greeted Ivan with a hefty pat on the back. 'I heard Elspeth had called by. Had to make myself known again. Such an age, such an age.' He studied Ivan's face as if he was unsure if he recognised him. 'You've changed. But then of course you have. Dash it all! What is it? Five, ten years ago?' But before Ivan could respond Kenneth had spun round to eye up Rodney in a similar manner. 'Have we met?'

Ivan, releasing Kenneth's surprisingly cool hand, introduced Rodney.

'Ah! Two lads from London!' And Kenneth laughed as at his own joke. 'I'm often up in town.' He clasped Rodney's hand. 'Taking in shows, jazz clubs. Are you into music, sir?'

'No, I'm afraid not,' an answer which would have pleased Gina.

'So, down for the weekend?'

'Yes,' Ivan was unsure what he ought to divulge. 'Gina has …'

'Ah, yes, my daughter. Where is she?' He looked up to the house. 'Should I go and find her? I often think she's hiding when I call round.'

'No, she's just putting on a dress, I think.' Ivan sensed that he ought to be guarding the home front. 'Are you still playing as much sport?' And aside to Rodney. 'Mr Simms is a keen sportsman.' And to Kenneth, 'Is it squash or golf?'

'Kenneth, please, call me Kenneth. And yes, both, though it was golf today. Course is very dry, I'm afraid, too fast balls, greens impossible to calculate.' His hair was slicked back, tinges of grey barely visible, the scent of aftershave powerful enough to rival the geraniums. 'We spent rather longer than usual at the 19th hole but that wasn't a bad thing.' He looked at the deckchairs ranged in a line as if at the seaside to observe the horizon. 'Those things are death traps,' he said. 'She ought to have got rid of them.' He ran his finger round the collar of his sports shirt. 'It's too hot out here, chaps. I'm going inside.'

The house was cooler, the deep blue curtains in the drawing room holding the heat at bay, the low light hiding the shabbiness of the brocade-covered sofa and armchairs.

'I'm intrigued by what you two do,' Kenneth's glance flicked between the two men. 'Your father's a journalist of some repute these days, Gina tells me,' singling out Ivan for an answer.

'Gustave, yes, he travels between his home country, Germany, and London. And I've just completed a Ph.d focusing on Russian literature. Some of my antecedents were Russian.'

'Oh my goodness! That seems rather rash. You know, our relationship with the Soviet Union. A bit of a no-go area I'd have thought.'

'It's their literary work which I've been studying. Not political relationships.' He glanced across to Rodney who was eyeing up the baby grand. 'We don't have to abandon the people and all that they've contributed to the world.'

He looked back at Kenneth who was obviously distracted, his attention drawn to his friend.

'Books, reading, can't say I do much of that myself. Prefer a play.' They all still stood as if characters on stage. 'Elspeth's the reader, when she's not rustling up more business. We've expanded enormously since my father's day. Three branches ranging over the county. Good thing Gina saw sense and came home.'

Ivan would have liked to refute the last statement on Gina's behalf but decided not to fight her corner. And anyway, it was undoubtedly a throw-away phrase ending with a nervous laugh.

'Where is she?' Kenneth peered into a small wall cabinet, 'Dad used to keep drink in here in my day. Mind you, wasn't like that during the War.' He turned to Rodney again, 'I was in the ROC before and then during, suddenly demobbed after VE Day. Did my bit though.' And with a rueful chuckle, 'Often have to bring my own booze with me these days.'

'Elspeth needs me as an ally at work but never normally comes here.' Gina sighed as Kenneth's car churned up the gravel, a dust cloud following the exhaust. 'But Kenneth uses any excuse to invite himself in for a drink,' She turned to Rodney. 'A failed marriage. I often wonder how I came to be born.'

'Why are you telling me this?' Bubbles roamed the kitchen as if unable to find a clean surface on which to land. Ivan had been far too liberal with the washing up liquid. She'd have been better off tackling it on her own when they'd both gone to bed.

'I only queried it. Your comment to Roland on the state of their marriage? Wouldn't it explain a lot?'

'Explain? Why do I need that?'

Ivan turned from the dishes, stood with dripping hands, 'To offer sympathy? A reason for your parents' unhappiness.'

'What's that to do with me?' She flung a tea towel at him. 'Dry your hands, you're dripping down your trousers.'

'I'm sorry, but I thought to understand his, their predicament might …'

'Might what? Might make up for the years of neglect, lack of love?' She sat down heavily on a wooden chair, one of four which had lived in the kitchen since it was built in 1912.

Ivan dried his hands.

'How do you know anyway?'

Placing the towel on the table he sat. 'They say, it takes one to know one, is all.'

Gina, already unnerved by the change of scene, the intimacy of Ivan bent over the sink, screwed up her eyes, peered at him as if he was a new and nasty specimen. 'And telling me right now? Was that so clever? Right now, when I'm struggling to get over the fact that you're not mine. Having to accept that you love someone else?'

Ivan looked at the floor. The floor where once Elspeth knelt to cradle George, to say, '*I love you.*' Slowly shaking his head, he said, 'I thought you'd got to grips with that. Years ago …, you accepted; I had to be honest. My best friend.' He waited but she said nothing. He spread his hands wide on the table, as if inviting her understanding. 'There's nothing worse than lies and pretence, is there?'

Gina closed her eyes which is what she'd done as a child, to ignore what she didn't understand, to close off the fear of what she wasn't allowed to know.

The fridge thrummed and juddered and righted itself to hum on.

'Gina, please!' Ivan begged. 'We've always said that we could share anything. I've relied on you for that. When Gustave went to live in London, when my mother died, then pretending to be a normal guy when I knew I wasn't. I've always known I could turn to you.'

She looked at him and in a whisper, 'Yes. But …' She picked up the tea towel and pressed it to her face. Through it she said, 'Do I really need to know that my father is homosexual, queer?'

'And that disgusts you?'

All the bubbles were gone and the sharp neon light left corners of darkness around them.

She took away the cloth and blotted her eyes. 'No. But he's my father.'

'A man like me.' This was a statement but it implied a question.

Gina shook her head. 'I didn't mean, of course I didn't mean…' She got up, looked over to the plates and glasses stacked on the draining board or soaking in the sink. 'I can't face this tonight. You must go to bed, check Rodney's okay.' She stood in front of him, rested her head on his mass of dark curls, drawing in his own dear smell of hempen sacks, as if he'd slept in a barn full of hay. 'Do you know, Ivan, I've learnt that some things are best not thought about if I can't do anything to change or accept them.'

Dear Ivan

Again I'm saying sorry.

My reaction to what you said about Kenneth being homosexual was unjustifiable, stupid and naive. It shouldn't have been a shock. But as I've never thought much about him, have little affection for him, it doesn't make any difference. In an odd way he seems proud to have me as a daughter, likes to play me off against my mother, which I ignore. But he's always been generous, buying me unsuitable clothes, happy when I like them.

I am truly sorry though that what I said in the heat of the moment might have reflected on you and Rodney. It does not. Who you love and how you love is only of concern to me if it makes you unhappy. You are the best man in the world - and always will be. But I promise not to flip out again!

And again thank you both for getting stuck in on Sunday. Clearing all that stuff to open out the veg patch was a blooming wonder. I am worried about Rodney's arms though; putting TCP on the scratches I thought was the proper treatment, except they did flare up horribly. Ruby would have known better what to do. Please take him to a chemist if they don't heal soon. Wrestling with those brambles was an act of immense bravery.

You can see I approve. A man who can almost outdo me playing Chopsticks is a hero.

Come again soon and I promise not to make you work so hard. I'd be interested in Rodney's ideas for refurbishing the house. And yours, of course.

Your always loving friend

Gina

Dear Ivan

Thank you for agreeing to give me away. With Rodney as my bridesmaid the ceremony will be perfect. He, of course, doesn't need to wear a frock. There will be no other guests at the registry office.

Bill and I are in complete agreement that we couldn't cope with the fuss that both Elspeth and Kenneth would wish for in different ways. It's strange, at times, to find that they have a similar stance on various issues, though usually coming from a different standpoint.

Our wedding is a mere formality, of course. A requirement in law to make sure that we're both covered if some disaster occurs. And that the child I'm carrying - early days - has socially decent parents.

I do love Bill - though, of course, you will always be my first! And he loves me too in a most generous and wholehearted way. It was a blessèd moment when he applied to the practice and charmed my mother into giving him a job. That he is a good divorce lawyer with all the new ideas of mediation, means that, for her, the marriage is made in heaven. For me his handiness with spatula and grill, enjoying the culinary arts, is a big bonus. Above all, that you approve and find him a likeable bloke makes me very happy.

It's such a relief that you are free on the 12th. We do need to get on with this before I become a talking point.

With love and kisses to my dearest friends

Gina

Kenneth 1982

Kenneth was propped up, pillows stacked behind him, his face grey, cheeks gaunt, the old furrows stretched out by lack of flesh. He'd been a handsome man, short and trim, blond hair and blue eyes, attractive to those men he desired, and, once upon a time, to her mother.

Gina hovered at the side of the bed. She'd come in response to Elspeth's call to say the diagnosis was terminal, the end not far off. She knew that she had to come but to see him here, gratefully acquiescing to the ministrations of the nursing home, was shocking; the metal frame 'cot', the oxygen tank, the medical chart hanging on the end of the bed.

'I'm so sorry,' she said.

'What for?' Kenneth's harsh whisper was defiant.

'That I didn't understand, or want to understand.' Gina was doubtful that this conversation would be helpful to either of them. Ivan, though, had insisted, *'Make your peace'*.

'I could have been kinder, more sympathetic,' she said.

'Huh! you warned me often enough.' His attempt at laughter provoked a cough which ended in a desperate dragging in of air.

How often had she accused of him of practising 'a filthy habit', forbidding any cigarettes entering her house, never joining him in a drink, even when he'd brought wine? She put her hand over his limp paw, the hand she'd avoided holding when a child. The silky white skin, the manicured nails, with no sign of unsightly ridges or tobacco stains. How had he kept them at bay?

'When did you start smoking? It was fashionable once, wasn't it?'

The silver cigarette case would flick open and clip closed, an affectation. The sharp click of the cigarette lighter, and the all pervading smell of cigarettes which she hated, announced his presence. Elspeth never commented though, perhaps believing it the least of his inadequacies.

'I remember your pipe,' she said. 'You and Frank Potter would light up together as if it were a special ceremony. I ran into the kitchen once to tell Ruby you were putting bonfires in your mouths.' She gave a little laugh hoping that he'd find it funny.

Instead his eyes welled up with tears. 'Ah, Frank, dear old Frank. Horrible, life like his cut short. Not even the War; just a bloody tractor taking a corner too wide.' He attempted a long breath and gasped out. 'Jack was doing his duty, fighting for …' but he couldn't finish. His chest heaved, tears dribbled down his cheeks.

She found the oxygen mask that lay beside his pillow, cupped it in his hand and guided it over his mouth. He didn't resist, breathed in little puffs, a sobbing sound, a childlike noise. To have provoked such grief wasn't her intention. Jack and Frank were her lead-in, a chance to talk of his curtailed love life, but it obviously hadn't helped him.

The room was bright with sunlight from a window looking out onto a garden. Hydrangeas and buddliea were banked at the back of a sweeping pristine lawn bringing in a loveliness that countered the sadness of those who had business in the building. Without the trappings of medicine and medical procedures, it might have been a pleasant room to lounge and talk.

His eyes were closed, the tears still wet on his cheeks, his breathing quieter as the oxygen filtered into his lungs. He held the mask and she sat down and waited. Had she been too hard on him? All her life he'd either annoyed or embarrassed. When she'd arrived this morning his first question had been to wonder where Elsa was. That she'd left her with Ruby as the nursery school was closed for most of August, amused him. 'The old girl seeing me out! Tough as old boots.' She wanted to rail against that description of Ruby who was frail at eighty-three, bowed down with arthritis, Ruby, who adoring Elsa, would be playing endless games of dressing up in clothes kept from when she, Gina, was a child; feathery boas and extravagant scarves, the provenance of which she had no notion.

Bill couldn't understand her hostility towards Kenneth, suffering his odd visits to their home, bottle in hand, with amused pity. 'He's lonely,' was the reason he gave for the time he spent listening to anecdotes of the War, what Kenneth and his comrades did to win victory. 'I understand that your mother can't put up with the repetitions, and her anger at his inability to lead his department, *and* that she can't replace him. But I'm sorry for him.'

Gina didn't argue. That her husband was uncomplicated and generous in his way with people was why she loved him. They'd never discussed the possibility that Kenneth was homosexual. She'd thought it irrelevant, which was what she had once said to Ivan.

A nurse came to take his temperature and pulse and had rearranged his bedding, all bustling efficiency. Kenneth, having abandoned his need for oxygen, was charming and deferential towards her, accepting obediently the orangeade he was required to drink through a straw. The nurse showed a fondness for him, chortling at a small joke he made about teaching her to play squash.

The brief intimacy established between father and daughter, though, was lost. Seeing him buttoned into his own striped pyjamas like a small boy was heartbreaking, the thick blue stripes reminding her of the blazer he'd once worn; a dandy not a clown. The sympathy she was prepared to give, an acknowledgment of the perverse life he'd had to lead, seemed more urgent than before.

'Have you had many visitors?' A banal question which he appeared not to hear. She tried another tack. 'Elspeth has contacted the rest of your old ROC squadron. She knew they'd want to know you were unwell.'

His eyes closed, he sat back, his arms limp on the coverlet. He couldn't have registered what she'd said. His breathing became regular, a benign expression on his face.

To sit in companionable silence was perhaps the most sensible thing to do. The armchair was comfortable, soothing petrol blue, its pair on the other side of the bed. Which side did Elspeth sit? For she'd come every day for the past week that he'd been here. That much Gina had established from the nurse on reception.

Elspeth told her that, 'He's been fighting this for months, carrying on as if nothing was wrong. Refused to go to the doctor even when I made the appointment.' That he'd rarely been to work hardly registered. He worked in a different branch and reports that he had a bad chest or was recovering on the golf course, raised no eyebrows. He had, though, called by to see them at home only recently. She'd found him regaling Bill with his opinion of the latest London show he'd been to see; Guys and Dolls. 'Spiffing show! Those Americans know how to put on a musical!' she'd heard him say to Bill.

The nursing home was a few miles out of town, a conversion of an older grander building. Was it the same place that Elspeth was brought when she'd damaged her arms all those years ago? The memory of those slug trail scars leapt back to Gina as clearly as that terrible journey in Grandpa's car under the cherry trees. And then Kenneth coming home soon after to tell them of Frank's accident, crying openly, another grown up behaving like a child, tears that she hadn't seen him shed for his own father; it'd been repellent. Bewildering too was Elspeth's stoic sympathy after her own collapse; Grandpa's death might never have happened. That was the day when Gina decided she'd prefer not to acknowledge Kenneth as her father.

Gina closed her eyes as if that would help her relax. Ivan was the first person she'd phoned on hearing Elspeth's message. He'd said, 'How do you feel?' To which she replied, 'You sound as if you're putting me on a couch. I was merely letting you know.' But, of course, he was right. She wanted him to tell her what she should do. He asked, 'What's worrying you?' And she was able to say,

'That he's a stranger and I am a daughter in name only.' And it was then that he said, 'Would it help if you told him that you knew of his homosexuality?' 'Heavens!' she said, 'That's a bit full on.' But lying awake last night it had seemed a good way to make up for her indifference, to recognise how he must have suffered.

The room was peaceful, few sounds to indicate what was happening outside the room. Kenneth's breathing a rhythmic wheeze, almost soporific. How long should she stay? Ruby couldn't be left too long with Elsa. She opened her eyes and was disconcerted to find him looking intently at her. 'Oh, you're awake! I nearly fell asleep.'

'Tell Elspeth no visitors,' he croaked.

She took his hand again. 'But if ...' How can she say it? 'Ivan sends his best wishes. He and his lovely boyfriend, Rodney. At least nowadays they can be open about being gay, loving each other.'

He didn't respond as she'd hoped and he'd stopped looking at her. But he squeezed her hand. 'Down there,' he indicated the bedside cupboard, 'a drink, your mother brought it in.'

A Lucozade bottle was tucked in alongside extra tissues and packets of sweets; a pale caramel colour, though it seemed to have lost its fizz. 'Do you want to use the straw or shall I ask the nurse for another glass?' she said but he shook his head and winked. 'Elspeth's no fool,' and he took a swig.

The remark and the smell told the truth. 'Should you be ...?' but it was a pointless question. He closed his eyes with a beatific smile.

He handed it back to her. 'Get the Polos. Don't want to be breathalysed.' Cheerful orders despite the wheeze and he pulled himself up on his propped pillows, settling as if rejuvenated, with a huffy laugh.

'It's your mother I'm sorry for,' he said. 'Tell her that when I've gone.'

'Daddy, don't!'

'What?' The drink's effect was extraordinary. He'd taken control. 'I've had a jolly good innings.' He smoothed the bedcovers. 'Got up to some terrific larks.' And again the mischievous smile that looked beyond her to memories he was happily recalling. The polo was finished with an impatient crunch. 'Only one regret.'

Gina said nothing. Ivan was wrong. Whatever had been missing in his life, it was not concerned with his homosexuality. And if they'd ever been able to talk freely, the life he'd led wouldn't have been acceptable to a child, a daughter. But her musing was brought to an abrupt end. His face crumpled, the gleeful expression gone to a grimace of pain.

'Daddy!' She leapt forward to grab the mask but he pushed her aside. His shoulders shook, his breathing quickened, his eyes wild. 'Shall I call the nurse?'

'No,' he gasped raising his hand to hold her back.

'But …'

'Shouldn't have hit him. Stupid.' He leant forward, flapping his hand at the side cabinet. 'Whisky.' A command, no more conspiracy.

She gave him the Lucozade bottle though this couldn't be right. But it was as if he'd pulled past whatever it was that troubled him. He quaffed the whisky ignoring her offer of tissues, his cheeks burning red.

'Hell of a mess.' He held the bottle to his lips, a child ready with its dummy, a soothing accomplice. He might have been talking to someone else. 'Took me for a sucker.'

'Who? When was this?' This wasn't what she'd come to hear, whatever that was. 'Who did you hit?'

He didn't answer, his eyes screwed up for another long sip.

'Dad and her, your mother,' he hissed. 'Canoodling in that damned greenhouse' He swigged and breathed more oxygen. He was no longer the poor invalid, some inner strength was lifting him up. His eyes bright, a dogged determination.

Gina pulled back from the bed, frightened by the ferocity of the way he spoke, what he was implying.

'Dad said sorry, but for what? Making me a cuckoo!' He spat out the words, his eyes wide, the bottle to his lips, and again to another audience. 'Didn't even fend me off. Just took it.'

Looking at him, the pumped up anger, one hand clutching the bottle, the other tight around the oxygen mask, gripped as if to do harm, was shocking. This wasn't fantasy, the whisky talking. It was some sort of appalling truth. The greenhouse, the glass panes shattered, Grandpa dead, Elspeth cut and crying. What she'd seen. 'Did you do that?' she asked for there was no other question.

His voice was hard, accusing. 'Their fault. Had to cover it up. Elspeth knew that.'

Gina stared at him, the man who she'd never known; his pampered hand clenched around the illicit bottle, his blue eyes narrowed as if for a fight. 'Bloody awful mess!' A quick gulp, the whisky fumes swirling around the bleached bed linen, he turned to see her at last, as if she would understand, be convinced. 'You're not my daughter, you know?'

A low glare from the sun sliced through the room, sharp light, a flame on her face. It burned through her, a searing truth. 'What?'

'Should have told you.' And he closed his eyes, dragged a breath and sank back, with what might be taken for a smile on the pouty lips.

'You're not my father?' Turned around it made sense except … 'Kenneth!' But he'd shut her out.

She drew back from the bed, She'd come to offer him compassion and affection. Instead he was burdening her with his need to relieve himself of guilt or take revenge. A last rite. None of it had been for her benefit. To tell her that she was not his daughter was an afterthought. There was no remorse or contrition. *'Had to cover it up,'* was what he'd said. Of hitting his father, or worse? Did he expect her to absolve him? It felt like spite. Pity gone, she was without words, a leaden weight in her stomach .

A knock at the door startled her. Kenneth was roused enough to push the bottle at her, the innocent Lucozade bottle. 'It's the padre, Mr Simms,' the nurse announced. 'I don't want to interrupt but he thought you might like to talk to him.'

'Please don't let me disturb you,' the priest directed this at Gina. 'You are …?' he began

Gina looked past the nurse with disbelief to this man who hovered at the door. Why hadn't he come earlier, this person whose vocation it was to hear confessions? Without acknowledgment, she skirted Kenneth's bed. 'I have to leave,' was all she could say. At the door she turned, 'I'm sorry, I'm so sorry!'

Nobody accosted the woman darting back and forth from one apparent exit to another. The labyrinthine linking routes through the two amalgamated buildings, old and new, were a challenge to visitors at the best of times. For Gina it seemed calculated to intensify the nightmare. Those who saw her would have been used to signs of distress from visitors, the coat carried over an arm but trailing on the ground, the shoulder bag dragging along beside her as if nothing mattered more than escape. None would see the Lucozade bottle clutched to her chest, the pain of its indentation on her ribs indistinguishable from the anguish his words had caused. Emerging finally through a side door, she threw the bottle of whisky into a litter bin, seeing as it flew from her hand that it was almost empty. He'd drunk the equivalent of two shots.

Elspeth. Gina stopped abruptly at the thought of her mother. Had Elspeth taken it in at his request? Had she been coerced or willing? Her powerful mother who rode serenely the storm of all difficulties and objections, who'd once said triumphantly, *'You and me, we'll make his wishes come true.'* What of her? Elspeth who'd loved George, obvious even to a child, apparent too from all the brittle focus on protecting his legacy, the breakdown after his death. And this? An affair, to be covered up? A daughter to be denied. Along with something more sinister?

The car was nowhere in sight, appearing to have moved from its original parking space, another part of the conspiracy to cause distress. Finally found and inside, the stuffiness heightening her nausea, she lay back in the seat. This had to be told, didn't it? A declaration of assault. Her beloved grandfather's death. His death that she'd never stopped mourning. Ivan's advice had come to nothing, worse. She was numb, paralysed to think who or what to tell.

Kenneth's funeral 1982

They stood side by side, Elspeth, Gina with Bill, and Jim Furland. In the pews behind ranged the other partners, associates and general staff, indistinguishably sombre in black. On the other side of the aisle were a surprising number of people, none of whom Gina knew. Elspeth had sent out the call, the notice of death in The Times and the local paper, discreet messages to those whose presence Kenneth would have appreciated. That he gave instructions that there should be no fuss - his ashes to be offered to the golf course - was not going to stop the occasion taking on a certain importance. 'It's an advertisement for the business, Elspeth says,' Gina informed Ivan.

He was out of the country speaking at a university in Russia so unable to attend. It was almost a relief for she feared his scrutiny; he knew her too well. What she wanted to say, to reveal, was too much for a blurred long distance call. She'd fobbed him off with the story of the whisky laden Lucozade bottle.

Bill hadn't questioned her distress when she'd arrived home that day, after all it was natural that she'd be upset at the sight of her fatally sick father.

She must speak to Elspeth. Kenneth had said, *'It's your mother I'm sorry for. Tell her that when I've gone.'* Then the statement that she wasn't his daughter. It had all come too quickly; pages flipped back, a whole history inverted. George, Grandpa was her father; that she could believe, wanted to believe. But why hadn't she been told long ago? And it had been spitefully said, as if she were the accused, along with the frightening admission of what he'd done to his father. The old pain of a box file of secrets lodged between her stomach and ribs was back. She was that child of eleven again, caught between pretending she hadn't heard, hadn't seen, and anger at those who'd covered up, denied her the truth.

Elspeth stood impassive at the end of the row. No one was surprised by her demeanour. A gracious acceptance of sympathy and good wishes, and those efficient arrangements for the funeral were in keeping with what they knew of her character. At sixty-two she was still a pretty woman though it wasn't an appropriate description of someone who neither wished to be seen as sweet and feminine nor as a coquette. Steel and elegance were adjectives evoked by her presence for staff, clients and acquaintances.

For Gina it was a bitter charade. How could Elspeth have carried on caring for a man who'd fatally assaulted the man she loved? But then Kenneth had said, '*Had to cover it up. Elspeth knew that.*'

Gina focused on the exquisite wreath of white gardenia resting on his coffin. A stark contrast to the bland decor of the crematorium. What had been the choice for his father? Kenneth wouldn't have cared. And she hadn't been there to see or say. Nobody spoke of it. Elspeth was away being mad.

The dirge of the electronic organ pumped out the final hymn, 'The Day though Gavest Lord is Ended.' A brave contralto warbled the top notes above the mumbled singing of the rest of the congregation.

Ruby was taking care of Elsa. Ruby who'd said quietly before they left for the funeral, her cheeks flushed, her eyes misty, 'His father was even younger, dreadful, not natural. He was the real gentleman.'

The organ struck up the RAF march as the coffin disappeared through the opening and closing curtains, the tempo out of time with the glide and final swish. Gina closed her eyes. Why had this man wanted to burden her with knowledge which was outrageous whether true or not?

In that brief period prior to the funeral she'd avoided talking to her mother whose phone call informed her of his death two days after her visit, and, later, the date of the funeral. How to broach the subject had preyed on sleepless nights. Where to start? Then, at the last moment, she'd been summoned to the house in Hinton Road. French and African marigolds blazoned the flower borders as they'd done every year since the garden was created, the stench overpowering. The sundial recording the hour. Nothing had changed since the day she left in 1961, furniture, wallpaper, and the faint smell of tobacco haunting the air.

Elspeth had led her into the dining room where papers were regimented into neat piles. 'Bill gave me the card from Elsa. I was very touched.' And from Elspeth's expression Gina saw that might be true. 'What I want to know, though, is if you would like to say something?'

Gina had stiffened, felt she'd been snared. She wasn't prepared; wasn't ready to ask whether Kenneth had told the truth; this wasn't the right time.

But Elspeth, who'd busied herself placing the picture on the sideboard for display with the other cards of commiseration, was already continuing with, 'Jim wants to say a few words which I think may pertain to how his father and George's father set up the firm,' her voice even and light. 'I've managed to find one of his ROC buddies who'll probably go on far too long, and Henry Carter, his golf partner, who promises to be brief.' She'd shrugged impatience, 'He said, *'Ken won't want us to delay getting to the 19th hole.'* The most incredible bore, but it has to be done.'

She'd turned back to Gina. 'Are you all right? You're incredibly pale,' and pressed her to sit down. 'I'm sorry that I didn't tell you earlier. Ken was so insistent that nobody should know.' She'd shrugged bafflement. 'I couldn't decide whether it was his desire to continue living as he'd always lived by camouflaging the problem. Or fear of death.'

'At the funeral?' Gina'd said, realising with relief what Elspeth meant. 'No, I don't think I have anything to say.' She'd swallowed. 'A glass of water is what I need, if you don't mind. I had to rush …' but the excuse wasn't needed for Elspeth was up, shaking her head.

'Of course. I should have offered you a cup of tea at the very least. I've nothing stronger. The alcohol went with him.'

'Just water, please.'

From the kitchen Gina heard the tap gushing and the opening of the fridge. Did Elspeth know of the priest's sudden entrance and her escape with the Lucozade bottle? A fly buzzed against the window pane and the telephone rang. From the hall she heard Elspeth's clipped tone. 'I don't mind where from. Just tell me honestly whether you can provide them or not.' A long pause. 'Please stop prevaricating. I want yes or no.' A short wait before Elspeth replaced the receiver and came back into the room saying: 'He expressly asked for gardenia. His love of fashion was one of the few things I admired about the man.' The glass of water was set carefully in front of Gina, ice cubes clinking against the glass. 'You understand that, don't you?' Gina met her mother's eyes. The old brittleness and tension were gone. 'You know that you were his last visitor before he slipped into his final sleep. The nurse told me he drifted off with a smile on his face.'

Elspeth headed the procession out to stand in the cloisters, accepting condolences and pressing everyone to join the family for refreshments. Gina clutched Bill's hand, evidence to him alone that her smile was a mask. The perfect husband, unquestioning, uncomplaining and his hand the perfect shape to accommodate hers. Wasn't she fortunate? She looked over to Elspeth, upright and gracious in the black cloche hat which flattered her neat chignon, the colour of her hair as true, it would seem, as the day she met this dead husband.

'I think it all went well,' she said, a note of triumph in her voice. 'Now we can enjoy the champagne!'

The room hummed. People chortling over their own anecdotes, Elspeth circling amongst them.

'She's an amazing woman!' Bill said. 'A diminutive figure amidst all those men, and yet she stands out, a lodestar.'

'Yes,' Gina agreed. 'A poor mother but the best schmoozer.' She leant against Bill, her champagne glass tipping dangerously. 'This stuff is very good,' and looking up at him, 'it's the best thing the wretched man has contributed to my whole life.'

He smiled indulgently, not taking her seriously. 'I hope she's going to be all right without him. You know, a gap in her life. Just keeping him in check …'

'For God's sake, Bill! You're far too gullible.' She drained her glass. 'I'll go and ask. Play the sweet, concerned daughter. She'll snap my head off, you'll see.'

Bill watched her go to the bar, request a refill, chatting and charming the waiters, as he knew she would. He'd never say it to her to face, but she was in some ways like her mother. Whatever she might pretend, this art of determinedly going for what she wanted, while making people think it was their idea, or, at least, the best proposition, had been passed on. Apart from their height and colouring, they sometimes seemed frighteningly similar.

Caught up in the swirl of people clustering around her to share their memories of Kenneth, Gina didn't reach Elspeth until nearly all the guests had left.

'Are you all right, Elspeth?' Gina looking down on her mother. Being so much taller was never an advantage. It meant she had to stoop deferentially to speak. 'Bill's worried that you'll be lonely without Kenneth.'

Elspeth laughed. 'That's what the majority of the guests were concerned to express. Not as bluntly, I may say.' A raised eyebrow. 'But you know better.'

Gina startled by this confidence, 'Do I?' and buoyed up with champagne bravado demanded, 'I need to talk to you. It's urgent.' No more prevarication.

Elspeth was reluctant to be diverted. 'Another time, Gina. I need to thank the staff and …'

'No, I have to know now.' Gina stood as a barrier, her empty glass clutched like a potential weapon or shield. 'Was George my father?'

'What?' But Elspeth wasn't paying attention, a half smile on her face as if to placate, a frown, her eyes focused on what was happening in the rest of the room.

Gina waved the glass to and fro in front of her mother's face, 'Kenneth said I'm not his daughter,' speaking as if in capital letters.

'Oh!' Elspeth reared back. 'When did he … ' But of course she knew the answer.

'It's true, isn't it?'

'Oh Gina!' Her hand had involuntarily gone to her throat as if under attack. 'I don't know why he did that.' Her eyes flitted around the room as if an answer might be out there. And then as if releasing a held breath, 'I didn't think he'd ever tell anyone. No!' She laughed feebly, a mocking laugh.

Gina stared. 'No? Why not? And what about me?'

'Yes, yes, I'm sorry. He shouldn't have …'

'No, that isn't the point. Why didn't *you* tell me?'

'I couldn't, could I?' Elspeth's tone was righteous at odds with her eyes which pleaded understanding.

'Why? I'm thirty nine, for goodness sake!'

'Shhh! Please!' And she looked fearfully across the room to where Bill was ushering out the last guests. 'Gina, I'm sorry you found out like this.' Again the imploring tone as she leant across to take Gina's hand and pull her down to sit beside her. 'I know it must be a shock. Perhaps I should have …' Pausing as if to assemble an argument she'd never thought to be making. 'You know George and I loved each other … You were an accident. And then …' She gripped Gina's unresponsive hand. 'That doesn't mean that we didn't want you. But…'

'Don't!' Gina flung aside her mother's hand, crying out, 'Don't!' as she stood up, her glass falling to the floor. A cold shudder took hold, as the room began to swirl and circle, the ceiling tumbling in and the floor falling away, the sound of her mother's voice calling, 'Gina!' receding. And then there was Bill carrying her to a taxi.

'You'll be all right, darling,' he was saying. 'A couple of Alka Selzter, a good night's sleep.'

'My mother!'

'Don't worry, Jim's gone home with her. She said that she'd pop in to see you in the morning. She was very concerned, quite upset, but I assured her that you don't usually drink like that. Hardly surprising.'

Elspeth looked out across the garden astonished by its beauty. A column of shade from the old sycamore cut diagonally across the two beds at the top of the terrace. Pink pelargoniums bordered by lobelia were untroubled by its intrusion. Mid morning, the sun blinking through clean-cut clouds, the summer heat kept at bay. She couldn't deny that it was as lovely as when he was here. His creation, once a perfect heaven.

She'd avoided coming here, or as rarely as possible, as a way of coping. Christmas Days she'd been forced to suffer lunch at Bill's behest, always a brittle affair with Kenneth in tow. Later in January she'd popped in for Elsa's birthday. The garden had been covered in snow.

A flock of sparrows swooped past disappearing into the hedge, twittering testily. Were they arguing or passing on gossip? That's what George would have said. She closed her eyes. No longer Kenneth's lawful wife; he'd gone, George was her rightful husband; she was his widow. Fanciful thoughts of little comfort.

Gina had ordered her out here with the promise of coffee. There were seats at the far end of the lawn, a cordoned row of apple trees at their back. She wandered down. How sensible that they'd netted the lily pond. A child could easily fall in. The side border was a mass of dazzling dahlias which she remembered and the spiky purple heads must be thistles, and those big yellow daisies. George had teased her, told her they were triffids.

Last night she hadn't slept trying to fathom why Kenneth had wanted to tell Gina that he wasn't her father. Stupid and perverse; a final taunt! All these years she'd spent concealing his *'little affairs'*; always *'sailing a bit close to the wind.'* Abiding by the pact she'd been forced to agree; the fear of scandal one of the few things they'd shared.

She turned back to see Gina coming towards her. Admitting the truth so abruptly hadn't been right. Without warning, no time to prepare. George, though, would be pleased that his daughter knew at last. He'd loved the child, longed to boast that she was their offspring. As he'd be overjoyed to see the garden that she'd kept, remade. Another part of his legacy.

It was odd, though, that Gina hadn't mentioned it before; Kenneth had been dead for nearly a fortnight. Of course it would have been a shock but she'd grown into a sensible woman, a trustworthy colleague, so she must have realised the implications of revealing this information. Talking it through with her was vital; none of this must go further.

Gina hadn't slept either. Lying beside Bill's solid back, barely a sound from his breathing, she'd silently raged, rehearsed again and again what she'd said, what Elspeth had said. And the hurt that George had deceived her. She'd always treasured the thought that he belonged to her alone. But, no, he'd been Elspeth's lover and couldn't acknowledge her.

But that wasn't the worst of it; she was at fault too. Her cowardice in not confronting Elspeth after visiting Kenneth. She ought to have gone immediately to find out the truth. Except what could she do with that truth? *'Their fault. Had to cover it up. Elspeth knew that.'* Was Elspeth really a part of it? Complicit in murder? Again wasn't she, herself, complicit? It all went back to what she'd seen and heard in the greenhouse, Elspeth's awful keening, her bleeding wrists, and George dead and she'd done nothing. Except, again, what was there to do?

The promptness of Elspeth's arrival had taken her by surprise. Bill had tactfully taken Elsa to the swimming baths, expecting, *'you'd like time with your mother on your own.'* He knew nothing of her childhood, she'd established herself in the firm, restored the house and garden by the time they met when she was thirty three years of age. How could she tell him any of this? She was caught again with the creeping fear of exposing any of it.

She'd managed to be forceful in sending Elspeth into the garden while she made coffee. Yet as she came out, stepping down the stone steps, the sight of her mother was startling. Standing alone, the tiny figure in a pink and blue patterned full skirted summer dress, appeared as young and vulnerable as when she would first have come here, a naive young bride.

Elspeth, hearing the chink of china, turned. 'This is perfect! The garden. As he always wanted it to be.'

Gina, caught off guard by this unexpected praise, clunked the tray heavily on to the slatted garden table. 'Oh, damn it! I …'

But Elspeth was not to be interrupted, saying, 'In the War, of course, he had to grow mainly vegetables. I remember leeks in those terrace beds and the border was full of potatoes and Brussels sprouts. It broke his heart but we were never short of food. Then when peace came the flowers were back, the vegetable garden and allotment enough to feed us, and more.' She was surprised to be happily reminiscing. And as she smoothed her skirt to sit down, she pointed, 'Those tall yellow flowers especially, a sort of daisy, came back with force. What are they called?'

'Rudbeckia laciniata,' Gina responded immediately which was hardly relevant and she felt highjacked by this bewildering overture. She needed to take hold of the conversation. 'He did know, didn't he?' she said. 'That I'm his daughter?'

'George, you mean?' Elspeth's voice changed, wary and sharp. 'Of course.'

'Then …'

'Of course he did! But Kenneth didn't, not until …' she clasped her hands as if to trap the end of the sentence. 'It couldn't be spoken of. So why he suddenly announced it to you I don't understand.'

'Spite?'

Elspeth ignored that possibility to carry on briskly with, 'Gina, I'm so sorry you learned the truth like this but you obviously understand, it was impossible then, the War, and

'…' her discomfort was masked by a regretful shrug. 'Kenneth should never have married me. I didn't realise and I suppose he didn't either. We never talked about it. I mean, in those days nobody did, it was illegal, a prison sentence,' she paused, unclasping her hands to let them lie limp in her lap, 'being queer.'

'That has nothing …' Gina began, cross at the partial inference that there was something wrong with being homosexual. But Elspeth had already put up a hand to stop any interruption.

'You have to understand. Marriage was a shield, a means to an end for him. Condemning us to live a life without the joy of true love. George and I found that together. That's the reality which could never be admitted.'

Gina stared at her, transfixed by this outburst, coming as if a prepared statement which, of course, it was, Elspeth's vindication and there was nothing that could be disputed. It's exactly what Ivan had trotted out once upon a time.

'Except that doesn't ….'

But Elspeth wasn't finished and knowing that she held the stage, she leant back, talking in an engaging tone as if at a board meeting. 'I've lived with this problem all my married life, Gina. Making sure Kenneth's indiscretions were out of sight. Poor man.'

Those last two words, as if implying sympathy for Kenneth, were too much. 'How *can* you say that? *Poor man*! Was he? To me he implied something very different.'

'Really?' Elspeth was helping herself to coffee, more relaxed now that she'd said her piece.

'He told me to say that he was sorry for you. What did he mean by that?'

Elspeth carried on pouring as if she hadn't heard. Gina, who was desperate to keep calm, to control her fury and fear, leant forward herself in an attempt to force Elspeth to look at her.

'This is important, Elspeth, because he made me think that a *crime* was committed.' She paused briefly for a reaction but Elspeth still appeared unfazed, adding milk to her cup, taking a spoon to stir and stir.

'A *crime*!' Gina repeated, taking hold of Elspeth's hand to stop the stirring. 'I need to know, don't you? What Kenneth said, raging at me he was, slurping the whisky you'd given him. Did he cause Grandpa's death?'

Elspeth snatched back her hand, massaging it as if she'd been hurt. But Gina wasn't going to stop. 'You have to tell me. He found you together, he said, you and Grandpa, in the greenhouse, 'canoodling' was his expression, said you'd made him a 'cuckold', or at least he said cuckoo, which was laughable but of course it wasn't, was it, because he was accusing George.' Gina didn't care how she sounded; no longer could this be unsaid. 'He hit George, didn't he? Hit him, and then what? Was it murder or manslaughter?'

A gentle breeze shuffled the leaves on the poplar trees at the boundary with the housing estate, a sound of anxious whispering as the two women sat side by side; Gina, her cheeks flushed, on the edge of her seat as if ready to pounce; Elspeth, outwardly unruffled, but with the old panic filling her lungs, breathing in long slow breaths. She'd suffered enough, braved too much to allow herself to crumple, descend into the lunacy of remembering because of Kenneth's stupidity, his infantile need for revenge. She turned to Gina calmly to say, 'You do realise that he was pumped full of morphine. The stuff which causes hallucinations?'

'But this wasn't …'

'No, buts.' She spoke precisely, a warning. 'That was a terrible time. And whisky must account for …'

'Yes, the whisky which he said you brought him, disguised in a Lucozade bottle. Was that right?'

Elspeth shook her head wearily, eyebrows raised. 'Gina, wouldn't you? If it were Bill? His favourite drink. He was dying, he had nothing to lose.'

'But what he said can't all be due to drugs and drink?'

'No, but we can't go through that again. It's in the past. What's important is that none of this goes further. I may not have loved him, but I'm not a monster. I've tried to maintain the facade of our marriage.' Her voice changed, the reasoning tone becoming autocratic, compelling. 'You must understand the scandal would have destroyed the business, marked George and I with the most vile gossip. Still would even now. And what for?'

'Honesty? Not to live with falsehood, or worse.'

But Elspeth was picking up her handbag as if about to leave. 'It has to be forgotten, Gina. I've had to, all of it. It mustn't go any further. Even Bill. You haven't told him, I hope?' And taking a handkerchief from her bag, she dabbed at her eyes.

Gina was appalled. Elspeth was crying. The effort to control the tears, the pent up composure gone. Her eyes closed, head bent to her lap she was balling the handkerchief tighter and tighter. Gina froze; should she reach out, take her hand, try to soothe the twisting and squeezing? But she can't. The strong mother, bereft of sentimental feelings, was the one she knew best. 'I'm sorry,' she said. And she was sorry. Tears were useless she'd been told, not the way to get what you wanted, and yet she knew they were natural, an impossibility to control in genuine grief. Here was Elspeth attempting to do so, not a ploy for sympathy.

The sun, high enough to drench the flower border with light and heat, blazed down. Bees drifted back and forth, delirious on nectar and pollen, the scent of lavender wafting sweetly on the air. From the house, the two women might have appeared to be in contented conversation. But nobody was there to judge, not George nor Ruby.

Elspeth, feeling the heat of midday on her back, was already pulling herself back from what she thought of as the brink. A last dab at each eye, and with a dismissive sniff she said, 'George's death was a tragedy which will always be hard to bear. You'll know that.' This was almost a question. 'But you also know that he wouldn't want us to suffer.' The certainty with which this was said impossible to deny so that when she carried on with, 'Any of this would still ruin us, Gina. People knowing the firm was built on a lie. That's all we have left, the legacy of what he'd built. And you've been part of that, we've carried it forward, haven't we? We've kept going what he left us.' And she even managed to sweep her hand to include the garden as if acknowledging it as in a final curtain call.

Gina said nothing. What was there to say? Elspeth wouldn't or couldn't bring herself to admit or even discuss what Kenneth had done. The woman was a tragic pawn, bound into an age-old deception. It was all too late.

Wholly recovered, the handkerchief back in her handbag, Elspeth drew in a deep breath and with a little deprecating laugh, said, 'I'm sorry. That was a ridiculous scene. I'm afraid I was a bit overwrought.' She straightened her back, turned to her cup of coffee. 'This is getting cold. Aren't you …'

'Elspeth, please, don't patronise me. I'm very troubled by what Kenneth implied. I always will be.'

'That I can understand, of course. But I've said nothing can be gained by digging up the past.' Her smile, the beguiling tone was impossible to deny. 'You can at least be content knowing George was your father and loved you greatly. That's surely enough?'

'Is it?' A question but turned around to a statement it was true. Part of her was relieved, for what more could she fight?

'Thank you.' Elspeth who reached across to take Gina's hand. 'It's essential we maintain the status quo.'

Gina

Ivan Schmidt 2017

Gina leant over the sink, the tap running cold water over her hands, blood dissolving to a thin coral stream down the plughole. The kitchen offered no explanation, no comfort. The red tiles, once linoleum covered, the white cabinet replacing the silver painted coke-fed boiler, were as remote to her predicament as the greenhouse appeared too close.

Wrapping a tea towel around the wounds, she sat at the table to think how best to approach what had to be done. Ivan? Could she ask Ivan to help? Bubble wrap to cover the greenhouse, fleece to shield the seedlings, the two of them could manage that together.

Ivan had come, of course, he'd come. Millie opened the door to him, all blushes and bobbing and wiping her hands on her apron, reserved ecstasy. 'Oh, Mr Ivan, all these years!' Neither knew whether the hug they each desired would be appropriate; Ivan concerned that not only his size but also decorum would make such an action crushing.

Instead he laid a hand on her shoulder. 'Where is she?'

'In the kitchen, said she's making us a cuppa.' And with a shy smile, 'It's lovely to see you, Mr Ivan, though I'm very sorry to hear of your loss. She told me how you've come to live down here, in the sticks is what she said.' The smile no longer shy, she positively beamed. 'It's good you're here after all these years and can give her a hand, what with this damage.' She looked him up and down, noted his walking stick. 'Mind you be careful though, glass is dangerous stuff.' Thrusting her hands into her apron pocket she pulled out a duster. 'Anyway I'd best be getting on with my work before she gives me a shout,' and giving him a little nudge, 'or the sack!' And she's off up the stairs laughing as she goes.

Ivan watched her go; Millie, her Aunt Ruby's replica, the loss of all those years gone by closing in.

'Your hands?' was the first thing he said. 'What have you done?' He gently lifted one to examine, saw the awkwardly bound plaster, heard the brisk intake of breath, as she attempted to withdraw from his grasp. 'Gina, these need proper dressing. A & E, or a chemist at least?'

'Stop fussing, man. I'm fine.'

'Huh! You don't look it.' He scrutinised her face. 'What's under that plaster? Let me re-bandage them. Two steady hands will be better than your cack-handed effort.'

'They're only cuts. I had to clear the glass away from the seedlings. I'm all right.'

But she left her hands in his as he carefully eased the plaster away for there was no good reason to refuse or take offence. Living in separate places, marriage to other people, hadn't diminished her desire for or trust in him.

'Thanks,' she said as he finished his careful re covering of her wounds. 'That does feel better. And now, come and see the greenhouse.' She glanced down at his stick. 'Do you need that?'

Thick dew glistened over the grass, a sheen of mirror droplets picking up the dull light. The only movement heard from the bypass, a deep thrum of traffic, momentarily cut through by the robin's claim for territory. How did she keep it like this, a museum piece? The winter pansies' bright expectant faces looked up at him, their petals as soft as his mother's cheeks, as Gustav once said; the pond a dark mystery at this time of year, the fish dug deep in the bottom mud; and beyond the herbaceous border, the greenhouse, a fine construction, built with pride to precise specifications more than a hundred years ago. Like an old church, it was in constant need of restoration, a concern expressed by Gina's daughter. *The money poured into that place would take you on a cruise around the world.'* Gina's response had been, *'I'd rather drown in my own pond.'*

Ivan followed her, cross that he was wearing his better trousers. Her telephone call at eight o'clock had been brief and acerbic. 'Good, you're home. I need your help.' No mention of the task, let alone the damage.

'Go and see,' she said. 'Don't touch the glass.'

He advanced cautiously. It had been forbidden territory to him as a child. Mr George let no one else care for the workings of his favourite sanctuary. Even Gustav Schmidt, as his gardener, knew that it was a place of refuge, private, verboten. *'I never go there, Ivan, and never must you.'*

He surveyed the damage, the panes missing from the door, two shattered on the side facing them, a couple of others cracked. Clearly it had been attacked by someone not a bird's unfortunate flight path. 'It must have been deliberate. Who'd do this?'

Gina shrugged. 'Lads from the estate?' An easy answer that came without thought.

'Then why haven't you called the police?'

Again she offered a defiant shrug.

He stepped further in. 'What did the vandals use as weapons?' He called back to her for she still hadn't come any closer. The glass scrunched under foot, and with his stick he poked aside the splinters and shards to look for the culprits but found nothing. 'No sign of anything here,' he called out but she appeared not to hear.

Ivan backed out of the mess. 'This needs more than my help. I'm calling a glazier before we do anything else.' He turned for a last look, to trays of seedlings neatly butting up to one another, pots in rows for maximum use of space on the benches, snug on either side, a schoolroom of obedient students. 'Perhaps we could cover the plants in newspaper or something,'

'No, they'll need fleece. A garden centre, we'll go in my car.'

'What, now?'

But Gina ignored his question turning instead to the bottom of the garden where a chain link fence was partially obscured by the trees planted when houses were built on the allotments soon after George died. Another tragedy which no one had opposed. The thought brought her sharply back to Ivan who was attempting to close the door of the greenhouse. 'Be careful.'

This is when he said, 'This wanton act ought to be reported.'

'No!' Gina snapped back, for how could she explain? It was the wanton act that Elspeth and Kenneth covered up which she'd just encountered. Buried for all these years and it'd now come back to haunt her. 'Come, it's too cold out here,' her voice falsely bright. 'You can find that glazier for me.'

The kitchen, familiar to Ivan even after the years of modernisation, had been a haven to the child he once was. The son of the gardener, Gina's playmate. Adulthood vanished, and an odd melancholy hovered, unsettling.

The throaty whistle of the kettle startled him out of his reverie. He pulled out his mobile phone, 'Do you have the number of a glazier or …' but Gina was in the hall calling up to Millie.

Coming back into the kitchen she said, 'You chat to Millie while I put decent clothes on and go get that fleece.'

'I said …' but she was off and Millie was coming through the door.

'How are you, Millie?' He said as she settled herself, stirring sugar into her tea. The similarities to her aunt were incredible; the voice, the wiry little body, even the way the chair moulded to her shape.

'Well, a few aches and pains but can't grumble, not at my age, can I?'

'Me too.' He indicated his stick. 'A dodgy hip. Need to get it sorted.' He took a sip of his coffee. 'Bad business, the greenhouse. Upsetting for Gina.'

Millie nodded, 'On top of everything else. There's enough to do out there without this. I mean she's a real task master, sir. Not with me, mind, with herself. I do worry that she'll wear herself to a frazzle.'

'I know. She's been helping me move into my new flat. Came up to London for a few days to help me pack.' He didn't add that she'd been particularly tetchy much of the time.

'Well, Mr Ivan …' Millie's quick backward glance to the door indicated that his feelings might be shared.

'Please, Millie, just Ivan, okay?'

Millie pursed her lips and he thought she wasn't going to say any more but looking again to see if they might be interrupted she carried on with, 'It isn't just because of this what's just happened. I think it's her mother what's disturbing her. Not that I like to say things about her but seeing as how you're almost family …' she leant into him. 'Mrs Simms, I mean, she's a lovely lady but she didn't often come round here before, having her own house, and with the business, and then being in that lovely hotel place, and, to be honest, no love lost.' Millie gripped his arm. 'Oh, I shouldn't be saying this, and I wouldn't to anyone else, but it's true.' A sad shake of her head, the grey perm unmoved, face powder picking out the pores on her nose and chin. No beauty, all heart.

'And now?'

'Well, I don't know,' she sipped her tea, her eyes, tiny blue crystals, reappraising what ought to be said. 'Not that I'm here every day, it's only Tuesday and Friday mornings, but I see her, Mrs Simms, most times and I know it's not that she's been invited. Well it doesn't seem like that.'

But Millie stopped abruptly at the sound of Gina coming down the stairs, calling out to Ivan as she came through the door. 'Have you found that glazier?'

'No, I've been chatting to Millie. Our aches and pains, old times, Ruby, who we all adored.' He couldn't quite think why he'd elaborated, except Gina's brusque attitude annoyed him.

But then she was saying, 'There've been two treasures in my life, Ivan, Ruby and Millie here.'

Millie beamed and blushed. 'Well, I'm not going to be that any more if I don't get a bit of dusting done.' And she was off, a wisp of a woman, a whippet let out of its trap.

Gina sat down, cradled her hands to her chest.

'They're not good are they?' Ivan leant across, looking up into her face. 'You ought to be resting.'

'Poof! There's too much to do. I'll go and get the fleece while you phone for a glazier. You'll find them advertised in the Yellow Pages.'

Ivan held up his phone. 'Modern man, the internet, lady.

Half an hour later he'd located a man to replace the glass but Gina was still not back. Millie had left; he'd watched as she wobbled her way down the road on her upright bicycle, the huge basket on the front threatening to upend the contraption. He'd wandered down to look again at the greenhouse. He gazed up at the glass roof to see that it was all intact which he thought odd as anyone chucking missiles in order to cause damage would have thrown high, overarm. But this damage would have been done by underarm shots or even someone standing close up to the glass.

A pale sun cut through the cloud casting a brighter light over the whole scene, pinpointing the snowdrops bunched round the stretch of apple trees which shielded the flower garden from the vegetables. How could anyone want to destroy such beauty?

He turned back towards the house to find a figure standing on the terrace. The woman was straight backed though diminutive. 'Who are you?' she called. But before he could answer, 'Where's my daughter?' Elspeth's high, authoritative tone reduced Ivan to a small child, the son of a foreigner.

'Mrs Simms,' he called back walking up to meet her. 'I'm Ivan, Ivan Schmidt, Gustave's son.

Ivan was a few feet away when Elspeth said, 'Oh, yes, of course,' though she still looked beyond him. 'My daughter, Mrs Gina Burton. Is she here?'

She stood imperious in small ankle boots, the fur collar of her bright blue coat turned up to ward off the chill spring air. Her hair, chestnut red that had been her pride and joy as a girl, was drawn back into a severe pleat; no one would have guessed her age.

'It's good to see you again,' Ivan leant forward as if he might be going to bow. 'Gina's fetching something to protect her plants. Her greenhouse was attacked last night.'

Ignoring his response she said, 'No, you're not the gardener, of course not.' She offered her hand. 'So nice that you've come. I think Gina did mention something about your visit.' Her eyes roamed his face. 'I don't know why she doesn't get a gardener. George always had one.'

Did she recognise him?

'Gina's told you that I've moved down from London, bought a small flat in the city?'

'Oh really!' She let go of his hand as if surprised it was still in her grasp. 'Are you staying for lunch?'

'It isn't planned but …'

'Oh, here she is. Gina!' Elspeth surveyed her daughter coming round from the front of the house. 'I was saying that you ought to get a gardener.'

'No, it's a glazier I need.' Gina looked from Ivan to her mother and back. 'They're out of fleece.' To her mother, 'Why have you come?'

Ivan, taken aback at Gina's blunt question, began, 'We were …' but Elspeth was smiling at them both as if they were sharing some sort of joke.

'Oh, I just popped in. Was thinking … well, it's of no consequence.' And with that she clasped Ivan's hand again. 'So good to meet you. You must come round to see me. I live in a hotel, you know. The house in Hinton Road I always hated so when Kenneth died I didn't stay long. Did you meet Kenneth? No, that was a long time ago. Funny to think back, before the War, and we didn't think there'd be a war.'

'It was that War which brought my father here, Gustave,' Ivan said, 'you will remember, I'm sure, he was your gardener.'

'That's a German name. But Ivan, that sounds Russian, doesn't it?' Her smile fixed on him, a queen pleasing her subject. 'George was wonderful in his knowledge, especially history. My father too.' And then turning to Gina. 'You remember, they were both Air Raid Wardens.'

'Yes,' Gina's clipped tone designed to put an end to the conversation.

'Ernest Smith, my father, died before George. How old were you, Gina?'

Gina ignored the question. 'Elspeth, Ivan and I have a job to do.'

'Oh, of course. I was only dropping by.' And letting go of Ivan's hand, 'You will promise to come and see me. Gina will bring you. Tomorrow, I'll expect you tomorrow. So good to reminisce.'

'Yes, of course.' Ivan, already perturbed by Gina's brusque dismissal of her mother offered to drive her home.

'Oh no! I have a taxi waiting for me.' And stretching up she placed her gloved hand against his cheek. 'Such a charming boy!'

Gina took hold of her mother's elbow. 'We'll see you to your car,'

'Don't fuss, Gina.' Though she made no more protest as Gina steered her round to the front drive, Ivan following. Climbing into the waiting taxi she called back, 'Tea tomorrow. Four o'clock. Gina knows the way.' And she was off.

To the receding taxi, Ivan said, 'She looks remarkable for her age. Remind me; ninety?'

'Ninety four.'

'Heavens! You'd never guess. And a hotel? Really? I thought …'

'It's her little joke. Sheltered accommodation, very upmarket, of course, but she deserves it, can afford it.'

'I'm pleased to hear you say that.'

'What?'

'She's not had an easy life - Kenneth?'

'Oh, for goodness sake, don't start! As she often said to me, '*You make your own bed* ….' She chose him.'

Ivan turned to see annoyance writ clearly in her frown. He tried again, 'I don't think she remembered me, do you? Is it so long since I've seen her?'

'I don't know. Can't remember. It could have been before Kenneth died.'

'Surely not, that's thirty plus years ago, isn't it?' Not waiting for an answer, 'Was that a one-off? I mean, she didn't appear to have a real reason for visiting.'

'No. I'm not sure what's going on.' She was already leading the way back to the kitchen. 'Tell me, the glazier? Any luck?'

'Yes, tomorrow morning.'

Gina stopped, turning on him angrily. 'That's not possible! My seedlings! They'll be shrivelled by morning!'

'Can't we …' but she'd already left him, stomping back up to the house.

He waited, then followed to find her blotting her eyes with kitchen paper.

'Hey! What's the matter?'

She sniffed and sniffed again.

He pulled a white folded handkerchief out of his pocket, shook it out. 'There's no need to worry, I can help. Maybe we could bring the plants inside?' And he leant forward to stroke the tears from her cheeks.

'Don't, Ivan!' She drew back taking the handkerchief for herself offering him a weak smile. 'Too much sympathy.' He'd borne all her bleats and grouses for nearly all her life, even at a distance. Except for this thing, this thing that was buried deep, couldn't be spoken of which Elspeth was churning up.

But there he was all concern, peering over his glasses, his thick black eyebrows scrunched up in a fierce frown. A grizzly bear is what she'd called him once upon a time, 'My big gruff, grizzly bear.'

'I'm being a fool,' and she sat down pulling him to the chair beside her. 'Old age. And Elspeth.' She could admit to that.

'Ah?' he said, pleased that Millie's intelligence was correct.

Gina stuffed the handkerchief up her cardigan sleeve. 'She keeps coming here as you saw, or phoning. Something she never did until a few months ago. Hadn't been in the garden since the day after Kenneth's funeral. I know that.' Something else she remembers too well. She shook her head in bewilderment. 'She's obsessed by the past.'

Ivan shifted his leg, felt immensely tired. 'That's normal at her age, our age even, isn't it? I love to reminisce about Rodney, our life …'

'Yes, I know, of course,' and she took hold of one of his hands, gently caressing it with both of hers. 'But it's not like her, a complete reversal. Before, any reflection was batted away with, *'It's maudlin to dwell on the past, a motto that my own mother taught me, never mope over your problems, solve them,'*

Ivan laughed, 'Does it matter? She must be quite lonely. Friends?'

'True. The few she had are gone, *'marched off to meet their maker which ever one that may be,'* is how she tells it. She has a wry sense of humour at times. Never a tear though.' A comb from her bun fell to dangle behind her ear. She let go of his hands to hitch it back in without much purpose, 'But come on, that's enough. The plants, an excellent idea. I'll make us some lunch first and then we can get started.'

'No, Gina, I'm ordering a takeaway,' and he got out his phone. 'Pizza or Chinese?'

Gina brightened when the trays of plants and individual plant pots were inside, ranged round the kitchen window sill, through to the dining room, newspaper laid for protection on the table and sideboard with some on the floor by the French windows. She allowed him again to re-plaster her hands, but then virtually ordered his attendance to oversee the glazier next day.

'Gina, I know nothing of glass and putty. And I've a hospital appointment with a specialist.

'Come early, then,' she demanded. 'Your astute eye - a third party to see if he's doing a good job or not. Ask pertinent questions.'

Ivan drove the country road back to his new flat. In an elegant block recently built in this elegant city close enough to the country and coast, and Gina, it seemed an ideal place to retire. Rodney may have craved the bucolic cottage with roses round the door and honeysuckle scrambling over a trellis, but that would have been for two men, younger men, fitter men. They'd both been London lovers, roots deep in the cosmopolitan life, a place from which Ivan could most easily travel for his work abroad.

That day with the first murmurings of spring in the hedgerows, green overcoming the brown and grey, the glint of sun polishing the tarmac, he was happy with his choice. But Gina, she worried him. She didn't look well; her appearance, if he's honest, shabby. Her hair, which she'd worn in a stylish bun for many years, was all over the place, strands wandering free, the whole unstable. And her clothes hung off her as if they didn't belong. Had she lost weight? Always a beanpole - her expression - so little flesh to lose without becoming a skeleton. But her manner, her whole demeanour was sour, her usual playful cynicism blunted.

She'd born the blow of Bill's sudden death six years ago with grit. *The best way to go, Ivan,'* she'd written in a letter to him. *'Not a moment's illness, or deterioration of mind, his body simply decided it had had enough. I must be grateful for that.'*

But this change was very recent, he was sure of that. In the last six months? When Rodney died which was almost a year ago, she'd been his rock, a cliché but true. She hadn't hassled him to move, merely nudged him to make decisions, keeping him company when he was most in need. She'd even accompanied him on a lecture tour to Germany pretending that, '*I don't want some buxom wench snaffling you up as an eligible widower*'. When had it started and why, this irritability? Was she regretting his move, cross that she'd encouraged him to live close by? Seeing him as another burden which she'd made clear was how she felt about her mother; reluctant even to accept Elspeth's invitation to tea, her whole demeanour hostile? That, too, was strange considering they'd worked closely and confidently together for decades, which long ago he'd forecast quite the reverse.

As soon as he was home, he took a bottle of wine out onto the small balcony, still wrapped in his winter coat. The courtyard garden below was lit by solar lights picking out each corner of the square. He poured himself a glass of wine thinking two might be needed. Rodney, who was teetotal, had never begrudged other people alcohol. He'd say; "*People may call me Pious Pope but when you've encountered a father who was saint and devil depending on what he'd drunk, you lose the temptation yourself.*"

He'd loved Gina too. He'd have advocated patience, '*look at it from her point of view.*'

'Impressive isn't it?' Gina remarked. 'A place appropriate to a person with an indomitable attitude.'

Laurel bushes bordering the entrance, the gloss black paintwork breathing authority, daffodils lining the drive to herald their approach.

Elspeth, already at the door to greet them, shot a disapproving glance at Ivan's stick as she guided him through to her flat. 'I've been remembering your father, Gusto. That's what he insisted Ruby call him.' This a confidential aside accompanied by an affectionate pat on his arm.

Ivan exclaimed, 'What a lovely room!' to Elspeth's obvious pleasure. Vases of tulips pick up the pink and green of the floral chair covers and as if to compliment Elspeth's cashmere cardigan, the colour of wild roses worn over a silky blouse. 'I'm so pleased you've come,' she said. 'Such a long time. So many memories.'

She drew a trolley forward and sat down indicating the chair opposite where he should sit. Tea was poured and distributed, slices of Battenburg cake offered before they could settle and Elspeth regard him with pleasure.

'Music is my main delight, you know,' indicating a large walnut cabinet polished to be the focus of attention. 'George and I were passionate music lovers. He knew so much and I knew very little when we first met.'

'Of course,' Ivan looked over to Gina who didn't appear to be listening. 'The baby grand was his, wasn't it? The one Gina plays.'

'Really?' A question to which she didn't require an answer. 'That's my radiogram. I have a large selection of records, many that we bought together, George and I.'

Ivan nodded. 'My father was a Schubert lover, especially Lieder.'

Gina stood at the window, staring out at the banks of shrubs, her height emphasised by the rigidity of her spine.

He'd been pleased to see that she'd dressed up for the occasion, her hair piled high, a silvery pewter, under control. There could never be rivalry as such between these women in figure or style but he wanted Gina to be shown as her mother's equal. A ridiculous thought left over from their childhood when one of Elspeth's disdainful remarks to his mother had bothered him. 'Gina is such a big child, so dark, it's difficult to credit.' That she'd inherited her grandfather's features, the tanned skin, the mass of dark curls and her height, was obvious but never celebrated.

'I was remembering your dear mother, Mareke,' Elspeth drew his attention back as if reading his thoughts, 'I was remembering the day when the idea came to me.'

Ivan wasn't sure what response might be appropriate but none was needed.

'George approved which was all that mattered. You'll understand that.' And again without waiting for his reply she said, 'A wonderful nanny for Gina. We will always be grateful. You will remember her, Gina?'

Gina turned briefly, a desperate glance.

'She was Dutch wasn't she?' Elspeth carried on as if she'd made a statement not asked a question. 'Kenneth was very silly, I remember that. My child being brought up by a foreigner, the wife of Dad's gardener, he said. Of course he was just trying to provoke, he didn't want me to go back to work. So old fashioned. Such a snob!' She abandoned her cup with a grimace. 'I should never have married him.'

Ivan looked down at his cup, wondered how to shift the conversation but Elspeth was intent on continuing. 'George was devastated when she was killed. Riding her bicycle wasn't it? Dreadful, dreadful. After that he forbade me cycling to work. We bought a car. My Morris Minor. Do you remember, Gina? Almond green.'

Gina glanced again at Ivan, a stricken expression. 'Is this …' but she didn't finish for there above Elspeth again, holding court, asking Ivan what music he liked.

To his reply that he preferred classical music like his father, she beamed. 'Ah, your father, your real father. I did tell Gina, though nobody else had to know. All so impossible.'

Gina came to sit beside Elspeth, frowning at Ivan. Had he picked up the oddity of what she'd said?

Elspeth appearing not to notice, held out the plate of Battenburg cake. 'Please have another slice, Ivan. Shop bought, I'm afraid, but delicious.'

Gina, however, was already gathering up the cups, saucers and plates onto the trolley. 'I'll take these through to the kitchen and rinse them quickly. Is there anything I can get you, Mother. Have you any supper prepared?'

'Don't fuss, Gina!' Elspeth closed her eyes as if to reinforce what she'd said. 'I am a little weary.' And she remained like that until all was cleared away. But when Ivan passed her chair to leave she caught hold of his hand. 'Thank you. You're a good boy. I always said so to George.'

An uncomfortable silence settled between them as Gina drove away. Ivan was baffled by his reaction to Elspeth's monologue, her determination to pursue memories of his mother, referring to her as 'a wonderful nanny'. Elspeth, an old lady after all, was doing her best to entertain someone she hadn't met for many years, putting on a good show. So why this feeling of desolation? It was decades since the bleak horror of his father telling him of the accident, weeping and holding him so tightly that he hadn't dared to cry. And why should it still sting to be taken back to the small boy aware of being someone lesser, an 'alien'. He'd heard the term, knew it had applied to his father, and him in turn.

He shifted his weight, the low slung seats of Gina's car plaguing his hip. She ought to get a different model, smaller, more up-to-date like his.

Gina muttered, 'I'm sorry.'

'Not your fault.'

'I didn't say it was,' sourness sneaking in.

Ivan ignored her retort saying, 'I see what you mean, though, wanting to talk about the past. Absurd to be upset, a grown man! And I'm sure that wasn't Elspeth's intention.'

'I did warn you. It was your idea to go.' Her original apology forgotten.

'It would have been rude not to take up her offer, surely.' An edge to his voice. 'Even though you said she hadn't remembered.' And he paused, looking out at the once familiar roads. 'How fit is she?'

Gina's gave a pained shrug.

'Well, I can't fault her memory, and I'm the first one who ought to understand. The value of remembering the past. Do you know the Maori saying? "*I walk backwards into the future with my eyes fixed on the past.*" The explanation revived him. 'Isn't that what makes us human beings, that we value our memories, live by them?' Adrift in his own philosophical discussion, getting no reaction from Gina, he dared to say: 'Why are you being uppity when I express an opinion? You told me the other day that she worried you.'

'Huh!' she swerved into her drive, fractionally missing the gatepost, wrenched the handbrake on and sat staring out of the windscreen. Finally she said, 'Because what you say sounds like sentimentality. Some things are best unsaid, as you discovered.' She swung open her door, and leapt out to inspect paintwork at the rear of the car, muttering, 'Damn!' as she polished the mudguard with the sleeve of her jacket.

'I'll ignore that,' Ivan called from inside the car. 'And I'd say, let her be. She seems pretty able for someone of her age, rejects your help anyway. And there's a warden, isn't there?'

'That's it is it?'

Ivan heaved out of the car, prised himself upright. 'Gina! Don't quarrel with me. I'd say she's not your responsibility.' He thrust forward his walking stick to gain pitch on the gravel. 'I'll phone in the morning.'

She stood and watched him drive his brand new car out of the drive, dainty and gleaming red. You wouldn't lose that in a car park. But she might lose him. At last after all these years, when he's near enough for real companionship, her bad temper could drive him away for ever. The thought overwhelmed her. And though knowing he wouldn't hear, she called after him, 'Isn't she?'

The greenhouse was empty, hollow air whisking out as she opened the door. No broken glass, the fresh panes ready to absorb the sunlight, to hold in the warmth. Whatever it was that triggered that awful moment of deja vu, had to be forgotten.

Dementia, or even that other illness that scrambles your brain, could that really be happening to Elspeth? She hadn't said that to Ivan and he didn't pick it up. The woman who'd run rings around any opposition in the past, built a business with branches in two cities and six adjacent towns, it was unbearable to admit that might be what's happening to her.

Making her way back to the house, the steps already indistinct in the fading light, she heard the telephone ring.

Elspeth's voice bright and clear, 'What a nice man! He must come again, Gina. When did he leave?'

Gina, her heart pumping from the sprint to reach the house and phone, asked, 'Leave where, Mother?'

'Here, when he left with his father, Gustave. He wasn't a gardener, you know.'

'Ivan went to London when he was eleven.'

'And now, where does he live? I'd like to see him again. He knew George.'

Elspeth peered through the glass of the greenhouse.

'Mother!' Gina called out from the terrace steps. 'What are you doing?' Nine o'clock; she'd come to open the greenhouse vents as a warm day was forecast. The perfect day for the outing with Ivan.

Elspeth didn't move and it was only when Gina close that she appeared to come to life as if from a trance. 'I was looking for ... oh, you know those pretty pink flowers that George grew. On his desk. They're fussy plants. Did you know that, Gina?'

Even at this early hour she was immaculate, the blue coat and a rose patterned scarf covering her head and tied under her chin. 'I can't see them.' Her nose on the glass.

'No, I don't grow them.' Pity crept out of nowhere, the childlike appeal of her mother's quest. 'I think they must be out of fashion.'

Elspeth didn't step back but tried to shield her eyes as if that might bring them into view. 'What are in all those pots then?'

Gina came closer to stand beside her mother. 'Flowers and veg. All things that my father grew.'

Elspeth turned slowly to study her daughter, in the same way as she'd searched for that pretty plant. 'You are like him. That was the worry.' Her hand fondled the fur collar of her coat. 'He was your father.'

'It's good to hear you say that.' Gina met her mother's gaze. 'It's not a secret any more?'

Elspeth ignored the question. 'Ruby called you 'a little throwback,' and clutching Gina's arm, 'Georgina, I chose the name. He always wanted to tell you. But we couldn't, could we?'

'That's what you said years ago.' Gina tried to ease the vice like grip of her mother's hand.

Elspeth held on, intent on her own reverie. 'Kenneth's fault.' Distress had overtaken her. 'I had to promise, didn't

I?' She pleaded, and looking back towards the house. she shivered. 'That man, you haven't told that man, have you? It would ruin us,' and tightening her hold, 'George would have forgiven.' The words were directed at Gina though she seemed to be talking to herself. 'I had no choice, did I?

Gina breathed in the smell of the new putty, a soothing nutty oil, saw the brighter colour around the repaired glass panes against the old. It would need a touch of paint when all this was over. She peeled her mother's hand from her arm, cupping it gently in her own. 'Why don't you come in for a cup of tea?'

'Will George be there?'

Ivan had already wasted one sachet in his coffee machine when the mug slid from its platform and emptied the contents on to the floor. Bending to mop up drew a sharp stab and lingering ache from his hip. He sank into a chair, tears welling. *'My beloved softie,'* Rodney would have said, *'for someone with your name, size and looks it's a surprise to find the vulnerable heart you hide.'* Has he made a mistake? The companionship with Gina which had always been as natural as when they were children racing down the slope of the Glebe Avenue garden, tumbling amongst grass clippings, was gone. Her unpleasant moods were dispiriting. Could she honestly be so upset by her mother? Elspeth was bound to be a bit erratic at her age.

The sun dodged behind the clouds and he took up his walking stick. The outing was her idea accompanied by another of the many apologies. Each time he'd called or they'd met over the last couple of months, she'd found some reason to be huffy or bitter, followed by justifications or pleas for forgiveness. It was becoming a dismal habit.

The Downs rolled out around them. A murmur of green touched fields and trees, streams snaked blithely through valleys, with blackthorn appearing like snow along the hedgerows. 'Not hawthorn,' Gina informed Ivan as if to be so mistaken would mar his day. They travelled in his car, 'which is a pity,' she'd said, 'as you won't be able to appreciate the view'.

Gina was still agitated after this morning's encounter with Elspeth. Elspeth had shaken off her offered hand walking back to the house, up crazy, crazy paving steps which were too old to repair, too familiar to replace, and on reaching the back door, had stared at the weathered paint as if assessing its need for a new coat and then turned sharply to say, 'George died years ago. I won't stay. If you'd be kind enough to call me a taxi.'

Gina smiled brightly at Ivan as they parked up at the pub. 'This is a celebration and to try to make up for my testy temper.' And over lunch they'd relaxed into easy talk, close friends with plans for what they could do over the summer, another future mapped out, the politics of the day chewed over with the fish and chips, kitchen disasters, plant progress drunk down with a glass of beer. Ivan became confident she'd be pleased to hear his news.

'I'm at the top of the list for the op,' he announced. 'The surgeon said to be ready as I could be called any day, which means soon.'

'When's soon?' Gina sharp reply overtook any expression of sympathy or reassurance. Her stomach clenched, as tight as her mother's grip on her arm that morning. At his age, under the surgeon's knife, hospitals rife with infection? She looked away. 'I'm sorry.'

The bar was full, voices suddenly louder, pitching back and forth under the low beamed ceilings, the heat rising, circulating the stale smell of fish and chips.

'Can we go outside?' Gina was already on her feet. 'Take coffee with us?' And she was off, leaving him to organise the order. Outside she breathed in deeply, the splash from a stream which tumbled through the garden, stirring up fresh air. Panic receded and when Ivan came out to join her, carefully carrying a tray with their cups of coffee she said, 'It's the chalk, you know, acts like a sponge to hold the rain which then bursts out as springs all over the place. Riddled with them we are in this part of the country.' Pleased to explain the virtues of where he's now living, and to forget her negative outburst.

He saw the water running over the stones of the shallow riverbed, heard the ripple and gurgle, a sound as calming as music, but was uncertain of where his news had taken them. Stirring sugar into his cup, he tried a different tack. 'What about bringing Elspeth here? You said that she's stuck with certain places she's willing to go. It must be stifling in her flat after a while, relying on taxis.'

An innocent enough remark he thought but Gina's cry shot through the air as if from a gun. 'Stuck! Stifling! Haven't you been listening?'

'Hang on! That's not fair.'

But *she* wasn't listening, the morning's encounter still vivid and raw. 'I can put up with the effects of old age, onset dementia maybe? But this is worse.' Her voice travelled the path back to the building where closed windows insulated the noise from inside and out. But how could she explain? *'You haven't told that man, have you?'* She pushed aside her cup of coffee. 'I don't know what she's going to say or do next. She's pestering me but also she's been to the main office, waltzed in to see if I'm there, even asked for Bill. It's demeaning to her.' But Gina knows this isn't the crux of it. It's the fear of what's been buried. And it's her fault, wanting it all just to go away. 'When you talk of the balm of memory, Ivan, I want to shout twaddle.'

'That's pretty harsh.' Ivan aghast at the venom of her attack could take no more. 'And please can you stop shouting at me. What have I done wrong? I've agreed it can't be easy.'

'Easy!' It was all broiling up inside her, the accumulated shame of carrying on with that status quo when Elspeth, herself, was pulling it apart. But it isn't Ivan she ought to be heckling.

A lone seagull flew across the fields beyond, trailing behind the echo of its mournful cry. A door flapped open from the pub kitchen and banged shut leaving a wider silence.

'Okay! What I've never told you. My father?' The question emphasised by a pause and fiercely raised eyebrow. 'I'm not Kenneth's child. George is my father!' The words were thrown out as if to challenge, her chin up ready to take a punch. 'My dark secret buried for all this time. A secret I wasn't allowed to tell even you!'

Ivan was caught off balance, not expecting this turn in her tirade, certain that to say, 'I know,' would add fuel to her fury. He looked at her, his beetle brows stressing concern as he said quietly, 'We did suspect. Gustave said something about seeing great love between Mr Simms and his daughter-in-law, *'a tragic love which tore my heart.'* A big softie was my dear Papa.'

'What?'

That admission hadn't lightened her attitude. He braced himself. 'As I say. And if you're going to accuse me of not telling you, think about your reaction when I told you I was gay.'

'That was different!'

'If you say so.' He paused before adding, 'Then tell me, when did you find out?'

'Kenneth's funeral. He'd told me before he died and she had to admit it.' Her note of triumph didn't fit with how she felt. 'Yes, thirty years I haven't been able to tell anyone, to enjoy, to celebrate.'

The wind was gusting stronger, fussing straggles of hair around her face, her bun coming loose. She pulled them back as if they were part of her fight. 'Ivan, I've been a pawn. Even my marriage certificate was invalid. And all this time I've obeyed her like a fool.'

'So why are you taking this out on me?'

'No! No! That's wrong.' She stared at him, so close and yet as if lost to her. Her head hurt, a pressure inside as if it would burst. Is she the one who's mad? Swinging round she pushed off the seat and strode out of the garden, disappearing behind a trellis leading to the carpark.

Ivan sat on, stunned at her sudden departure. But then having gone back into the pub to pay the bill, went out to the carpark thinking that he'd find her waiting beside his car.

She walked on the road keeping close to the hedges, not bothering to think which side would be less dangerous with passing traffic. The continuous winding downhill quickened her steps, speeding the space between her and the pub. Cars shot by, letting fly angry honks, adding to her sense of injustice.

Spits of rain dotted the surface of the road. Her legs ached with the steep descent, her heart plucking at her chest, her lungs stretched taut as her pace picked up faster and faster. The distance travelled, the wet in her face, the tarmac taking her away from it all, was somehow exhilarating.

By the time he caught up with her, she'd reached a village, where, despite a pavement, she continued to walk on the road.

'Get in!' He shouted pulling up beside her. 'Do you want to get killed?'

She stood undecided. Her hair fell in soggy strands, her jacket a cold compress on her back. The poison was still inside her, the desire to escape as urgent. And here he was shouting commands.

'You look a mess, Gina!,' he called out. 'Do you really want the police to pick you up as a tramp!'

She dithered. His fierceness was quite compelling.

A car swerved round them, a pedestrian called out, 'You're on double yellows, man.'

'Get in before you catch your death and I have a heart attack.' Ivan was cruising beside her. 'Bad temper's one thing, death another. And I don't propose to be party to either. So get in now or I'll think you've gone mad!'

She kept walking, his comment on her state of mind, a catalyst to galvanise her again. Taking to the pavement as he inched along the road beside her, a trail of traffic building up behind on this two-way road. What did they look like? A kerb crawler and a bedraggled pensioner; she imagined the headline, the story unravelling beneath. Their names and addresses would appear in the third or fourth paragraph. What could she say to the reporter?

But Ivan was again shouting, 'Whatever's the matter with you, get in the car so we can get it sorted out.'

'Sorted out!' Like a lit match, her anger flared but then looking at him, his fierce scowl, it died. She wanted to laugh.

'Right,' he said as they pulled away and he'd slipped the car into fourth gear, 'the first thing to get straight is that you owe me £27.50, your share. Fish, chips, wine, coffee and the tip.' He glanced across at her. If she was suffering from depression this brutal approach was probably wrong. And rows weren't in his repertoire. 'Tell me where I've failed.'

Gina pursed her lips, dragged the comb out of her hair where it'd dangled since leaving the pub. 'Not you, not your fault,' she muttered.

'No?' He kept his eyes on the road. 'Lack of interest, lack of affront, lack of empathy in your dealings with your mother, too much sympathy for her?'

Gina shivered; the wet and cold of her clothes brought out by the heat inside the car. 'All of those.' But placing her hand on his warm thigh, she offered a sorrowful smile.

Lime trees lined the verges of Glebe Avenue; on warm days for a brief period in late June the scent hung heavy and sweet. The end of April, though, the leaves were mere red buds. Ivan slid the car to a halt.

'I'm not going home and nor are you until we make sense of what this is all about.' He released his seat belt. 'And if you're thinking of doing another runner, I've activated the child lock on your door.'

Gina shrugged as if in pain. 'It isn't that easy.'

'Apparently.' He spoke as to the windscreen, as if pondering his own thoughts rather than asking or telling her. 'Elspeth; to find her losing track of life is hard to admit. The lie about your real father is shocking, but I think it's not so rare. Other people, wartime romances, these ancestry online sites making difficult discoveries. Dare I say, at least you knew the man and loved him. Own up.' He took up the hand she'd lain on his leg, squeezed it gently between his own. 'So, what else? I'm not upset you didn't tell me, I understand, as I do their dilemma, the scandal. Is that so devastating? But I can't take any more pummelling.' The rain battered on the roof of the car, the windscreen misting up, oblivious to the steady rhythm of the windscreen wipers to-ing and fro-ing. 'Why can't you trust me?'

She shook her head, guilt swooping in. 'I do, but … it goes so far back.' She closed her eyes as if not wanting to see what she had to say. 'George's death, Ivan. It wasn't natural. I'm sure of that. But what Kenneth told me she denied.' She shivered, her whole body taking hold and shaking uncontrollably.

Ivan turned the key to start the engine and drove the last few yards up the road and into the driveway of her house. Coming to a halt outside the front door, he said, 'Shall we go inside? I'm no Freud as you've told me on more than one occasion, but I'd prefer to be sitting in a comfortable chair to hear you out.' He released the child lock on her door. 'You have to explain, Gina.'

On the hall table the answerphone flashed two messages. Gina automatically pressed the recall button. Elspeth's voice rang out. 'I just popped in. I was thinking of George's gramophone records. Millie said you were out with that man. Can you phone to let me know?'

The second was from Elsa. 'Hi Mum, I've just had Grandma on the phone wanting to know if I have any of Great Grandpa's records. I have no idea what she's talking about. Insisted I come and see her this weekend. It's not convenient but I'll try to make it on Sunday afternoon, if that's okay.'

Gina looked up at Ivan and shook her head.

He said, 'Ignore them! I'll make a cup of tea while you have a hot bath.' He was already taking off his coat. 'And promise not to drown yourself because I've not strength enough to carry out CPR or whatever it's called.'

Gina stayed with her hand on the telephone. She was as stiff as a rake. How could she climb the stairs let alone do something as normal as sitting in a bath while Ivan fiddled in her kitchen? He was leaning on the newel post at the bottom of the stairs, plainly exhausted. 'How is it, my old love, that you don't lose your sense of humour?' she said.

'Please go,' he said, 'or as Ruby used to say, you'll be the death of me.'

They sat on the sofa which had once been covered in blue brocade, where once Kenneth had lounged with his feet on the fragile silk, testing his father's patience.

'You remember the path that ran from the new house, through the old allotments to the back gate leading into this garden?' Gina began.

He knew, of course he knew, but not how much that scrubby, rutted track meant to the girl who skipped and sang her way to see her grandfather. To be his helper, his mate, to be the one who loved him most of all because his wife had long since died and was forgotten and he was alone except for Ruby, but she didn't count.

Kenneth had gone to play golf, it was Sunday. Elspeth was out too, leaving instructions to turn on the oven at eleven o'clock, which she'd done.

Passing the dug-over beds of the allotment plots where one man called out 'Good day', where the blossom of the blackthorn frothed white against a bright blue sky, and the sheds of wood and corrugated iron were even more ramshackle after the winter frosts. The latch on the back gate was loose; she'd thought to tell Grandpa. 'I heard her first, bleating like sheep. I peeked inside the greenhouse, saw the blood and Grandpa lying on the ground. I thought she'd killed him.' Gina, perched on the edge of the sofa, glanced back at Ivan. 'I don't know why I thought that. She was the one who was bleeding.' Admitting this brought her back to the child who hadn't dared to go into the house to tell Ruby. 'I didn't want to be there or anywhere, I didn't want it to be true. I ran away hoping it wasn't.'

He laid a hand on her back but said nothing.

'If I'd called the police?' She turned fully to face him. 'I've sometimes wondered what would have happened if I'd done that.'

He remembered her letters to him, very matter of fact, and his own feelings as an awkward adolescent who didn't know how to sympathise when she was being given a huge house and garden and he was living in a one bedroom flat. 'I phoned you but was no help!'

'No, don't. No recriminations, those are all mine. But can you see why I didn't blurt out that my mother had killed George and gone mad?' With his hand on her back, explaining out loud as much to herself as to him, was strangely simple. 'I couldn't tell anyone, I didn't know what was truth or lie. Kenneth coming and saying that Grandpa had died of a heart attack and Elspeth was in hospital as she'd hurt herself on some glass. No one knew what I saw.'

'But Ruby?'

'Yes, Ruby, who I didn't see until a long time after. She came to visit me but neither of us could talk about it.'

And for a few moments neither of them wanted to say anything either. There was just the hushed purr of the electric log fire flaming in the grate.

Gina finally said, 'If I'd loved my parents, as I thought of them then, might it have been different?' But any answer they both knew would have been irrelevant. 'They both wanted the whole thing hushed up, so I wasn't going to admit what I'd seen, or ask questions. I was too scared to even think let alone talk about it to anyone. And then when Kenneth was dying … his confession.'

None of this Ivan knew so his query, 'Confession?' meant another apology, and going back to that morning when her identity changed and the suspicion of a crime became real.

'I'm a coward, Ivan' she said after telling the whole ordeal. 'I think I wanted Elspeth to deny it for, if it was true which I'm sure it was, there was nothing I could have done about it. He was dead.'

She looked across to the piano, sheet music stacked haphazardly on the rack, waiting to be shuffled through, ready for her to lift the lid and touch the keys into life. He'd stood beside her so many times, as she'd fingered her way through a new melody. Her father. Never in doubt of his approval even when he'd placed his big hands on the keyboard saying, '*Try it like this*,' and then lifted perfect sound from mere dots on a page.

'I loved him so much, Ivan, you know that, even Elspeth recognised it one time in something she said. But Kenneth … and now Elspeth?' She turned to Ivan a stricken expression. 'I don't want to be disturbed, don't want to remember. I can't cope with her meanderings, face up to what worries her. After all her denials! How can I?'

The room was almost in darkness; the old standard lamp, the wall lights chosen by Rodney, the one overhead hanging from the original central rose, unlit.

She took his hand from her back, leant back and wound it around her shoulder. 'Thank you,' she said. 'I wish I'd done this years ago. Made you my accomplice.'

Ivan nodded. 'So do I.' And pulling her closer, he leant his head against hers. 'I am your accomplice, always have been, but in nothing untoward, mind.'

'Oh you sweet man!' Nestling in to him. 'I put you through too much. It's as if I've carried around a box file of deceit, lies squashed down, thought I'd buried, to be forgotten.'

'But Elspeth?'

'Not now, I'm too tired.' And wrenching herself from his hold she was up and on her feet. 'Come on, I've exhausted you.' And already at the door, 'Light, we need light!' switched the switch. 'That's better. I can see you.' She looked down at him, surprised to think that he knew it all but, 'We don't need to say anything else tonight. It's enough that I've told you. Go! I'll call you in the morning.'

Stained glass May

Gina stood with her back to the front door, calm settling over her, part exhaustion, part reprieve. The ranting and bitterness might have been performed by another woman. Her pent up secrets she'd given to Ivan, the man she should have told years ago. She wanted to both laugh and cry, but she'd done enough of that.

The outside lamp shone through the door's small stained glass window painting pools of amber on the parquet floor. The grandfather clock ticked as if a beating heart. But the gilded mirror hanging on the opposite wall reflected back a woman she didn't recognise. What had become of her?

What would her father think if he were here now? The father who'd left her this house and garden to care for. Not to his son or to the woman he loved, but to her, his child. He'd loved and trusted her to hold all this dear, and she'd done that, the garden the proof. But he'd been her mother's lover, loving her enough to risk his reputation. The woman who had wanted to kill herself rather than live without him and yet had gone on to increase his reputation, dedicating her life in that cause. That could not be doubted. Gustave was right; a tragic love.

And now she was ill.

Elspeth's denial that she'd called and left a message didn't surprise. Elsa's comment, 'If Grandma's being a bit odd, perhaps you should see the warden at the home.' Gina accepted as wise advice. 'A bit of dementia is to be expected at her age,' was a typical response from the forthright young woman who resembled her grandmother in many ways.

Next morning she reported to Ivan. 'Elsa spoke of dementia as if it were a bout of 'flu.'

'Perhaps Elspeth should see a doctor?' Ivan suggested.

'You and who else is going to drag her there?'

The warden was unprepared to speak without 'my client's knowledge'. Gina faced up to her, listing the many journeys Elspeth was making in a taxi at odd times of day, the frequency of her visits. 'That's her choice,' the woman asserted. That Elspeth was forgetful, not recognising her own granddaughter's name, talking of the past as if it were the present, was dismissed. The warden insisted that Mrs Simms seemed very positive, visiting the restaurant often, always smartly dressed. She levelled a steely smile at Gina. 'We keep a close eye on our residents. If I have any concerns I'll call her doctor.'

Gina reported to Ivan, 'Once again, Elspeth's got the better of me,'

Weeks went by, Elspeth's visits became more frequent, similar requests each time. Always asking for, waiting for George. Gina accepted that her offers were refused, wasn't upset when she was told, 'Your hair looks awful! Why do you wear it like that? You never used to. It's Kenneth's fault.'

'It gave me the impetus,' Gina told Ivan when they met in his city, 'your new patch' as she gaily called it. Having invited him to meet her saying, 'I have a surprise for you', there she was, sitting in the window of a café turning her head this way and that, with the aloof air of a fashion model. 'I thought you should be the first person to see,' she said as he bent to kiss her. 'The Twiggy cut, remember? The rage when I first met Rodney.'

'Good grief, Gina! You look amazing.' He suppressed his first thought, isn't this a bit drastic?

'Not a whim, Ivan, as you're thinking, or frivolous. See, I've got curls again?' True, they bounced on top of her head, unfettered by combs, in charge of themselves. 'Elspeth was right, intimated it was a mess and that it was Kenneth's fault.' Ivan was shocked at the gaiety with which this was said but she shrugged extravagantly, 'Don't worry,

I'm accepting her odd outbursts. Can manage them without getting cross. I even asked whether she'd like to come and live with me - at least, I said, 'in this house', not to make her feel I was trying to take her over.'

'My, that was generous!'

'No, foolish. Her reply as I expected, 'What a strange thing to say!"

Being able to openly 'off load' to him took the sting out of it, she'd already acknowledged to him. Being kind and tolerant she had said, 'Is work in progress. George would have wanted this, wouldn't he?'

Two days later the sight of the pink flowers against a surreal blue sky made Ivan want to weep; the grounds of the hospital enhanced by this one tree. To share with Rodney such joy was what he missed most. Gina's response to his, 'Oh that's beautiful,' was a bland 'Yes, Magnolia Soulangeana', as if that were important.

'I'm sorry,' he said. 'But I couldn't say 'no'.'

'Of course not.'

'They can't have many cancellations. Getting rid of pain must be most people's priority.'

She didn't reply.

He persisted, 'You can't still be angry because I argued that I was quite capable of managing on my own.'

'No,' but she was. His insistence that he could go back to his flat when he came out of hospital, was one of those silly tiffs which ought never to have come about. She'd asked for his help, why couldn't he accept hers?

The drop-off point was already full. 'You go in. I'll park and bring your case,' she said.

He didn't move. 'Nobody likes being knocked out and cut about, but I'll be the better for it.'

Gina ignored him, concerned that she was blocking ambulances.

'Look, I'm not going in there with the possibility of meeting my maker and you in this mood.'

'Stop it! You'll be fine.' Which was not how she felt, her reaction to what was essentially good news for him. An earlier slot to get his hip fixed.

'Exactly. You're like the toy weather-house you had as a child, which I coveted I may add.'

'What?'

'The woman out when it's sunny, the man when it's wet.'

'Damn it, Ivan! You'll make me cry.'

'If that's what it takes.'

'I always thought they were Elspeth and Kenneth.'

To which he laughed. 'You'll keep your pecker up, won't you?'

She leant across to undo his seat belt. 'Go!' And she brushed her cheek against his. 'Millie asked me to tell you that the stars are with you. Her sister checked your horoscope and it says, *'a good week to sort out those big problems'.*'

She drove back from the hospital unrepentant at her bad temper. The fear that she'd lose Ivan and the dread thought of how to manage her mother overwhelmed her again. Elspeth had never inspired compassion so how to rustle it up now?

And there she was, at the front door as if about to ring the bell. 'Oh, I wondered where you were.'

'Taking Ivan to hospital for his hip operation.'

'Oh, that's good. Ivan, I remember he's the one with the walking stick.'

Encouraged Gina said, 'I'm worried. He's seventy seven, too old to be having an anaesthetic.,'

'Really?' Elspeth's frown indicating surprise rather than sympathy.'

Gina irritated asked, 'How can I help you today?'

'I don't know.' Elspeth's eyes searched the hall as if the reason would pop out at her. 'Do you know where Kenneth is?'

'What do you mean? His remains?'

'No, no. it was something I was trying to remember. Something wrong that I have to …' pausing and pointing as they stood in the doorway into the lounge. 'That's George's chair and I used to sit over there. Kenneth spoiled it. All wrong. He was very wrong and I shouldn't have given in to him, should I?' Gripping Gina's arm. 'You don't know, nobody knows.'

Wresting her mother's claw like hold on her arm, Gina said, 'Why don't we go outside, into the sunshine? There's nothing to fear out there.'

'No, of course not.' A sharp answer.

They sat on the seat under the sycamore tree, the leaves unfurling vivid green, the old gnarled branches reclothed. Gina smoothing the armrest, the wood polished by many hands, could this be the right time to challenge her mother? That crisp response having been from the woman she knew. 'I often think of what this seat has witnessed, happiness and unhappiness.'

Elspeth's response, 'We often sat on this seat,' wasn't quite what Gina hoped for.

'Ivan says that memories should never be buried, because one day they'll come back to make our life hell.'

'What?'

'That's easier said than done, isn't it?'

'What is?'

Gina persisted. 'I can't forget what happened when I was eleven and George died. It will always haunt me.'

'George?' Another fierce clipped response.

'Yes. I came to see him, but you were there, sitting with your arms bleeding and Grandpa on the floor. I thought you'd killed him.'

'What do you mean?' Elspeth sounding righteous her attention now solely on Gina.

'I was terrified, I ran away. I couldn't tell anyone, and you and Kenneth wouldn't tell me anything. Never have. But I saw you sitting on the floor crying.'

'No, that was Ruby who came, not you.' Elspeth shrank back, tucked her chin into the collar of her coat. 'Don't!'

But Gina dared to go on. 'Yes, Ruby rescued you, you told me that, but nothing else. Your cuts, the scars, why?' Her voice had risen to a pitch that was too loud, not how she'd intended but it was impossible to stop her despair rising not diminishing. 'You said that you'd tell me when you came back from the hospital, you said when I was old enough but you never have.' At last she'd made the accusation of the cruelty caused when no one would speak about what happened. 'I just wanted the truth, still do. And then Kenneth …'

'No! Don't!' Elspeth began shouting over and over, as if to drown Gina's voice, 'Stop it, stop it! Ruby! Where's Ruby!'

'Ruby died years ago!' Gina shouted back. She hadn't meant to but here she was taking hold of Elspeth's shoulders, might have shaken her. 'Listen. listen. George didn't die from a heart attack. Kenneth hit him. I told you that years ago but you wouldn't listen.'

'No!' Elspeth struggled to be free. 'It wasn't my fault!'

'I know but we need to talk about it.' Her mother's shoulders, the thin bones under a thick wool coat, felt as if they might easily break. She let go.

Elspeth cowered, her hands wrestled with each other, twisting and turning.

'If we could just talk about it.' Deflated Gina waited; this isn't what she'd intended to happen. Except what had she expected? 'Please, something worries you and I want to help. If we could remember it together, perhaps?'

But Elspeth's eyes were closed, the words shut off. Silence, a chasm opened out between them.

The tulips in the beds in front of them flamed a vivid red, the petals abandoning their goblet shape to parade the yellow and black interior, the landing pad for foraging bees. Tulipa apeldorn. A blackbird sang a long song above their heads, a song that was for another bird, a mate.

Gina tentatively put her hand on top of her mother's to quieten the agitation and was not dismissed. They sat on.

George was dead, love destroyed, so much dishonesty. And yet? It was such a lovely day.

'Is that man coming back?' Elspeth suddenly said. 'He had a walking stick. I thought that was a good idea. Where can I get one, Gina?'

Ivan called late that evening. 'I'm on my mobile. All done. A bit groggy but I thought you'd want to know, I'm still here, in the land of the living.'

Elspeth suddenly appeared on the doorstep with her suitcase saying, 'I can't remember why I was at that other place.' It was two days after Ivan's operation. She swept past Gina who'd opened the door, saying, 'Thank you, Ruby,' and climbed the stairs to the room which would have been hers sixty years before. Gina didn't disagree with her, merely asked if she was happy to be back. Was this the result of the row, if it could be called that?

Wind was harrying the magnolia tree, flinging its petals to moulder on the driveway when Gina collected Ivan from the hospital. 'Your room's ready,' she said. 'The only surprise is that Elspeth has moved in.'

Elspeth sat on the bed, the candlewick bedspread a troubling thing. She traced her fingers along the swirling line of blue tufts, mesmerised by the circling round and along and back. But this wasn't hers. Where had Ruby found this strange thing? Where was the pink counterpane, that belonged to her, an heirloom of crewel work?

She lay back, quite tired with all that packing. It had been hard to press her clothes into one case, so many jackets and skirts, dresses and shoes. Why they'd all been taken to that place she couldn't remember. Was it for a holiday? Someone would have to go and pick up the rest. She needed to tell George.

She greeted them in the hall. 'I can't find my things, Gina.' That was the woman's name. Yesterday, was it yesterday? Everything had been very blurry, something had happened. It had been upsetting. But … 'Oh, who's this?' The light was dim coming through the little window with the orange flowers in the glass.

'It's Ivan, Mrs Simms,' as he lurched forward on crutches. 'Back from the hospital, having my hip replaced. You remember?'

Did she? Ivan, a Russian name. Gustave is German. 'Of course, of course! It's just that it's so dark in here. I mentioned it to George but he seems to have forgotten.'

'We're much later than I expected. Takes them ages to sort out a discharge. You'd think …' Gina broke off to close the door and guide Ivan to sit down. 'You go into the drawing room, Mother. Ivan will join you while I …' but the rest of the thought was lost as she saw what Elspeth was wearing. 'You're ready for bed? Don't you want supper?'

Elspeth blinked. 'Supper? Haven't I eaten already?'

The woman was quite forceful, but kind. The woman who was Gina, her daughter. The tray of food had been good; some sort of fish. She had been hungry. And it was nice to sit in the rocking chair by the window of her bedroom looking out over the garden which was what she'd often done when George was here. George; he was dead. She must remember, but every time it was a blow, a hammer striking her heart, her chest crushed. It was better to forget.

Gina shot out of bed at the first shriek, stumbled from the spare room where she'd been sleeping, to the sound coming from her own room where Ivan had been put to bed.

The bedside lamp was enough to show Ivan sitting up with Elspeth lying across the bed, her head pressed into the duvet. 'It's all right,' Ivan was murmuring, his hand patting the small body, 'I didn't expect …there, there!'

Gina stared at what might have been a comical sight if it hadn't been for the noise and Ivan's expression of pain as he continued to comfort the prostrate woman. Gina didn't need to ask; Elspeth had come to find George.

'Ivan, leave her!' the command as shocking as the sudden blast of brightness as she switched on the overhead light. 'Lie down, you shouldn't be sitting like that. Mother!'

Elspeth curled up as if to make herself disappear. Ivan swung his legs carefully over the side of the bed. 'It's all right,' he said. 'I need to go to the lavatory.'

Gina handed him his sticks. 'Can I help you?'

He shook his head. 'This I've practised.'

Ivan gone, Elspeth lay quiet and still, white silk pyjamas, loose hair, thinner, paler, her small feet. Gina climbed onto the bed beside her. 'You've had a shock, Mother. This is the wrong room. Let me take you back to your bed?' carefully unwinding her mother's arms which were clasped tightly around her body she tried to twine them around her own neck.

But Elspeth shrank back, crawling to the far side of the bed. 'This is George's room. What are you doing in here?' Authoritative even in her dishevelled state.

'No, George is dead, remember?'

'George is dead?'

'Let me take you back to your room, your own bed.'

'Her deterioration has been remarkably quick,' Ivan said as she drove him to the physiotherapist. 'Are you sure we shouldn't ask for a doctor's opinion?'

'What for?

'There might be pills, counselling sessions?'

Gina merely raised her eyebrows.

'But you can't be getting much sleep, patrolling the landing.'

'That's not what I'm doing. Locking your door helped.' It wasn't a tactic she was proud of, or telling Elspeth that George would come to her. Treating her as a child, somebody to be duped, wasn't right. Except it worked. This woman who'd come back to live with her was not the mother she'd known. This was Elspeth as a shy bride, or later when George and she had declared their love for one another.

'We're too much for you,' was what Ivan had already said several times in the last couple of weeks. 'I really can go back to the flat, you know.'

'Please don't.' She was driving his car, had acquiesced immediately to his request. Even told him, 'this is jolly nippy.' It was striking, this change in her humour. No longer did he need to carefully couch his questions or opinion. Rarely the woman who flitted between impatience and gratitude. 'A hot coal that can't rest in your palm,' as he'd told her.

Elspeth seemed to have forgotten that she'd ever lived anywhere else, and apart from the confused frown she sometimes wore, it appeared that she was pleased with the arrangement.

The wind danced shadows on the white wood of the greenhouse, the sun polishing the glass. Was there someone inside? Elspeth looked again, saw movement flickering back and forth. Was it him? Prowling around, trying to catch them? She crept closer. She had to get rid of him. 'Kenneth!' Bravely she stepped forward, screwing up her eyes to see who was there. Or could it be George?

'Mrs Simms? Elspeth?' Ivan called in a low voice, standing well back. He didn't want to startle her. Never quite knowing, after all these months, how to address her. 'Lovely day, isn't it? I'm going to need my hat with this heat.'

Elspeth spun round, weapon in hand.

'Good idea,' he nodded at the small furled umbrella she was holding up as if in defence. 'A parasol. Black, probably the best colour to keep off the heat.'

Who was this man? She did know him but why?

'Are you a friend of George?'

'It's Ivan, your Russian friend, our little joke!'

She leant forward rather than walk the few paces to see him better. 'Oh, yes,' and she laughed, 'Yes, of course, I know you. I was rather distracted,' looking at the umbrella as if surprised to find it still in her hand. She glanced back at the greenhouse. 'Is there anyone in there?'

'No, Gina's gone shopping.' He was by her side. 'Would you like to come and sit in the shade?' He offered his arm. 'We could have a cold drink.'

'How kind.' She put her arm through his but still looked back at the greenhouse. 'Can you see someone in there?'

Ivan had to bend forward, almost doubled up to her height to figure out what she was seeing. 'Ah! That's what you mean. The reflection of the trees swaying, the light imprinting a moving pattern; an interesting phenomenon.' It was easy to understand why she'd been lured into believing there was an intruder; this apparent from the way in which she was brandishing her umbrella. 'Who did you think it was?'

'Kenneth, I thought it was him. I can't get rid of him.'

Ought he to say that he was dead and buried long ago? What would reassure her? Gina was much better at this. 'Kenneth's not here,' he finally said. 'You don't need to worry about him.' And holding her tightly to him, he pulled her round to walk slowly up the lawn to the terrace. 'The shade of the sycamore is what we need and then I'll make us a cool drink.'

Together they carefully negotiated the steps up to the house. As if to distract her he said, 'These are dangerous, need replacing. I've said as much to Gina. A death trap for those of less firm footing.'

'No! No! George wouldn't like that. They were here before I came, you know.' And she patted his arm. 'Of course, you wouldn't know that being a stranger.'

Gina returned to find them chatting on the seat, could even hear laughter as she came to join them. Ivan pandering to Elspeth's whims, no longer annoyed her.

'Ah, who is this?' Elspeth said to Ivan.

'Your daughter.' Gina laughed as if her mother were playing a game. 'I see you've already cracked open the champagne.'

'Don't be silly, this is lemonade!' Elspeth held up her glass. 'This nice man made it for me. Would you like some?'

'Yes. And his name is Ivan. You remember he lives here too.'

'Oh,' Elspeth studied him closely, 'you're not the gardener.'

After supper that day, Ivan and Gina walked around the garden which had become a pleasing ritual. Standing outside the greenhouse he said, 'I hardly dare suggest this, but could Elspeth have attacked the greenhouse, back in March?'

Gina looked from Ivan to the greenhouse and back. 'How? When?' This hadn't been a consideration. Not at all. Her greatest fear was that she'd done it herself, driven to a sleepwalking madness by Elspeth's progressively weird behaviour. 'Really?'

'I don't know, but her attitude, the way she brandished the umbrella as if about to attack somebody. She thought Kenneth was in there, I'm sure of that.'

'Possible but still hard to believe. You think she was ready to attack Kenneth?'

'I don't know. But the way the panes of glass were broken back in March, could have been achieved by someone hitting them hard with something like an umbrella.'

'Would she have had the strength? But I don't think it matters any more.' One day she'd tell him of the other worse scenario she'd imagined. 'As long as she doesn't do it again.'

Her untroubled response surprised him as did so much of her changed attitude to Elspeth. He said, 'This morning she chastised me for mentioning your rickety paving stones need replacing. Heirlooms in her opinion, which you would endorse I seem to think.'

She pushed up against him, the solid weight of him a joy to be cherished, not to be argued with. Layers of grey clouds scowled overhead, rain could be expected any time. But the ripple and splash of the pump in the pond soothed and refreshed, and the runner beans in the vegetable patch promised an excellent crop. She dared to hope that he'd never go away, live with her here for ever.

Floating free August

This wasn't what Gina had come for, never expected. She'd arrived with the intention of clearing the last of Elspeth's possessions from the flat, dusting and cleaning, to leave it in proper order. She'd discussed with Ivan the need to decide what to do about the property; letting it furnished or selling empty; the problem being the need for Elspeth's signature.

The box was tucked far back in the radiogram, behind the racks which had once held records. A stout cardboard box, the top flaps folded in on themselves, no tape to remove. She sat on the floor, tired out by the stifling heat of a room unaired, eager to finish. It was heavier than she expected. One large plastic barrel jar was bolstered by newspaper, the faded print on the label reading; 'Remains of the Deceased' and below in block capital letters, 'GEORGE EVERLEY SIMMS'. Breath balled in her chest; could this really be him? Wresting it from the crunched up paper, she raised it carefully, felt the weight, knew that it was full, the seal on the lid unbroken. The date, as faint as it was distant, 25th March 1955, two weeks after his death. This must have been when his funeral took place, the funeral to which she hadn't been taken. Standing it reverently on the carpet beside her, Gina waited for her breathing to calm, her racing heart to slow.

Beside it, inside that nest of paper, she found two envelopes and a small jeweller's box, the latter containing his initialled gold cufflinks. The slim envelope held a one page letter from the funeral directors asking Mr Kenneth Simms to collect his father's remains. From the date when written and the brief phrase, 'as we wrote to you previously a year ago, we would appreciate collection …,' it was immediately apparent, as to why they were in Elspeth's possession. She would have intercepted, taken charge, brought them back to keep, to cherish, to hold as hers. Tears of unbounded pity trickled down Gina's face. They didn't need to be wiped away. Again she waited while the full implications of this discovery crept over her. How had Elspeth borne that grief, that loss, with no one to share it? Locked inside her, never able to express.

Finally Gina opened the fat foolscap envelope which contained three photographs from her childhood that she'd never seen. George was standing beside the pond, a small girl nestled into his legs, his hand folding her to him. He was smiling at the person behind the camera, his happiness leaping out of the picture, as the child smiled up at him. Gina breathed, 'Me!' In the second photo they were both sitting on those crazy paving steps, a flower pot, trowel and small fork at their feet, laughing gleefully up at the person who took the shot. The last was of Elspeth, posed with her feet apart, hands demurely clasped to keep her skirt from lifting in the wind, her hair loose and flying free, smiling provocatively at the camera.

'Oh, my!' Is all Gina could say, again and again.

Time stopped, the pink carpet floated beneath her, the box was no longer plain and functional as any cardboard box for it held priceless treasure.

'How do I do this?' Gina sat with Ivan at the kitchen table the box between them. 'This is her secret trove, not mine.'

In the last two months Elspeth had regressed, it seemed, to the time during the War when she'd first come to live at the house in Glebe Avenue. She, George and Ruby on their own in the place which she believed was her home. She happily drifted in and out of those memories, rarely recognising Gina, unworried that she needed to be nudged to remember. 'Oh, yes, of course!' she'd exclaim as if of no consequence. Ivan was greeted with, 'Ah, here's the gardener again,' and a little laugh which could have meant anything. Millie accepted that she'd become Ruby. Fear of Kenneth and the circumstances of George's death appeared to have receded. 'I think it's the routine, having us both here to talk to, and being back in the place where she was happiest.' Gina had decided.

To introduce what had been concealed privately was something that needed thinking through. 'I don't want to upset her, but I can't keep it to myself can I?'

Ivan blew his nose on one of his fabled handkerchiefs. 'How has she managed all these years? The front she presented to the world.' He blotted tears from his cheeks. 'It's heart breaking. Holding on to his ashes.' He thought of Rodney, his ashes safely strewn in Hackney's Victoria Park, where they'd first held clandestine hands, declared their love and then been married.

'Yes, well, I know, but come on, Ivan. It's important to get this right.

Gina sat on the edge of the bed, fearful of damaging the tattered bedspread, the heirloom she'd retrieved from the attic. The pink with blue and green threads looped in chains, circled and swirled not going anywhere, never joining up. The candlewick had been sturdier but this beautiful thing pleased Elspeth. 'I knew Ruby had put it in the wrong place,' she'd said.

A slice of sunlight focused on the object on the floor, the box placed on the carpet, Elspeth sitting in the rocking chair by the bedroom window.

'I found this, Elspeth,' Gina said leaning forward as if to lift a flap. 'I knew you'd want to have it.'

Elspeth jerked upright, as if strings had been tugged, her hands covering her mouth, her cry of, 'Don't touch,' commanding.

'You remember what's inside?'

'Don't touch!'

'No, I won't touch. I know it's yours. I rescued it for you.' Ivan was downstairs. it's what they'd discussed, to keep it gentle and calm. 'Will you show me?'

'Why have you taken it?'

'No, I brought it back for you.'

Elspeth kicked away the stool on which she'd rested her legs, tried to prise herself out of her chair. 'Dratted thing!'

'Do you want me to help?'

But Elspeth batted her away. 'Don't!'

'No, I won't touch you or it, but this is stupid. I've looked inside. I know what's in there. The photographs, you, George and me. I'd never seen them before.' She paused. Elspeth hunched forward, was not taking her eyes off the box. 'Why can't you show me, talk about them? They make me happy.'

Elspeth was quiet again, ferocity overtaken by bewilderment. 'Who are you?'

'I'm your daughter, George's child.' Her patience was ebbing with a need for, what? To be treated as someone capable of understanding, to share the man they both loved? 'Here!' Gina lifted the box onto her mother's lap.

Elspeth instantly wrapped her arms tight around the box, closed her eyes. 'I don't know who your are. Go away, Kenneth! You don't scare me, it wasn't my fault.' Her words again belligerent. 'He's mine, he's safe.'

Gina stood over her, all resolutions forgotten. 'This has got nothing to do with Kenneth. He's not here. I've told you. This is my home, he's dead.' And she prised the box free enough to pull the envelope with photos out. 'Look! That's me with him, my father, isn't it? And you, see you look lovely, don't you? George took the picture, didn't he?'

Elspeth tentatively opened her eyes, glanced up at Gina, and down at the pictures in her hand. It was her and that was him. 'Yes, George! That is you, of course.' And she looked up at Gina again. 'Thank you,'

'I wish,' Gina said to Ivan as they sat in the garden that evening, a low sun gilding the spent tops of the cardoon thistles, 'but that wish is a wish too far.'

'She's all right, is she?'

She'd left Elspeth earlier, apparently asleep, holding her treasure, but when she'd gone back later, knocked on the door, she was greeted with, 'Ah, it's Gina, isn't it? I was just coming down for the Proms,' the box nowhere to be seen.

'As right as she'll ever be. But I have picture proof of my father's love; what more can I want?' She looked to

Ivan and back down her garden where gnats danced dizzily in front of them. He was living with her, had done for all these months, making no attempt to leave, mowing the grass, cooking and he'd even made a brief reference to letting his flat. 'And,' she added, 'I won't ask or tell but I can scatter their ashes together when the time comes. That would make them both happy.'

Going inside they found Elspeth sitting at the piano. 'Those people,' pointing at the television, 'make far too much noise.' Smoothing her hands over the shiny piano lid, pride in her voice. 'We knew Myra Hess, you know! She played The Moonlight Sonata at The National Gallery during the War.'

Gina opened the door to the shock of the body, crumpled and propped against one of the legs of the staging. 'Elspeth? Elspeth!' Panic at her back, she knelt to gather the floppy frail weight into her arms, the body still warm; she was alive. 'What are you doing out here?' Seven o'clock, the dawn chorus barely over.

Elspeth's eyes blinked open, 'George?' her voice dreamy, her eyes closing again as she sank back into sleep. Beside her lay a black umbrella.

'Let me help you inside, Elspeth, you can't sleep out here.'

The words drifted past her for she was so tired, too tired to stand. The sacks were gone, the sacks that he'd lain on the hard cold slabs, someone had taken them away. Her skirt would be dirty but he wouldn't care. He'd say, as he always said, 'You've come!' as if it were a miracle, and she'd be uplifted as in that painting he'd shown her; together, flying above the houses and trees, free as birds.

'How long have you been here?'

The voice floated in and out, how long, how long. Her watch would be able to tell, a dainty thing of marcasite that the man in the shop said couldn't be repaired. The woman with her had said, 'You might like a new one, Mother,' and she'd snatched her wrist away for it wouldn't be right.

But there was that voice again whispering, 'Mother, I'm Georgina, you chose my name.'

Elspeth opened her eyes. 'Yes, that's right. George, he was so pleased.'

'I know, my father.'

Elspeth struggled to pull herself upright. 'Kenneth isn't here, is he?' She drew in a deep breath letting it out with a great sigh. 'He was wrong, you know. I had to pull him away to save George.' Her eyelids closed for they were so heavy, leaning in to the warmth of being held. 'George will forgive me.'

'Yes,' Gina's answer came without thinking, an answer that must be true. 'If there was anything to forgive.' She stroked her mother's cheek, soft and cold. Had she been out here all night?

Elspeth lay back; the gentle touch so soothing, and the calm and quiet, just the birds singing, sweet and joyful and the smell of something she can't remember. Except, 'Someone's taken the sacks. Was it you?' she said.

'No,' a lie as easy and necessary as those that had been told all those years ago. 'George will know where they are.'

'Of course.' Elspeth smiled,. 'I expect he'll be here soon.'

'Yes, but shall we go into the house to wait?'

The scent from the new pink rose that rambled over the kitchen window was unbelievably lovely as Gina walked Elspeth slowly back to the house. 'The Generous Gardener', a gift from Ivan. He'd be home soon, back from finalising the letting of his flat.

'What would you like for breakfast, Elspeth? Scrambled eggs?'

Elspeth smiled, her hand still holding on to her daughter. 'Yes, that's right.' And inside the house, as she let go to sit down at the kitchen table, she looked about her with an exultant cry, 'This is my home!' And smoothing her hand over the surface of the table as if to take back possession she said, 'I might go upstairs first for a short nap. I am very tired.' But she remained seated, surveying the cupboards and walls. 'There's a picture, I wonder where it is? It was painted by a Russian man, I remember. Like your friend.' Her face bright with delight. 'He likes music too, you know. 'The Moonlight Sonata'. It was one of our favourites, George and I.'

Elspeth lay on the bed. Someone was playing the piano. George, of course, of course! She closed her eyes and let the music take her body, lift it up into the air, floating and free with George.

Acknowledgements

I owe an enormous debt of gratitude to my writing group, Sandra Horn in particular. Her excellent editing skills throughout the writing process as well as her encouragement and love which have kept me writing for thirty plus years.

I have also to thank those who are in our group at present, Lisa Conway and Penny Langford who experienced the second half of The Greenhouse Legacy, and previously, Jayne Woodhouse.

Finally, this novel would not have come to publication without the dedication, advice and skill of Drew Westcott and Innes Richens. My heartfelt thanks go to them.

www.drewwestcott.co.uk

www.innesrichens.co.uk